ABOUT THE AUTHOR

Jackie Kinsella is an 'ex' international athlete, who traded in her running shoes for a pair of shiny high heels to work as a long-haul flight attendant. Having discovered a passion for writing at an early age, Jackie dreamed that one day she would write a funny, sexy, story that would make readers laugh out loud and touch the souls of hopeless romantics everywhere. A strong believer in the Universe and Divine Counterparts, Jackie hopes this story will bring a smile to your face, love into your heart, and a reminder that…

"No matter the distance, no matter the circumstances, what is meant for you will find you."

Beth Saunders

The Secret Life of a Flight Attendant

JACKIE KINSELLA

Dedicated to my Mum and Dad.
The two shining lights in my life, who taught
me the true meaning of unconditional love.
I miss you both every day.

And to my beautiful children...
Thank you for choosing me to be your Mumma.
You have my heart and soul.

CONTENTS

INTRODUCTION

After saying goodbye to the remaining passengers, I drank a much-needed glass of champagne and slumped down into one of the first-class seats.

My mind wandered back to yesterday, his hands gently caressing my breasts. How I gave out a small moan as his warm breath brushed against my inner thighs. I could almost feel the sensation as I remembered how his eager tongue explored between my legs, probing deeper and deeper, until I felt the intense vibrations of every nerve and fibre in my body.

'Oy oy sleepy head, wakey-wakey it's time to get off.'

I opened my eyes to find the captain staring at me, 'Ere, I don't know what you've just been dreamin' about luv, but you looked like the cat that got the cream, didn't she?' he said elbowing an amused first officer.

I felt myself blushing, so I lifted my exhausted body off the seat, quickly grabbed my bag and headed out of the aircraft door.

If only they knew.

From a very young age there was never any doubt in my mind about the career path I wanted to take and receiving my airline wings was one of the proudest moments of my life.

Growing up I had been fortunate enough to travel the world with my parents and flight attendants had always intrigued me. While we sat at the airport, I loved to watch the beautifully groomed cabin crew float by, and to pass the time I would play a game where I would give each of them a story. Some had secret lives; others simply had adventures on their trips to far and distant places. In my eyes, flight attendants were the embodiment of mystery, and I always knew that one day it would be my head held high, my feet clicking along in heels, my body in a uniform that clings in just the right places, and my face displaying mysterious eyes and that never fading lipstick smile.

What I did not know, was that by working for one of the best airlines in the world, my life would transcend into something where I could be anyone I wanted to be, have secrets, tell lies, make huge amounts of money, and most of all…enjoy every minute of it!

Thinking back, I have been living a lie most of my life. I grew up as a single child in a moderate size, middle class home, in a small, picturesque village in the south of England. The majority of our neighbours were extremely wealthy and although both my parents had lucrative careers, they could never match the exorbitant lifestyle of our fellow villagers. Nonetheless, we played along, and we were accepted into the thriving social scene of England's finest blue bloods. No one asked questions and we did not tell.

However, despite my parent's acceptance of the situation, I was determined to find a way of becoming a genuine member of what I called, 'The SES' (Sussex Elite Society). When I first stepped inside my friend Henri's sprawling home at the age of thirteen, I knew that I wanted my life to be different from that of my parents. I wanted Henri's life and all the trimmings that came with it. Every weekend in the summer, we would ride his horses, go sailing on his parents' boat or escape to the huge attic room that overlooked the ocean. When I wasn't looking out of the window, I would lay on the bed for hours and stare at the old wooden beamed ceilings daydreaming about the future.

One particular day a storm raged outside. The ocean was wild, and as I listened to the howling wind and the rain pelting on the windowpanes, I had never felt so alive…or so in love. I wanted this house, I wanted money, lots of money, and I knew that one day I would get everything I wanted…I just didn't know how!

I had no idea that one evening in March, fourteen years later, my life would take a major detour from the "norm" and bring me closer to my dreams than I had ever imagined. The Universe was steering me towards a different path, one that would open my world up to lies, deceit, sex and money, and I knew that once I took my first step onto that path, my life would never be the same again.

My parents call me "Elizabeth."

My friends call me "Beth."

My men call me "Kat."

1

HONG KONG: LIFE IN THE FAST LANE

I felt a wave of excitement as we touched down into Hong Kong Airport. I have always found Hong Kong to be a city unlike anywhere else that I have experienced. With its vibrant mix of cultures and wealth, it is a city that literally never sleeps.

As businessmen and women leave the office, it is easy to be tempted by the multitude of bars and restaurants that litter the streets. Late dinners are often followed by even later drinks, and as a few early morning revellers meander around the maze of Soho streets looking for a cab to take them home, they are often shown the way by the friendly market stall holders setting up for the day's trade.

For some, life in Hong Kong is like a fantasy. Out of the box business ideas often become an instant success. Sex, like alcohol, is easily accessible, and most things, including work, are done in excess. Fast paced living is complemented by peaceful islands and nature trails for those wanting to escape the bright lights and hustle of the city. Personally, I always think of Hong Kong as a place where anything can happen, and usually does!

While I was checking into the crew hotel, I bumped into my friend Joe who was very excited about a party he was invited to. His enthusiasm to go to the "Party of the Year" at Sky 100, was so contagious that I didn't need much tempting when he insisted that I join him.

A couple of hours later, we were inside the lobby of the International Commerce Centre and I was captivated by the design of the building.

Joe grabbed my hand, 'Amazing isn't it? You are going to die when you see upstairs!'

We stepped inside the high-speed elevator and watched on a screen as we climbed almost 400 meters within sixty seconds. When the doors opened we were greeted by two beautiful women who handed us both a gift bag containing hundreds of dollars worth of beauty products, a disposable camera and ten thousand dollars of fake gambling money.

'How bloody unbelievable is this Beth?' said Joe bursting with excitement.

We followed a neon path that led us to the observation deck, where models wandered the floor dressed as "Vegas Showgirls," closely followed by jugglers and fire-eaters.

'This is so surreal,' I said, as a man walking a tiger walked past.

'I told you it was the party of the year! Oh my fucking god, there he is...got to go love. See you later!'

Joe had spotted his latest crush, so I took a glass of champagne off a passing waiter and walked over to the window to admire the magnificent view of the City.

After a couple of hours of polite exchanges with strangers and still no sign of Joe, I decided to leave when someone tapped me on the shoulder. I turned to see a devilishly handsome man smiling at me.

'I couldn't help but notice that ye are alone. Would ye like some company?'

Before I had time to answer, he clicked his fingers at a passing waitress, took my empty champagne glass and substituted it with a full one.

'John,' he said giving me a very sexy wink. 'So, what brings a beautiful girl like yerself to a borin' party like this?'

'Actually, I was considering leaving...and now I'm *definitely* going.'

Leaning close to me, he gently brushed his hand against my thigh and whispered, 'Now why would ye go and do somethin' like that?'

Maybe, it's because you seem like an arrogant arsehole, who clicks his fingers at people.

He looked amused, 'Why don't ye stay a little longer so we can get acquainted?' As I stood up to leave, he put his hand on mine and softened his tone, 'Don't go! I'm sorry if I gave ye the wrong impression, I would love it if ye stay and have a drink with me.'

Cockiness aside, it was undeniable how handsome he was, and his soft Irish accent was hypnotising. I guessed that he was in his late thirties; his square jaw and strong features were framed by a mop of thick, wavy, black hair and he had the most unbelievable dark blue eyes that I had ever seen. I decided to give "Baileys" (as he was just as Irish and just as smooth) the benefit of the doubt and sat back down.

For the next hour, Baileys delighted in talking about his favourite topic…himself! Despite the fact that he had not asked me one question about my life, not even my name, I was so mesmerised by the intensity of his eyes that I was surprisingly happy to listen. I was also getting a pretty clear picture of his life. From what I gathered he went to the gym at seven am, worked from nine am until nine pm, partied till dawn, had lots of random sex, slept a little, and then did it all again the next day… and of course, earned lots of money.

After my third drink, it was undeniable that despite his cocky, self-assured exterior, he was quite charming and I was starting to warm to him when he asked, 'So gorgeous girlie, do ye want to get out of here and fuck me brains out?'

Oh dear, if only he wouldn't talk!

He saw my silence as a challenge, 'Come on, let's say we both leave and have a little fun together. Ye are hot and ye have great tits.'

Please stop talking!

I rolled my eyes, but he wouldn't give up. He ran his finger down the side of my arm, giving me chills, 'Ah come on. I promise I won't do anythin' too naughty.'

Although he had piqued my curiosity, I refused his advances which only served to motivate him more. After a few moments of silence, a slow grin spread across his face as his eyes bore into mine.

My god, he has to be the sexiest man I have ever met.

'What's yer price?'

I wasn't sure if he was serious, but I decided to play him at his own game, 'What are you suggesting?'

He leaned in and whispered seductively into my ear, 'What would it cost me to take yer gorgeous arse off to a room, slip off yer panties, kiss ye all over, and make love to ye till ye come?'

Suppressing a giggle and starting to believe that maybe you can get anything you want in Hong Kong at a price, I played along, 'I think we both know that we won't be "making love" and although it sounds very tempting there's a flaw in your plan,' I teased.

'Oh yeah, and what would that be?'

I leant into him so he could feel my breath on his neck, 'I'm not wearing panties.'

I let my comment linger.

He groaned, 'Three thousand dollars.'

Quickly calculating in my head that he was offering me three hundred pounds, I scoffed at the suggestion, 'No way! You'd have to pay at least double to get these legs wrapped around you.'

I hitched up my skirt just enough to give him a view of where my knickers should have been and opened my legs a little.

He groaned again, 'Okay, okay, let's go,' he said. 'Six grand it is!'

'Seven!'

He smiled and took my hand, 'Seven!'

'Wait!' I yelled, as he pulled me through the throngs of partygoers. 'Where are you taking me?'

He didn't answer.

When we stepped into the elevator Baileys ushered me to the back, and as people crammed inside Baileys moved behind me, his hand working its way under my skirt, his fingers teasing me between my legs. When the elevator stopped on the ground floor, Baileys smiled, took my hand and led me outside to catch a cab. After ten minutes of long, sensuous kisses, we pulled up in front of a luxurious apartment building.

'Don't worry,' he said taking my hand, 'this place is very discreet, and I promise I'll look after ye.'

The receptionist welcomed Baileys with a flirty smile as she handed him a key and an envelope. I on the other hand was not so lucky; my smile was met with an evil glare.

'Do you know her?' I asked when we got inside the elevator.

'Yeah, she's a right dirty bitch that one. But it's good for me because I get me cock sucked on a regular basis and a huge discount on the room.'

Bloody hell, I hope he has condoms!

Once inside the apartment, all my fears disappeared as it was stacked with condoms, lubricant and even a wide selection of porn. Baileys excused himself and went into the bathroom, so I took it upon myself to put on a DVD and get undressed.

I wish I'd put on some nice underwear.

When Baileys appeared from the bathroom I gasped. He had a beautiful body to match his beautiful face. Those hours in the gym had certainly paid off as his washboard abs framed the most beautiful, proud piece of manhood that I had ever seen. Looking very pleased to see me naked, he slowly started to rub himself as he walked towards me. I kissed his enormous erection and then pulled him down onto the bed, and as we listened to the unmistakable sound of background porn, we started our own show.

Slowly and tenderly, he kissed my face, neck, and breasts, and as he made his way down my body, his tongue explored every part of me. Moaning with pleasure, I selfishly basked in his unwavering attention until I was brought back to the present when Baileys said, 'Suck me cock.'

I repaid the favour and worked my way down his body, teasing him with bites and sucks until I finally did as he asked. Catching glimpses of the girls on TV, I copied them with vigour and worked it like never before. Baileys started to lose control, 'That's a girl,' he yelled, 'keep suckin'. Argh…that's so fuckin' good.'

'Are you ready to…'

'Don't stop,' he pleaded, 'just keep goin'.'

Obediently I got back to the "job" and within minutes he exploded…all over my face! Reeling backward, I wiped my eyes and stared at him in disbelief, 'What did you do that for?' I said slightly annoyed at his lack of warning. 'I thought we were going to…you know….'

'Fuck!'

'Exactly!'

'No, I mean…fuck me! That usually doesn't happen.' He fell back and covered his face with his hands, 'Fuck…oh fuck!'

I did not know what was worse, the fact that I had semen all over my face or that I was not going to get a "Fuck." Disappointed, I stood up and headed to the bathroom.

'Wait! Don't go.' He gestured for me to come back, 'Let me do somethin' for ye.'

When I had finished wiping my face, Baileys grabbed me and threw me onto the bed. His hands wandered down my body as he kissed me passionately, his fingers doing things to my senses that I didn't think possible. Keeping his mouth seductively close to mine, but not quite touching, he gently caressed my clitoris with his thumb as he pushed a couple of fingers inside me. His eyes not leaving mine as he began circling, pressing and pushing, until my body was flooded with an erotic sensation that was so intense I thought I was going to pass out. The moment I screamed, Baileys placed his lips on mine, catching my hot breath in his mouth as my body gave in to the spiralling vibrations rising within me.

Baileys smiled, 'That was unbelievable. Are ye free tomorrow? I would love to give ye the real deal.'

That would be nice.

He read my hesitation wrong, 'Don't worry... I'll pay ye seven grand for tonight and seven for tomorrow. How's that?'

What?

Any romantic notions I had evaporated in seconds, and after he handed me the envelope containing the cash, I watched in stunned silence while he dressed. When Baileys had put on his shoes, he came over to the bed and handed me a business card, 'Take ye time. I'm heading off. Somewhere to be and all that! I'll meet ye outside tomorrow at six.'

I nodded but found it strange that he still did not know anything about me. As if reading my mind, he turned before opening the door, 'Hey, what's ye name?'

For a second I hesitated, 'Kat.'

He smiled.

And so…. Kat was born!

Back at my hotel, I found it hard to stop smiling. I could not believe I had just been paid for a blowjob and a great orgasm. However, my pleasure was short lived as it didn't take long for the guilt to creep in. As I tried to go to sleep, I battled with my conscience until I finally drifted off.

Baileys Part Two

When I woke the following morning to see the seven thousand dollars in an envelope on the bedside table the reality hit me.

Oh my god, it really happened. I actually had sex for money… well sort of, and I'm doing it again today!

As the time neared six o'clock, I was getting excited. Despite the niggling feeling that I was doing something wrong, I wanted to see Baileys again. I didn't know what he thought about me, but deep down I was hoping there might be more to it than a simple business transaction. After a little self-pampering, I put on some sexy underwear and a cute little silver dress, checked my makeup and then went outside to get a cab.

At six pm sharp my cab pulled up outside the apartment building and I could see "Blow Job Bitchzilla" working at the reception desk. When she saw me, she gave me her signature glare, and I was glad Baileys had asked me to meet him outside. After twenty minutes and still no sign of Baileys, I realised that I had been stood up. Feeling disappointed at being let down again, I pulled out my phone to call a cab when the doorman approached me, 'Excuse me miss. Is your name Katie?'

I shook my head 'No,' and then realising my mistake, I quickly turned to him, 'Oh wait! Sorry yes! That's me. I'm Katie.'

With a raised eyebrow he handed me a sealed envelope and walked away. I glanced inside the foyer to see "Bitchzilla" laughing. Feeling slightly paranoid, my imagination suddenly ran wild and I started to panic as I scanned the area to see if anyone was watching me.

Shit! What if I am being secretly filmed by a new reality TV show that is going to expose me to the whole world as a hooker?

I felt sick.

What if it's a police sting operation and the letter is a summons to appear in court for prostitution charges?

I started shaking, my nerves had gotten the better of me and I was frozen to the spot.

Breathe Beth, just breathe!

I tentatively opened the envelope.

> *Kat*
> *Something's come up and I can't make our session as planned. I'm sure being such a pro (pardon the pun) you charge for late cancellations, so here's 50% of our agreed amount. Shame, but I'll just have to imagine your gorgeous mouth wrapped around my throbbing cock.*
>
> *JD*
>
> *P.S. I've enclosed another business card in case you fancy rescheduling, but I'm going away with the wife and kids next week, so make it in a couple of weeks' time.*

Folding his note back into the envelope I felt as though I had been punched in the stomach, and this time it was not about the money.

Going away with the wife and kids! What wife? How many kids does he have? Where were they in the conversation yesterday, or come to think of it, while he was preoccupied south of my border? Bastard!

I could not believe it. When did life get so easy that someone could hand over three thousand dollars to a complete stranger for doing absolutely nothing, cheat on his wife and seem to have no conscience about it at all?

Feeling slightly used, not to mention, stupid, I decided to walk for a while to clear my head and make sense of what I had done. When I was too exhausted to walk any further, I hailed a cab and sank into the back seat. I took a deep breath and closed my eyes.

I can't believe I thought he might actually like me.

Back at the hotel, I put on a movie, but it was no use because my mind kept wandering back to Baileys. Frustrated, I accepted that he saw our liaison as a simple business transaction and told myself that I should too. I had called his bluff and it happened to pay off. Nobody got hurt, and it *definitely* would not happen again.

When I finally closed my eyes there was one thing leaving a bad taste in my mouth and a worse feeling in my stomach... he called me a "Pro!"

2

FRANKY PANKY
"YOU CAN TEACH AN OLD DOG NEW TRICKS"

After an hour sitting in my hotel room staring at my "Pro" cash, I decided I needed to do something to take my mind off yesterday, so I went downstairs to the bar, ordered a Mojito and tried to relax.

'Are you alone?' came a voice from behind me.

Can't a girl have a drink in peace?

I turned to see an older gentleman take the seat next to me, 'Do you mind if I join you?'

He looked sweet so I humoured him, 'Not at all. What brings a dashing young man like yourself to a town like this?'

'Cute!' he chuckled. 'Frank's the name,' he said extending his hand, 'I'm from the good 'ole USA.'

'Well, pleasure to meet you Frank from the USA. What are you doing so far from home?'

'I come here once in a while for work but it can get a little lonely for an 'ole guy like me, so it's nice to chat to a pretty young lady.'

'Well, thank you,' I said in my best American accent. 'What do you do here?'

'Finance. I live in New York, but my company has branches all over the world.'

'Sounds interesting.'

'Not really,' he chuckled, 'I send the young guns here mostly, but occasionally I tag along for the ride.'

The conversation with Frank was easy; he had a great sense of humour and a mischievous glint in his eyes. I told him that my name was Kat and that I was a fabric buyer for a clothing chain from the UK. I travelled a lot, and spent most of my time between Hong Kong, Singapore and China. He told me that he was seventy-six, and that he divorced twenty years ago. His three children were all grown and living happy, successful lives and despite his wealth, Frank confessed that he was very lonely. After almost two hours and a further three drinks, he invited me to dinner.

'I'm sorry Frank,' I said with honest regret, 'I already have plans.'

He sighed, 'That's a shame sweet pea, it's been lovely chatting with you.'

I smiled, 'Same.'

Suddenly he sprang to life, 'Say, what are your plans to-morrow evening? I have a boring 'ole work function and I hate to go to those things alone. What d'ya say we go together?' His eyes sparkled, 'we can spice it up a bit and pretend we are lovers,' he chuckled.

I was flattered, but I didn't really want to get stuck having dinner with a bunch of old men.

'Seriously, I'd be honoured if you accompany me. It would make my 'ole buddies real jealous,' he laughed.

I hesitated.

'I'll make it worth your while. Now please don't take this the wrong way, but I'm very, very rich, and it would give me great pleasure to pay you for your time if you'll be so kind as to escort me to the function.'

This can't be happening again…surely!

'Frank, I'm not an escort.'

'Don't be upset sweet pea, I'm not suggesting any hanky panky, just plain 'ole companionship, conversation, and lots of good food.'

Confused, I continued to stare at him, not quite sure if I was being filmed. I scanned the bar but did not notice any cameras or suspicious people listening in on us.

'How does a thousand US take your fancy?'

OMG. This is happening again! Is it me, or does everything literally have a price in Hong Kong?

I looked at Frank and his cheeky laughing eyes.

'You're serious about no hanky panky?'

'Absolutely.'

'You're definitely not expecting anything else?'

'No…no…of course not.'

I notice that he had his fingers crossed, 'Frank?'

He started to laugh, 'An 'ole man can dream can't he?' he winked and laughed so much that he almost fell off the stool.

I considered the offer as Frank continued to chuckle to himself. He was clearly amused, I on the other hand did not know whether to laugh or cry! Once Frank had stopped laughing, he placed his hand on mine, 'I'm sorry. I have a naughty sense of humour, and I understand if you say no.'

There go those heartstrings again! Why do I always feel sorry for people?

I looked at his hopeful eyes, 'Okay! What time do you need me?'

Frank's face lit up, 'Really sweet pea...you're gonna come?'

'Yes, I'm gonna come,' I smiled mimicking his accent. 'Do you have a business card, just in case something comes up and I can't make it?'

Frank handed me his card, we confirmed a time to meet and I left him a very happy man.

After a day of pampering, I met Frank at seven for our little rendezvous. He looked very dapper in his black suit, despite his white tube socks showing under his trousers. Linking arms, we walked into the function room and Frank found it hard to contain his excitement. He had concocted a story about how we had met online, and that he had been writing me love letters. I went along with his game, after all, I was the master at making up stories about people, and it made him so happy that I did not want to ruin his fun.

Four hours and lots of hand holding later, I was ready to leave, 'Frank, thank you for a wonderful evening. I'm going to call it a night.'

'Oh sweet pea, I've had an amazing time. How'd ya like to make an ole man really happy,' he asked as he pinched my bottom. 'What'd ya say we take this love affair upstairs? I don't bite ye know!

And there go the heartstrings again.

'Frank, you promised...no hanky panky!'

He looked sad.

'Frank, can I ask you a personal question?'

'Sure gorgeous, anythin' you want...shoot!'

'When did you last make love to a woman?'

'Oh now, sweet pea, let me think. I'm seventy-six,' his mind wandered off and I could see the sadness etched in his eyes. 'Huh, well that would be nineteen years ago, just after ma wife left me. Wanted to prove I still had it ye know? But it didn't last, I wanted love and she was just after ma money.'

I felt so sorry for him. I couldn't imagine living for nineteen years without the touch of another person and I was suddenly overwhelmed with an urge to give him that. He was so lovely, and he deserved some happiness, so I took his hand and led him into the elevator.

Inside his room, I told Frank to sit on the edge of the bed and then I walked over to him and planted a kiss on the top of his head, 'What do you want?'

'Can you take your clothes off?'

His eyes nearly popped out of his head as I slowly started to undress and teasingly lowered my knickers. I stood in front of him fully naked and took one of his hands. I guided his hand across my breasts and down to my crotch, placing it between my legs, allowing Frank to explore. Suddenly, he pulled away and started ripping his clothes off.

'Slow down tiger, we don't want you having a heart attack now do we?' I said half serious as I helped him to undress.

As Frank lay on the bed naked, I was pleasantly surprised with his physique. For an older man, I could see evidence of a muscular youth and although his penis was rather small, I considered it cute. I let my hands wander and starting at his chest I traced my fingers around his nipples before gently kissing each one. Finally trailing down to his groin, I found "little Frankie" which was very hard. When I clasped little

Frankie in my hand, I heard a gentle sob. I looked up and found that Frank had tears spilling down his cheeks, 'Frank what's wrong? Did I hurt you?'

'No angel, you're doing everythin' just right; I'm a soft 'ole man. You just keep doing your thing sweet pea.'

Still holding on to little Frankie, I placed my head back down between Frank's legs and started to kiss his inner thighs. After a couple of minutes of hand and mouth coordination, I held one of his little balls in my hand and just as I was about to move on Frank lost control.

Relieved to have narrowly escaped another "Semengate" incident, and to have avoided a potential heart attack situation, I couldn't help but feel a little sad that Frank had still not had sex. Frank on the other hand was overjoyed; he said he had not experienced anything like that before. I was sure he had; he probably just couldn't remember!

After a little cuddle, we took a shower together and I was soaping Frank the inevitable happened…he came again!

We both dressed and true to his word Frank gave me my money, plus extra for my handy work in the bedroom. We said our goodbyes and as I left Frank's hotel, I actually felt good. I had made an old man very happy, received two thousand US dollars and once again had not had sex!

Later that night I contemplated just what I was getting myself into. The money was amazing, but my moral conscience was not happy. So, after much thought I decided that this trip was a one-off, and having sex with random strangers for money would definitely *never* happen again.

3

GRANDMA: BOOBS AND BAUBLES

I threw my bag down and started to run a bath. The first day home after a trip is pretty much a write off, which is not good when you only have one day to rest. However, lucky for me I had three days off, so I planned to spend one day with my crazy, eccentric grandma.

I should tell you a little about Matilda Worthington, my beautiful gran. She is seventy-three years old, and you would never believe it. She zooms around town in a Mercedes convertible, works as a real estate agent, writes short stories for the local newspaper and knows everything about everyone in Sussex. Gran is the most fun, interesting, flamboyant, slightly eccentric person I know, and I love her dearly.

For the past thirty years, Gran has religiously spent every Thursday night in London with a girlfriend. Last week she was almost arrested for speeding and flirting with the police officer, but her efforts were wasted because he was gay. It was only when she mentioned that her handsome nephew was looking for a new partner, that he stopped writing her ticket!

Gran has always been a little wild. When Grandad was alive she would drive him crazy with her ever-changing plans to make money. One time, without telling him, Gran bought a farmhouse in Ireland. When Grandad asked her what gave her such a ludicrous idea, Gran's reply was, 'Stop being a stick in the mud darling! Ireland is so pretty and one day we can move there to dance and sing with the Irish folk. In the meantime, we can rent it out for pocket money.'

Grandad had to remind her that he was in his seventies and that he had no intention of moving to Ireland to dance with anyone! Despite this setback, it did not deter Gran. To appease Grandad, she sold the farmhouse but failed to tell him that she had invested the money in a ski chalet in France.

The following winter, when Gran finally confessed, Grandad reluctantly agreed to go and test it out. Gran hadn't skied in years but after five ski lessons with the most attractive instructor she could find, she was flying down the slopes. Unfortunately, there were a few casualties due to her uncontrollable speed, however a few mulled wines and apologies later Gran was in everyone's good books again. Grandad did have a chuckle when he told me that the resort put up a warning notice the next day asking skiers to: *Please consider your fellow skiers and ski with caution*. Then he whispered, 'Especially if you see a small grey-haired lady flying down the slope yelling, 'Oh darling isn't this wonderful.'

I loved my grandad but sadly a couple of years later he passed away unexpectedly, and I think that was a turning point for Gran. She had a new determination to live life, throw caution to the wind and have some fun. The first thing she did was sign up to study for her real estate license. I believe that the board let her do it thinking she was just a crazy old lady, but Gran surprised everyone, and within a year she had made the most sales out of all the agents in Sussex.

'Darling, how are you?' she beamed when she opened the door. 'Come inside dear and tell me all about your trip to Hong Kong.'

I gave Gran a hug and noticed there was something different about her, but I could not put my finger on it, 'Hi Gran, you look amazing. What have you been up to?'

'Well, it's funny you should mention it, one of my clients is a hairdresser and he's put some honey streaks in my hair, what do you think?'

'Your hair is beautiful, but it's not that. Let me look at you. I don't know...you just look...different?'

It's your boobs!

'I'm not sure what you are talking about darling,' she said turning away and sticking out her chest like a peacock!

'Gran! Oh my God! I knew it! You've had a boob job!' I screamed. 'Wow...look at the size of them!'

'Now now dear, don't get all in a tizzy. I'm just experimenting.'

'Gran this isn't something you just "experiment" with. I mean, they look fantastic but are you sure you *needed* them?'

'Darling, you know that your grandaddy and I didn't have much of a sex life. Well, since he's been gone, I have been itching to get out there and see what all the fuss is about.'

Oh gosh, I'm not sure I want to hear this.

'One does not want to embark on a new love affair with breasts that say hello to one's belly button darling! Anyway, a dear friend suggested a "lift" and as you can see the results are amazing...I'm not even wearing a bra!'

Slightly bewildered, I followed Gran into her conservatory.

'Darling stop looking so worried. I'm very excited about dating again, and I have been reading some interesting things on the internet about the two P's.'

Two P's?

Gran noticed my confused expression, 'Durr! Positions and piercing! My lord, who would think one would pierce one's clitoris?' she said as though talking about a clitoris to your granddaughter was the most natural thing in the world. 'Isn't that amazing dear? I know what a clitoris is! Your poor grandaddy would have thought that it was a new form of arthritis! Poor darling!'

Don't listen Grandad.

'Anyway, apparently a clitoral orgasm is incredible. I've heard that your whole body shudders like an electric shock,' she giggled. 'Oh darling listen to me, you probably know exactly what I'm talking about, a young girl like you. I bet you've had to straighten your hair you've had so many!'

Not until recently.

'Not quite!'

'Oh dear, having a bit of a dry spell are we darling? Tell me about something else then; you know how I love to hear stories about your trips. Did you meet anyone in Hong Kong?'

In some strange way, I think that my gran has been living her sex life vicariously through me over the years. Now that I look back, she always asks me to tell her everything that happens to me on a date and I mean everything! (I obviously forgot to mention all the earth-shattering orgasms I have been having!) I indulge her because I know it makes her happy, and I often elaborate to make it a bit more interesting.

As we headed off to our favourite little restaurant for lunch, I considered telling Gran the truth about my trip, but

I decided it was best only to tell her a little about Frank, 'So anyway, he invited me to a corporate event and told everyone that I was his lover. We had so much fun Gran and at the end of the night he asked me up to his room.'

Her eyes were like saucers, 'Darling how adventurous! Tell me what happened next, did you see it?'

'Did I see what?'

'You know! His…. thingy.'

'Gran if you're going to have sex with men, you'll have to stop calling a penis a thingy,' I laughed. 'Yes, he did take his clothes off, and before I could do anything he sort of… you know!'

'Know what dear?'

'Came.'

'Came where?'

Oh dear.

The penny dropped, 'Oh, he ejaculated?'

'Yes Gran.'

'Silly me, of course! The poor, poor little man. How awful to have a beautiful girl like you ready for action and then failing to deliver the goods. Well, he certainly delivered, but a little early wouldn't you say?'

'Oh Gran stop it! He was so cute. You know, he hasn't made love for almost twenty years?'

'Oh that's interesting, twenty years you say? Do you have his number darling?' she said with a wink.

You would eat him alive.

'Don't look at me like that darling. You never know, I may fancy a bit of that myself. Mind you, I doubt he'd know where the clitoris is either and that's all I need…an early starter trying to find my little bean of ecstasy,' she sighed.

I nearly choked on my champagne, 'Gran what have you been reading?' We both laughed so hard that I had to grab her before she fell off her chair.

After lunch we headed back to Gran's house. I fixed my hair (she insists on driving at ninety mph with the top down), kissed her goodbye and promised to see her when I got back from Los Angeles.

4

LA: FLIGHT OF FANCY

I love L.A! Every time I go to Los Angeles something exciting happens to me, so when I left for the airport and my stomach started to tingle, I wasn't surprised.

Walking into the cabin crew briefing room I felt excitement in the air, 'Gary what's going on?'

'Just the usual! Silly girls getting all in a tizzy about a VIP.'

I was about to ask him who it was when the supervisor popped her head out of the briefing room, 'Everybody come in and sit down please. I have an important announcement.'

Once we were all seated, she continued, 'If you haven't already heard, we have Mr Thorsen on board today. So, it goes without saying that I want you *all* on your best behaviour.'

'Sex on legs Thorsen!' giggled Amanda. 'Yummy!'

Stacey was just as excited, 'Do you think he's staying in our hotel? I wouldn't mind getting myself a bit of Aussie meat.' She turned to Amanda and whispered, 'Did you hear that he slept with that Laura girl from Leeds and apparently paid her ten thousand quid to keep quiet?'

The supervisor glared at the girls to silence them, and then looked at me, 'Beth, you are on top today.'

Stacey burst out laughing, 'I bet miss frigid arse would like to be on top.'

A chorus of giggles ran through the room until the supervisor clapped her hands, 'Everyone calm down please! Stacey, you are skating on thin ice.' She looked at me, 'Beth, I know that I can count on *your* discretion and professionalism to take care of Mr Thorsen. On the other hand, Stacey, Amanda, you two are down the back and I don't want you to take one step into First Class unless you have to. Do you understand?'

Both girls nodded and Amanda elbowed Stacey, 'Bloody hell, you should have kept your mouth shut.'

I suddenly felt nervous. Usually I don't get flustered meeting our VIPs but let me tell you a little about James Thorsen. Although we are a British run Airline, Jay (as he likes to be called) is a real, grow 'em big and strong Australian. An ex-triathlete and all-time superstar, he decided to switch careers at the age of thirty-five and after applying the same dedication and commitment that he had given to his sport, he became a huge success in Australian aviation.

Jay is six feet two inches of pure gorgeousness. Being an ex-athlete, he has square shoulders, long legs and strong arms. With a tan of a surfer, his sun-kissed, light brown hair curls at the bottom, and his green, almond-shaped eyes remind me of a tiger. His full juicy lips compliment beautiful straight teeth, and his strong jaw could rival Brad Pitts any day. Jay exudes masculinity, he is confident but not arrogant and people love him. Overall, he's the most beautiful man that I have ever seen and I'm not the only one to think so. He has held the top spot on the UK and Australian list of "most eligible bachelors" for a couple of years running, although technically he isn't eligible. It's well known that he has been in a relationship with his girlfriend since high school.

Jay's personality won him global celebrity status, and with his looks and obvious charm he very quickly became the "face of the airline." Renowned for always being up for a laugh, he gets involved in some pretty unusual promotional campaigns.

When I first saw Jay, I was mesmerised. I was working as part of the public relations team at a promotional event in Sydney and even though I didn't actually speak to him that night, our eyes met across the room for about ten seconds. It felt magnetic how his eyes drew me in, and I experienced a strange sensation as if we were both suspended in time despite everything else moving around us. I had never encountered anything like it before and my attraction to him took me by such surprise that I made a conscious effort to avoid him for the rest of the evening. Just thinking about it gave me goose-bumps and explained my sudden bout of nervousness.

When we boarded the plane, I left the crew to their pre-flight duties and went upstairs to check on the flight deck. The Captain smiled at me, 'We've got the big boss on board today Beth, you ready for him?'

'Sure,' I lied. 'A passenger is a passenger to me, doesn't matter who it is. It'll be a breeze.'

'Well, that's if you can keep the rest of the crew away from him it will be,' he laughed.

The first officer joined in, 'Yeah, good luck with that. He's a babe magnet!'

I pretended to be cross, 'Come on you two, it's bad enough I've got the crew gossiping and drooling over him without you both stirring the pot.'

Once I had my orders from the flight crew, I left them laughing amongst themselves, closed the door behind me and made my way to the stairs. I was just about to step down onto the second step when my heel caught on a loose thread in the carpet, and suddenly I couldn't stop myself from falling. I screamed and tried to grab the rail but missed and grabbed onto the shoulders of the passenger coming up the stairs. He had his head down so didn't see me coming, but he certainly felt me because within seconds we were both at the bottom of the stairs and I had flattened him!

'Whoa, what in the…?' he started to say, sounding a little frustrated.

As I struggled to get off him, I kept my eyes closed and my head down. My head-on collision had an Australian accent.

Oh no! Please don't let it be him.

His tone softened, 'Just a minute, stop wriggling, we seem to be tangled somewhere.'

'Oh gosh, I'm so sorry sir,' I murmured too embarrassed to look up.

He managed to free my belt buckle from his trousers, 'Do you greet all your passengers like that, or am I just special?' he said, pulling me up.

I tentatively opened one eye, then the other, and was confronted by the whitest set of teeth that I had ever seen. I stared at his lips.

'Are you alright mate?' he asked sounding a little concerned.

Oh my god, I could kiss those lips all day.

I looked up and found myself staring into the same tiger eyes that I had seen before.

Those eyes!

'Wait a minute…I know who you are,' he said with a huge grin, 'Beth, right?'

I was shaken out of my trance, 'Oh gosh, yes sir. I really am so sorry. I caught my heel on the carpet and…'

He seemed amused, 'Hey, no worries! I don't think anything is broken and luckily it was me who you landed on and not some other poor unsuspecting passenger.'

My eyes wandered back to his lips.

'Besides, it's quite nice to have someone like you throwing themselves my way.'

Is he flirting with me?

I looked into his eyes that were twinkling with mischief, 'You aren't hurt are you?'

He laughed, 'We build 'em strong in Australia you know; it would take more than a little tumble to hurt a fella like me! But thanks for asking. Now you head off to wherever it was you were going. I'm sure I can find my seat.'

I turned to walk away, and he put his hand on my arm, 'Oh, and Beth.'

'Yes?'

His eyes burned into mine as he lowered his voice to a whisper, 'Please try not to fall on anyone else today!'

I was mesmerised.

Gary clapped his hands, making me jump, 'Beth, you heard Mr Thorsen! Now get a move on!'

Mortified by what had happened and a little confused as to how Jay knew who I was, I hadn't noticed that the back of my skirt had wrapped itself up around my waist.

'Bloody hell Beth, sort yourself out! You're showing your arse to half of B Zone,' laughed Gary.

I quickly dived into the nearest toilet to regain my composure.

That could only happen to me...why the hell hadn't I put any knickers on today of all days?

I looked in the mirror and mimicked my mother, 'You know Elizabeth; one should always wear clean underwear. One just never knows when one may have an accident and you really don't want to be caught without a good pair of clean briefs.'

When I came out of the toilet, it was to the applause of all the passengers that had no doubt seen my bum, so I decided it was better to face it with a curtsy rather than to get defensive about it. That seemed to go down well until someone shouted, 'Now show us ye tits love.'

'Great!' I mumbled as I retreated into the galley.

'Sweetie, you really should at least wear a G-string. I mean, who do you think you are, a bleedin' celebrity? It's enough to put me off my lunch. And by the way, your runway could do with a trim!'

'Oh shut up Gary!'

When I sat down for take-off, I ignored the giggles of the passengers facing me and I started to daydream about Jay; his piercing green eyes, his lips, and the energy I felt rush through my body when his hand touched my arm. I was brought back down to earth by the ringing of the phone next to me. It was Gary, 'Beth, stop bleedin' daydreaming and get on with the service announcement. I don't know what's gotten into you today but get your act together....and keep your legs shut!'

I could hear his laugh echoing through the cabin as I slammed the phone down.

Eight hours later, with only a couple of hours left before we reached Los Angeles, I went downstairs to make myself a cup of tea in the galley. My thoughts turned to Jay. I hadn't seen much of him during the flight because every time I walked past to check on the flight deck, he had his head buried in his laptop.

I wonder what it would be like to be in a relationship with James Thorsen. Would he ever put me before his work, or even have time for sex? Oh my God, that would be depressing to be with someone as hot as him and not have much sex.

'There you are!'

His voice startled me. I jumped and spilled my tea on my hand.

Shit!

'Struth mate, are you okay? Here, let me help you.'

Jay took my hand and held it under the cold tap. Shockwaves ran through my body when he placed his other hand on my lower back. I couldn't bring myself to look at him, but I could feel his eyes searching my face. After a couple of minutes, I found the intensity of our chemistry too much and pulled away, 'Thanks, I think I'm okay now.'

'Come here,' he said, smiling as he took my wet hand and dried it with a towel.

Just being so close to him was making me feel dizzy, so I kept my eyes fixed on his chest, watching it rise and fall with every breath. It was hypnotic.

When Jay finished drying my hand, he placed the towel on the galley bench and turned to look at me.

Why are you just standing there staring at me?

'Was there something you needed Mr Thorsen?'

His lips curled up into a sexy smile, 'No.'

'No?'

He stepped closer to me, not taking his eyes off mine, naughtiness dancing in his pupils, 'I got *everything* I needed… thanks.'

When Jay pulled the curtain back and left the galley, Gary rushed in, 'What the bloody hell was that?'

'You heard that?'

'Of course I bloody did. I saw it too! I couldn't come into the galley for fear of electrocution. The energy was insane! I thought for a minute he was going to rip your knickers off right here.'

'Gary, don't be so stupid.'

'True story! But then I remembered…'

'Remembered what?'

'You aren't bleedin' wearing any!'

After clearing customs, I stepped onto the crew bus for the short fifteen-minute ride to our hotel and I was ready for a drink. The mood was light, and not surprisingly my bum was the butt of all the jokes, but I didn't mind because my mind was on someone else…Jay Thorsen!

Once I checked into the hotel, I walked into my room and was surprised to see the little message light flashing on my phone. I dialled 0.

'Hi, (pause) Beth it's Jay here. Oh, sorry, Mr. Thorsen.'

Nooo way!

'I'm attending an event at the Skybar in West Hollywood tonight and I would like to invite the crew along. It starts at eight, but you guys can come anytime. (Pause) It would be nice to see you all there. You can get the address from reception. It's casual so no need to dress up. See you later (pause) hopefully!'

My stomach did a flip!

This is insane! Why is he calling me and not the supervisor? Shit, maybe Gary is right!

I jumped in the shower feeling like a ridiculously giddy teenager, and despite Jay saying it was casual, I decided to make a bit of an effort and dress up. Once I was ready, I headed downstairs to tell the crew.

'Fanbloodytastic! Free drinks tonight!' squealed a delighted Scott.

'I'm not going; we've just worked our arses off for ten bleedin' hours,' moaned Gary.

'Come on spoilsport, please come with us. It'll be fun, and if it's boring we'll take off and head back to a bar in Santa Monica,' I said as enthusiastically as I could without sounding too keen.

'Well, I'm definitely going,' smirked Amanda. 'I wouldn't mind getting myself some prime Aussie meat tonight.'

'No way biatch, if anyone's getting a piece of his arse tonight, it'll be me,' retorted Stacey.

While we waited for the girls to get changed into something more "fitting for the occasion," I tried to persuade Gary to join us, 'Come on Gary, if anything, just watching Amanda and Stacey will be entertaining enough.'

'Sad bitches…if only they knew that he was in love with you,' he smirked.

'Stop it! He has a girlfriend!'

Gary looked at me with a smug look on his face, 'Well… maybe it's time he found a *wife*!'

When we arrived at the bar we were immediately escorted inside and given our own private booth in the VIP area. The view of Los Angeles twinkling in the night sky was incredible and as a live band played on the stage nearby, I soaked up the vibrant atmosphere. Within minutes a man dressed in black and wearing a small earpiece approached our booth. He had a thick Southern accent, 'Hi y'all. I'm Brad and I'll be your server for this evening. Would y'all like some Champagne?'

Gary jumped out of his seat, 'I think I speak for all of us when I say yes, yes and yes please.'

Brad smiled, 'I'll be right back.'

Six bottles of champagne later, Gary was ignoring me in favour of talking to Brad, so I decided to take a walk. We had been at the party for over two hours and I still hadn't caught sight of Jay. One thing I had noticed was that Stacey and Amanda had disappeared about thirty minutes after we arrived, and I was sure that when I found them, I would most likely find Jay!

My attempt to tell Gary I was going for a walk fell on deaf ears, so I ventured out into the pool area. At the other end of the pool, I entered a small doorway that led into a huge garden terrace. It was beautiful; fairy lights complimented the flowering walls, and guests sat in little nooks scattered around the terrace. As a blues band played softly in the background, I couldn't help but think that I had stepped into a secret, magical garden. I wandered around for a few minutes and found a little spot with a spectacular view of the Los Angeles night sky. Accepting a glass of champagne from a passing waiter, I took a moment to appreciate my life and thought once again about how fortunate I was to be doing my job.

Suddenly I felt butterflies in my stomach, and I sensed him coming before I heard his now familiar voice, 'Are you enjoying yourself?'

Feeling Jay's breath on my neck sent a tingle down my spine. I turned and smiled, 'It's a wonderful party. Thanks for the invite,' I averted his eyes for fear of giving something away. 'The crew are really enjoying themselves too.'

'Well, sometimes these things need a little spicing up and I figured you guys would do that this evening. Mind you, it's pretty lively out there anyway.' He leant into me and whispered, 'You know I have a huge bruise on my arse from our little fall today.'

Shocked and surprised at his comment, I quickly turned and almost headbutted him.

'Whoa, easy tiger,' he said stepping back.

'Sorry...I didn't mean to...' I could feel myself blushing, 'Are you serious about the bruise? Is it painful? I've never fallen before and...'

'Beth, relax! I'm just yankin' your chain. I'm fine. I'm actually more worried about you. Maybe I should have uniforms look at those high heels they have you girls in and change them. We don't want you just falling on anybody do we?'

There it is again, that cheeky "do you think I'm the sexiest man alive" glint in his eye.

'Oh, no, we certainly don't want that!'

Only if it's you.

I finally relaxed as we both stood in silence looking at the view. It was strange how comfortable it felt standing next to him; it was as though I was safe now, protected in some way. I hadn't felt anything like this before with anyone and I was wondering if Jay felt the same way. He interrupted my thoughts, 'You know I actually really like LA. I always have fun here. What about you Beth, what do you like?'

I told Jay about my love for the ocean and my dream of one day waking up every morning to the sound of the waves. He talked about the beaches in Australia, and how much he loved going home; he told me about his childhood and asked me about mine. When I told him stories about my gran he laughed out loud, 'I'd love to meet her one day.'

I looked into his eyes and just as I was about to reply, we were interrupted.

'Eeeeliiiizzzzabbetthhhhhh.... I can see you.'

We both turned to see Stacey heading towards us.

'HEY, what are *you* doing over there with Mr Thorsen?' Stacey stood in-between Jay and I and placed her hand on Jay's chest, 'Well, hello boss! Thanks for the partaaay, it's fab!'

Jay looked amused but Stacey didn't seem to notice, 'You look bloody lovely tonight Mr Thorsen. Do you want to come back to my...?'

'Stacey! Move away from the steak, he's mine!'

Amanda!

Jay raised his eyebrows, 'Steak?' he mouthed to me.

I shrugged my shoulders, 'Girls, that's enough!' I said stepping in front of Jay, 'I think it's time I got you both out of here.'

'But I'm hungry,' Stacey said winking at Jay.

'No, you're not!' I said almost too defensively. 'You need a strong coffee...and a cold shower. Come on!' I said pulling them both away.

Amanda tried to break free, 'Who are you? The sex Police?'

'In this case...YES!'

I could hear Jay laughing as I marched them off, and just as we approached the door I turned around and mouthed goodnight. He winked and mouthed, 'Thank you.'

Oh, my heart.

As we made our way through the pool area, I caught sight of Gary in the corner making out with beautiful Brad, so the girls and I left the party and got into a cab.

The ride home was a blur because all I could think about was the undeniable chemistry that I had felt between Jay and I...and this time it wasn't just sexual. The strong sense of peace I felt when we were standing together in silence, was intense!

'Oy Beth, what were you and sex on legs talking about?' asked Stacey.

Amanda sounded angry, 'Yeah, you seemed pretty cosy back there. Anything you want to tell us miss frigid arse?'

I looked at both of them, 'Just keeping it professional girls...someone has to!'

Once the girls were back in their rooms, I thought about going back to the party. Jay had told me that he was leaving for Las Vegas the following morning and I had no idea when I would see him again. I looked at the clock and it was one am. I doubted he would even still be there, so I decided against going. Instead, I took a shower, climbed into bed, and as my head hit the pillow, one face kept coming into my mind...Jay Thorsen!

5

RUBY: BFF

Back in the UK, I caught up with my best friend Ruby. Coming from a very privileged background, the constant rebel almost lost her inheritance at seventeen when she declared she was going to be a flight attendant. To appease her disgruntled grandparents, she finished her degree in public relations, however, the very next day she marched straight into her favourite airline's head office, and told *them* why she should have a job... and basically wouldn't leave until they gave her one.

Ruby likes to portray a tough exterior to the outside world and she has an air of aloofness about her that not many people understand. Physically blessed with a perfect body and exquisite looks, she answers to no one and leaves a trail of broken hearts wherever she goes. She picks her friends wisely, doesn't suffer fools gladly, and she is definitely not someone that you would want to cross.

Ruby and I have been best friends for seventeen years and despite her toughness, I happen to know the *real* Ruby. The Ruby that only a chosen few get to see; the vulnerable, kind woman with a heart of gold, high morals, and someone who is fiercely loyal and protective of the people she loves.

Despite the family wealth, Ruby's childhood was challenging due to her mother remarrying five times. Her biological father left before she was born, and Ruby fell totally in love with her first stepfather. When the marriage broke down after nine years, Ruby was broken-hearted and left feeling totally abandoned. From that day on, the other men did not stand a chance. She built a wall around her heart and at the tender age of ten years old Ruby declared that she would never love another man for the rest of her life.

When it comes to her job, Ruby is the ultimate professional who takes her role as supervisor very seriously. Despite her tough love approach to the crew, she is well liked and respected in the company. Privately, I consider her the drama queen of flying because every time I see her after a trip she delights me with her tales of "Hellish passengers and drunken crew."

After the latest dramas were unveiled, we headed off to the gym. Ruby is bordering on fanatical when it comes to exercise and she is devoted to maintaining her, self-labelled, 'beautifully crafted body.' She detests laziness and is very opinionated when it comes to people taking care of themselves.

One of the craziest memories I have of this is when we were in Miami together and we saw an obese man eating a cheeseburger at a bar. Ruby was so disgusted that she refused to get in a cab home and instead, insisted on running two kilometres back to the hotel, 'If that fat bastard won't do something about it, then I bloody well will,' she ranted. 'Beth, get out of the fucking cab and run! I saw how many margaritas you had tonight. Do you know how many calories are in those things?' After a few tunes of Rocky and a succession of air punches she finally lost it, 'Stop laughing at me and get out!

Did you see how disgusting he was? He should be having a tummy tuck, not a bloody cheeseburger!'

Highly amused, I asked the cab driver to stay with her until we reached our hotel. I was exhausted just hanging out the window, but not Ruby, 'There,' she said as I paid the driver, 'that's burnt off a couple of hundred calories. I'm not happy with *you* young lady, so I'll see you tomorrow. Gym at seven! No excuses…and Beth…NO sneaking to breakfast before!'

When we finally reached the gym, Ruby looked at me slightly concerned, 'Beth, we are going to work hard today. I didn't want to mention it but you're getting a bit of a muffin top, and if you're going to be seen with me *that's* got to go… get it?'

Ignoring her remarks, I walked towards the weights room only to be pulled in the direction of the cardio equipment and ordered to get on a treadmill.

'This first!'

I decided not to argue with her, after all, things never changed with Ruby, I often thought she'd missed her vocation in life and that she should be heading up some military operation somewhere, kicking guy's arses, swearing her head off and shagging everyone on the side.

I saluted her as I stepped on the treadmill, 'Bloody hell Rubes do we have to go this fast? I'm not as fit as you remember?'

'Stop whinging! Do you think I look this good by whinging? No! I work hard! Stop being so bloody soft Beth,' she yelled.

The women in front turned around and looked at me sympathetically.

'Now pay attention. As you run, I want you to visualise your muffin top disappearing and at the same time say the words, "My fat is melting, my muffin top is gone!" That can be your new mantra.'

I pushed the stop button to catch my breath, 'Are you serious? I haven't got the energy to run, never mind talk to myself as I do, besides people are staring at us.'

'Who cares? Let them stare! I AM A GODDESS with a beautiful body,' she yelled even louder.

'Yeah and you've got a mouth that dribbles shit,' came a voice from the treadmill behind.

We both turned to see Alex, his chiselled body dripping sweat. Ruby had fancied Alex for almost a year now and despite flirting outrageously with one another, neither of them had dared to do anything about it. I found this very strange on Ruby's part because usually when she sees someone she likes, she attacks her target in five minutes and she has more notches on her bedpost than any man I have ever met.

Excellent! My excuse to do a quick exit.

'Why don't you two just cut the crap and go and have a shag?' I said as I grabbed my towel and ran in the direction of the changing rooms, leaving Ruby with Alex to sort it out.

Ruby came into the changing rooms five minutes later, 'Got a date then?' I asked.

'Of course.'

'About bloody time!'

'Don't they say that the best things come to those that wait?'

'He's okay, but I wouldn't say he's the best,' I laughed.

'Not him darling…me!'

We spent the evening at Ruby's sitting in our PJ's, drinking wine and chatting. At this point I did not know how much I could confide in Ruby about everything going on in my life. I mean, how do you tell your best friend, 'Hey guess what happened to me, I sort of had sex with two men for money. Oh, and by the way, I'm falling in love with our boss, yes, you know the one, big hunky Aussie with a girlfriend!'

I weighed up my options and decided that being judged by Ruby was not on my agenda just yet. I still had to get my own mind around what I had done, and what I was possibly about to do, so I kept quiet.

At midnight we both fell into bed, happy, relaxed and a little tipsy.

The next two weeks passed rather uneventfully, except that Ruby was well and truly over Alex, who she had renamed, 'The prick with a dick!' Apparently after they did the deed, he bragged about it to all the guys in the gym and showed them photos that he had taken with a secret camera.

Ruby was beyond livid, 'Now I'll have to change gyms because of that fucking moron. I mean who bloody well does that? I can't believe he had a fucking secret camera. I should sue his scheming hairy arse...did I tell you he looked like a fucking gorilla from the waist down?' Ruby always likes to express herself but today she was really letting off steam, 'I've got a good mind to go down to that gym and take a picture of his little dick. You know it's not *all that*.'

'Rubes don't lower yourself to his standard. Maybe look on the bright side, at least now everybody knows that you have an awesome body.'

'That's not the point *Beth!* I say who sees my body, not a fucking hairy loser with a small dick!'

After listening to Ruby rant on for another ten minutes, I hung up the phone and started to think about relationships and what direction I wanted to take my life in. Despite always dreaming of being in a happy marriage, having kids and a lovely home, I was starting to question whether I really wanted a serious relationship with anyone, let alone my boss.

My experience in Hong Kong had opened up a world of new possibilities, a world that excited me. I now had the ability to make lots of money, have sex with no commitment, no dramas, and no questions asked.

I closed my eyes and imagined how my life could be. However, no matter how enticing it seemed, I knew that I was fighting an internal battle; I wasn't fully convinced that I could live with my moral conscience and pull off a secret life.

When I finally turned off my lamp, one face came into my mind...the one thing I couldn't seem to turn off at the moment...Jay Thorsen!

6

NEW YORK, NEW YORK
SO GOOD I CAME TWICE

Two days later I was back on board and on my way to New York. The flight had been a little challenging due to take off delays, so after dealing with angry passengers and sick children, I was relieved when we finally arrived.

Inside my hotel room, I noticed an envelope sitting on my bedside table. I opened it and my mood quickly changed; It was an invitation to a party being held by one of the Airlines corporate clients. I quickly called the other crew members to ask who was coming and arranged for everyone to meet downstairs in one hour to share a cab.

When the cab pulled up at the address, we were all a little surprised, as it didn't look like the usual venue for corporate events; it looked like a scary old house. Not really sure what to do, we decided to check it out. After standing at the gate for a minute, I noticed an intercom and decided to push the button.

A threatening voice boomed out of the intercom, 'Password?'

We all jumped.

I cleared my throat, 'Sorry to disturb you, but we have an invitation for the party tonight and...'

'Bottom right-hand corner of the invitation, five-digit code, what is it?'

I turned to the crew, 'Does anyone have the invitation with them?'

'Here, I've got mine,' said Pip, 'it says S 3 X Y.'

'But that's only four digits.' I said.

Scary Voice softened his tone, 'It means you guys are VIPs. Come through the gate, walk up to the door on the left side of the house and get your stamp.'

Excited, and a little apprehensive, we walked toward what I would now call a mansion and were met at the door by two of the biggest security men that I have ever seen. They gave us each a bracelet to wear, which enabled access into all the VIP areas and unlimited free drinks.

The exterior of the mansion betrayed the beautifully decorated interior, and I was keen to explore. As Pip and I wandered from floor to floor we discovered that each floor had a different vibe.

The dark and sultry looking basement had lots of small, round tables, scattered around a tiny stage area, where the band was playing blues music.

The first floor was dedicated to the 1970s, where partygoers danced under the glow of a huge disco ball.

On the second floor, we found ourselves surrounded by couples making out on lush sofas with huge, red, velvet cushions. The air smelled of sweat as people gyrated slowly together to the sound of RnB.

The vibe on the third floor was intense and this was where the action was really happening... Salsa! Men threw women around the dance floor with passion, and the sexual tension in the air was palpable. This was by far my favourite floor, so I made a mental note to come back later.

When we reached the fourth floor, two guards stood at the base of the stairs. Bouncer one stepped forward, stopping us in our tracks, 'Can we help you ladies?'

'What's up there?' asked Pip.

He smirked, 'This is what we call our "private" area.'

I wiggled my bracelet, 'That's okay, we are VIPs.'

He leant down towards my face and whispered, 'It's reserved for *other types* of guests, if you know what I mean!'

I had no idea what he meant, 'Not really! Can we take a look?'

'Let me make myself clear, unless you girls want some "action" this place ain't for you. Do you get my drift?'

Bouncer two laughed.

Pip was getting bored and wanted to head back downstairs, 'Come on Beth, let's go. B1 and B2 clearly want us to leave.'

I told Pip that I would catch her up, and after she left I continued with my interrogation, 'Are people having sex up there...or doing drugs?'

B1 shook his head, 'Little lady, take my advice and scoot back to where the good girls hang out.'

'Why won't you tell me what's going on up there?'

'Why do you want to know?'

'Just curious that's all.'

'Don't you know that curiosity killed the cat?'

'Actually, *this* Kat has nine lives,' I said, smiling to myself.

His tone turned serious, 'Well if you wanna keep it that way, take your pretty, little, curious ass off with your friend, and don't worry about this floor okay?'

Feeling defeated, I retreated gracefully and made my way back to the Salsa room, but my curiosity was getting the better of me and I was itching to know what was going on upstairs. I decided to poke around a bit and look for someone who may be able to tell me.

About an hour later, I sat next to an extremely drunk girl who was trying to get someone to take her home...or so I thought.

'Are you okay, do you need a ride somewhere?' I asked.

'Nope. I need to get upstairs... that's what I need.'

'What *is* upstairs?'

She took another sip of her drink, 'The answer to my bills honey.'

I was getting frustrated, 'Why won't anyone give me a straight answer?'

She eyed me suspiciously, 'You ain't a cop are you?'

'No, absolutely not, I'm a flight attendant.'

'A trolley dolly hey? You wouldn't happen to know any wealthy first-class flyers here that may want to take me upstairs for some first-class fun, would you?'

Upstairs must be some type of brothel.

'You're a prostitute?'

'Not exactly, I'm a lawyer! Well, I will be when I graduate.'

'But you have sex for money?'

'Doesn't make me a prostitute honey. I prefer to call myself an escort.'

'Isn't it the same thing?'

'Like I said, not exactly. Now if you do meet any fancy men who want some fun, send 'em my way. I need the money.'

'How much are we talking here?'

'What's it to you honey? Are you interested?' she said, checking me out. 'I don't usually do pussy but desperate times call for desperate measures. You hear me?'

'Actually I'm not interested, I'm just curious.'

'Well, you know what they say.... curiosity killed the cat.'

'So I've heard,' I said dryly.

Suddenly her face lit up, 'Hey, we could do a threesome.'

'I don't think so.'

'Why?' she said pursing her lips in my face. 'Aren't I hot enough for you? We could split it, five hundred each.'

'You get a *thousand dollars* for sex?'

'No, that's for two girls, single is usually five hundred to seven hundred, depending on if you'll do anal.'

I was disgusted and intrigued at the same time.

'Why all these questions honey? Are *you* a Pro?'

Apparently, according to Baileys!

'No. Like I said, I'm just curious.'

'Sure you are dolly...now if you're not interested, quit wasting my time and let me find a man.'

I decided to go back to B1 and ask him a few more questions. He shook his head when he saw me approach, 'Didn't I make myself clear before?'

'Yes, but now I know what goes on up here and I want to know what a girl needs to do to get some action?'

Realising that I wasn't going to go away he obliged, 'Well, you can bring your own client and give the management ten per cent for the room, or you can speak to someone about getting clients, but then they kinda own you, so it's not a good idea 'cos they take fifty per cent of your earnings.'

'I see! And is there a number I need to call to book a room?'

'Nope, you just show up. If the room's available it's yours, if it's not…it's not.'

Satisfied, but not quite sure why I was so interested, I returned to Pip and the rest of the crew on the RnB floor.

Two hours later, I fancied a change of scenery and went alone to Salsa.

'Hey trolley dolly!'

I turned to see the girl I was talking to earlier coming towards me.

Bloody wish I hadn't told her my job!

'There you are! I found a guy who wants a threesome. Look, the sexy Latino over there.' She pointed at a beautiful looking man, 'Is he hot or what?'

Wow!

'Yes he is, but I've never had a threesome before, or been with a girl for that matter.'

'It's okay; you don't have to do anything to me. I'll do all the work, I promise! Like I said, I really need the cash. Besides, I think you're kinda hot.'

I laughed, 'Thanks…I think!'

She took my arm, 'We only have the room for an hour, so we better get going. By the way, my name's Julia.'

I tried to mutter an objection, but it was too late, within seconds I was shaking hands with the 'Latino.'

'Yeah she'll do,' he said looking me up and down.

She'll do? Cheeky bastard!

Julia noticed my reaction to his comment and quickly whispered, 'Don't take offence, they all say that!'

As we walked past B1 and his sidekick at the bottom of the steps, I shrugged my shoulders. B1 shook his head and laughed.

Julia turned to me, 'Hey! I forgot to ask...what's your name?'

I hesitated for a fraction, 'Kat...my name is Kat!'

She laughed, 'Meowwwwww!'

Inside the room I was pleasantly surprised. The interior was luxurious, and mirrors surrounded a huge circular bed in the centre of the room. Julia took my hand and as she led me towards the shower she whispered, 'Red button on the left-hand side of the bed...see it?'

'Yes.'

'If *anything* turns nasty, I mean *anything*, you push that button okay? Don't think about it... just push it. But don't worry, the "Sams" who usually come here are pretty good boys, they like to come back. It's just for an emergency.'

A bit more frightened than I was two minutes before, I was told to undress and pushed into a huge shower room. After a couple of minutes, I started to relax as the three of us exchanged a few kisses between lathery strokes. Admittedly, I was very aroused as I discovered that being washed by somebody who wasn't in his seventies was quite erotic. By the time we made it to the bed I was eager to try something new.

Julia took control and pushed me onto the bed on my back. Taking me by surprise, she kissed me passionately on the lips then let her mouth find my nipples and work their way down to my "pussy" as she calls it. I could see that Mr Latino was getting quite excited by our display, and as I laid back and enjoyed Julia, he took advantage of her from behind. I was enjoying it so much that I had an orgasm straight away.

Julia removed herself from the Latino and lay down on the bed. She continued to direct me, and as we moved from position to position, I couldn't believe how erotic it was. When

Mr Latino entered me, Julia fondled my breasts and continued to kiss me passionately on the mouth. I felt wave after wave of ecstasy surge through my body as I had my second orgasm.

Julia decided she wanted what I was getting, so she promptly positioned herself in front of Latino's face and whispered for me to, 'Finish him off with a hand job.' I had to hand it to her, she knew what she wanted, and she wasn't afraid to ask.

The sex was fantastic because Mr Latino was an incredibly experienced lover, and Julia was true to her word that I didn't have to go near her, except to touch her breasts occasionally to make it look authentic.

At the end of the hour I'd had great sex, two orgasms and made four hundred and fifty dollars! In the real-world people like Ruby did that for free, so I didn't feel bad, just very excited and pretty happy about my decision to give it a go.

As we left the room, Julia asked if I was in town the following night because she wanted to hook me up with someone as a "Thank you." (Apparently, Latino wouldn't do it without another girl and if I hadn't been there she wouldn't have been able to pay her rent). Still drunk and on a bit of a post coital high, I said yes and agreed to meet Julia at the club at seven pm the following evening for a few drinks beforehand.

I walked back to the crew and just caught them as they were leaving. Pip looked concerned, 'Hey Beth, I've been looking everywhere for you. I was worried, where did you go?'

I smiled to myself. 'I was upstairs doing salsa with a local Latino.'

She linked my arm, 'Was he hot?'

'Scorching!'

New York...The good, the bad, and the ugly.

The following night I met Julia outside the club as arranged. She told me that the regular girls get a special password F.3.C.K. (*very original*) and that they are allowed in all the VIP areas but not allowed free drinks. I was curious to know more about Julia, so I bought her a drink. Julia told me that she had been coming to the mansion for two years and had a regular supply of "Sams" (sex and mysterious strangers – as she calls them). Apparently last night was one of her dry nights, which she claimed happened from time to time. Usually, she earned about $2,000 a week and if she did a double shift, she could earn between $4,000 — $6,000 a week. The girls with managers had to give fifty per cent of their money away, so Julia preferred to work alone, 'I ain't gonna give my hard-earned cash to anyone, besides I only wanna work a few nights a week, so I can keep up with my study.'

'So you do this to pay for your tuition fees?'

'Yeah, lots of girls do. Law school ain't cheap.'

When Julia was sober I saw a completely different side to her, she was well educated and a really nice girl. We talked about her upbringing in Tucson, Arizona and why she chose to study in New York. When it came to talk about me, I evaded the questions or lied, and then swiftly steered the conversation back to Julia. I did ask her to forget my profession though, as I didn't want anyone to know.

'I can do that for you sweetie. Your secret is safe with me!' she winked.

After a couple of hours and quite a few drinks later she told me about my "Sam" for the night, 'Now listen, as it was such short notice I could only get you Roger.'

I don't like the sound of that!

'What do you mean; you could *only* get me Roger?'

'Well, he's not exactly a looker like our Latino friend, but he's sweet and he'll be very quick. You should be finished in half an hour.'

'What happens for the other thirty minutes?'

'That's up to you. You get the room for an hour regardless. Sometimes it's better to do someone like Roger and get out of there pronto, than to spend the full hour with a hottie who can't come!'

I wasn't sure if I agreed with her, but I decided to bite the bullet and stood up to leave.

'Hey, one more thing before you go. Roger can be a bit… excitable!'

'Excitable? What do you mean?'

She laughed, 'You'll see.'

I sat on the edge of the bed waiting for Roger to arrive and when he opened the door I had to catch my breath. Julia telling me that he wasn't exactly a looker was an understatement. Everything about him immediately made my skin crawl but I knew that I couldn't let my disappointment show because he looked really happy.

'Hey honey, you're preeetttty…woooo…YEAH!'

Okay, so now I know what she meant by excitable.

'Come to Roger and let me give you the *FUCK OF YOUR LIFE*!'

Oh dear!

I was starting to wonder what I had gotten myself into. I should have realised it wasn't going to be all fun and games. Who was I kidding to think that everyone who pays for sex is going to be as beautiful as Baileys, or as sexy as Mr Latino!

When Roger started to paw at my thighs, I decided that I needed to do whatever I could to make him come and get it over with as quickly as possible. I started to probe at his crotch.

'Yeah BABY, that's a girl. RUB IT. Yeah, rub it, OOOOH YEAH, rub it, rub it, rub it... rub it...'

I stifled a giggle as he was so vocal, and I wondered if the room was soundproof. While Roger eagerly took off my top, I tried desperately to cling onto the bulge in his trousers and keep him hard. He moved my hand away aggressively, abruptly dived between my legs, and all hell broke loose. He was really going for it and pretty soon his salivating jowls were headed for my face. In an attempt to turn away he caught the side of my cheek and began to lick and kiss me.

'Hey.... NO kissing!' I yelled as I desperately tried to move away from him.

'Whatever you say BABY...AHHH, lick, OOOOH, lick, YEAH, lick, lick, lick...!'

Thankfully, Roger stood up and started to undress. If I thought it couldn't get any worse, I was wrong. Roger was extremely hairy and underneath his huge stomach was a mound of thick, black pubic hair. As he walked towards me, I couldn't help but wonder where his penis was.

'On your knees baby!' he commanded.

I decided not to argue, as that would make the whole experience even more distressing, so I did as I was told.

'Show me what you've got BABY...come on, suck it!'

I wasn't exactly sure what I was supposed to suck until Roger lifted up his stomach and revealed his small, very fat penis! When he grabbed my head and started to push his hips back and forth, I found it difficult to keep it inside my mouth.

'Roger,' I spluttered between gasping for air, 'Why don't we go to the bed?'

'Soon Baby! A few more rounds, one, oh, two, oh, three, oh, YEAH!'

Thankfully after a count of ten, he pulled me to my feet and laid me on the bed. Grabbing the back of my knees, he lifted my legs into the air spreading me like a Christmas turkey. I wasn't sure what was coming next; I hoped that it was Roger, but no such luck. With one swift movement his tongue was licking me again, and after another count to ten, he finally entered me. I couldn't really feel it, but I knew it was in there because Roger was faithfully letting me, and no doubt the rest of the floor know that he was riding high, 'Oh my sweet dear Lord, what a PUSSY! YEAH BABY, you are HOT and TIGHT! OOHHHH, one, yeah, two, yeah, three, yeah.' And off he went.

This time when he got to ten it was more like, 'Tennnnnnnnnnowwwweeeeeeeee.'

'Wow, that was great Roger,' I lied.

'It ain't over yet BABY!'

It's not?

'Roger is gonna take you to HEAVEN!'

Before I could protest his tongue was between my legs again. I enjoy a bit of oral, but he seemed to miss the point (literally), so I decided the best thing to do was to fake my own orgasm and at least let him feel good about himself. After a couple of minutes of writhing, moaning and oohing I pretended to climax and told Roger that he was, 'AMAZING BABY!' It seemed to do the trick as within minutes he was dressed and out of the room, leaving behind six hundred dollars and a business card for, 'Next time!'

Never again will I let anyone decide who I sleep with…ever!

After taking a much-needed shower, I closed the door behind me and walked past the two security guards at the bottom of the stairs. They both erupted into laughter, 'Good night BABEEEE,' mocked B1.

I turned to face them, 'Oh fuck off!' I said trying to sound defensive, but as I walked away I could not help but laugh too.

7

CLOSE SHAVE IN CANNES

Back home, I decided to give Ruby a call, 'Rubes it's Beth… pick up, pick up wherever you are.'

'This…pant…had better…pant…be…a…pant…fucking emergency…pant, pant.'

'Caught you at a bad time?' I laughed.

'It's eight-thirty in the morning…One…HELLOOO?… Two…what happens at eight-thirty Beth? Three…. CIRCUIT TRAINING Beth.' CLUNK!

Oh bugger!

Ruby hates being interrupted while she's exercising. It's like interrupting the pope during one of his sermons…you just don't do it! Feeling like a naughty child, I made myself a cup of tea and sat down to watch "Friends." An hour later, someone started banging on my front door.

'Took you bloody long enough! Get packing darling…we are going on a "Frip."'

(Ruby's favourite way of saying fun trip.)

'What's going on?' I asked confused as Ruby marched through my front door.

'My bloody phone wouldn't stop ringing this morning! After you called, I got a call from work.'

I followed her down the hall, 'I hope you were nicer to them than you were to me.'

Ruby laughed, 'Well honestly, how is anyone supposed to get anything done when the bloody phone won't stop ringing? Anyway, they requested that I work on a promotion with A and A, and when they asked if I could recommend anyone else...well of course I chose you darling.'

'A and A? Who's that?'

'Arse and fucking Abs! Durrr! Think bronzed, tight arse, sexy in a "throw ye clothes on the Barbie" sort of way.' Ruby stared at me like I was a one-year-old trying to say my first word, 'Earth to fucking Ditsy Dora!'

'Jay?'

'Look at your face! If you're shocked now, wait until you hear where we are going.'

The words stumbled out of my mouth, 'Where?'

'San-tra-bleedin-Tropez!' she screamed. 'Can you believe it? We have three days in Cannes. Beautiful people Beth! Beautiful, beautiful bodies!'

'Isn't Cannes north of San Tropez?'

'Who cares if it's bloody north of San Tropez, smart arse! It's all France sweetie, ooh la fucking la. I love French men and their sexy accents.'

'Rubes, what men don't you love? Anyway, as amazing as it sounds, I can't go. I have a flight tomorrow.'

'That's where you're wrong sweetie. It's all been taken care of by moi, and we are *both* flying our sweet little derrières to France at five o'clock today.'

'But...'

'Stop bloody whinging! I'll help you pack, now come on... chop chop.'

I saluted her as she pushed me up the stairs.

'And less of your cheek young lady! Now show me your shoes!'

Just like a new recruit to the academy, I let Ruby take control. Apart from the fact that I was getting scared of her, my head was in a spin. All I could think about was the fact that for the next four nights and three days, I would be with C.H.A.D (my new name for Jay…Cute, Hot and Dangerous).

The rest of the day was crazy; last minute manicures and pedicures were just one small part of it. Ruby did a great job of rallying the troops to find me a decent wardrobe to take: Jeans - NO, flip-flops - NO, boob covering tops - definite NO! Everything had to be glamorous, slinky and very sexy. By three o'clock we were on our way to the airport.

Two bottles of Champagne later, we arrived in Cannes. With its pristine tree-lined avenues and glamorous hotels, the whole town looked and smelt like money. As we drove down Rue d'Antibes, designer labels whizzed by in designer cars, and I couldn't help but notice that even the dogs looked posh.

'Fan-bleedin-tastic Beth. This is the life! Hey maybe we can find a nice, rich sugar daddy while we are here. A youngish one though, not one of those old wrinkly dicks with a pot belly.'

I instantly thought of Frank, and just as quickly I un-thought about him when I caught sight of a half-naked hunk jogging along the sidewalk.

'Cor! Bloody hell; get a load of his abs. Woo hoo, hey, what's your name gorgeous?' yelled a "not so classy" Ruby. 'Get in the car, I'll give you a workout!'

'Rubes, what are you doing? People are staring!'

'Beth, did you see him? Did you see that body?'

'Yes I ......'

'That's it. I'm getting laid tonight!'

'When are we working?'

'Not until tomorrow. We have to be at the boat harbour at 12 pm sharp, so plenty of time for a lie in.'

The car pulled up outside Le Majestic Hotel on the Boulevard de la Croisette and Ruby looked as surprised as me. It was the most beautiful hotel I had ever seen. We made our way through the foyer and for once Ruby was lost for words. On the way up to our room, Ruby finally spoke, 'I'm not surprised that we are sharing a room, this must be costing a bloody fortune.'

We opened the door and both our jaws dropped. I looked at Ruby, 'Rubes, this isn't a room...it's a suite!'

While Ruby ran around checking out the rest of the rooms, I opened the champagne that was on ice, poured a couple of glasses and melted into the huge sofa.

'Beth this is fucking amazing! Listen, I'm going to take the master bedroom, and when I pull tonight I'll put a scarf over the handle of my door, so you know I've got company.'

'I don't think I'll need a scarf to tell me that! I've heard you before. Anyway, you always get the big bed! What if I pull?'

She burst out laughing, 'Yeah right! Sorry darling, but when have you ever had a one-night stand? Ever since I've known you, you've been tighter than a nun's arse.'

'I have not! What about Simon?'

'Darling, a kiss and a bit of a feel doesn't count. Just face it; you're much more of a relationship junkie. Don't be ashamed of that! I'm just more of an "act on animal instinct" kind of girl… if I want a shag, I'll get one! Simple!'

I was about to defend myself and tell her, 'Well that's where you are wrong,' but I couldn't. Despite my recent sex for money sagas, Ruby was right about the Beth she knew, and I wasn't about to tell her about Kat...not yet anyway!

An hour later there was a knock on the door, 'Message for Elizabeth Saunders.'

I took the envelope, secretly hoping it was a note from C.H.A.D, but it was our itinerary for the following few days. When Ruby read it, she looked confused, 'This can't be right!'

'Why?'

'For starters, it says we are included for all the dinners and to dress smart casual. We *never* get invited to eat with the guests and we don't even have to wear our uniform, except for the advertisement awards!'

'That's odd.'

'Very fucking suspect if you ask me, but hey, I'm not complaining! I'm always up for a free lunch. Now come on, let's get ready to parrrtayyyy!'

Glammed up, we wandered the streets of Cannes, trying out various bars, until we reached a bar that had a really fun vibe.

'Two o'clock! Blue shirt, killer arse!'

'Who?' I yelled over the music, 'The long-haired guy with the disgusting ponytail?'

Ruby rolled her eyes, 'Seriously Beth! Do you know me at all? The other one! Shorter hair...biggish nose.'

'You mean the one coming over here right now with the bob?'

I watched as the skinny man, with a girl's hairstyle, headed straight for Ruby.

'Ciao Bella. Sono Paolo,' the words almost dripped out of his mouth as he grabbed Ruby's hand and gave it a seductive kiss.

'Cheeeooow Paolo! Sono Ruby. This is...'

'So Rubeee,' he interrupted, 'You are from England no? I love the beautiful English girls, but you look more, how do you say, eegzotic?' He ran his finger down Ruby's arm, 'I am very happy to meet with you.'

Ruby seemed very pleased with herself, 'Not as happy as I am gorgeous! You are *very* sexy!'

Paolo slowly licked his lips as his eyes scanned Ruby's body, 'I would very much like it to take you home with me. In Italia we like to eat the good food, drink the good wine and make lots of the sexa.'

Bloody hell, this is like watching a bad porn movie.

I elbowed Ruby and giggled, 'Listen to him, bloody Italians are so ...'

'Oh la fucking laaaaa...Beth darling, I'm off. He's turning me on just listening to him.'

I pulled Ruby aside, 'Are you seriously falling for his dribble?'

'Now now darling, don't be jealous. I'll be quiet...I promise!'

'You're leaving me here?'

Ruby rolled her eyes, 'Come on Beth, you're a big girl! Talk to his friend with the ponytail or something.' She grabbed Paolo's hand, 'We're off. Ciao.'

I can't believe she just did that!

Feeling a little deflated at being abandoned, and with no intention of talking to "ponytail," I was contemplating my next move when I heard a familiar voice behind me, 'That didn't seem very fair, leaving you all alone?'

I could not possibly be this lucky!

I turned to see C.H.A.D smiling at me. I smiled back.

'I saw your friend disappear with that guy...or was it a girl?' he smiled, 'and thought you may need a rescue.'

My heart was pounding in my chest.

Jay looked over at a group of people laughing at a table, 'I'm having drinks with some friends; would you like to join us?'

Yes, yes, yes, yes.

'That's so nice of you to offer Mr Thorson, but I think I'll go back to the hotel.'

'Right Beth, let's get a few things straight. Firstly, I insist that you call me Jay. Secondly, nobody comes to Cannes and looks at it from a hotel room!'

I hesitated.

'We won't bite,' he winked.

I almost fainted, 'Well if you're sure.'

'Absolutely!'

Jay took my hand and led me towards his party, and I felt like an excited schoolgirl with a crush. At the table he made room for me next to him and introduced me to his friends. I was surprised at how easy it was to talk to everyone, especially Jay, and the next few hours flew by. At eleven pm I told him that I was leaving.

'Don't go!' he said in a whisper. 'Why don't you chill out for a while longer...unless you're not enjoying yourself that is!'

'Oh, it's not that! I'm having an awesome time. I just don't want to outstay my welcome that's all.'

He smiled, 'No worries there Beth...not going to happen! Just relax.'

One hour (and a few funny stories about my gran) later, the mood in the bar changed. I was so engrossed in my conversation with Jay that I hadn't noticed that all of his friends had left the table to dance.

'Well, Beth you know what they say! When in Rome.'

Before I had time to reply, Jay pulled me up to my feet and headed for the dance floor. Wrapping me in his arms, I instinctively put my head on his chest, and I couldn't remember ever feeling so happy. When the song finished, I looked up to see Jay smiling down at me and as I started to pull away, his strong grip pulled me back in, 'Steady on Beth, not so fast.'

I was back in the safety zone. I closed my eyes and snuggled into Jay's shoulder as we both swayed to the music. I could feel his breath on my face; the beat of his heart, and it was perfect the way our bodies seemed to mould into one another.

If this is a dream, I don't want to wake up.

Suddenly, I was wide awake when we were interrupted by Jay's friend Paul, 'Jay mate, we're heading off. Beth, it was nice to meet you. Bye.'

After we broke apart, Jay shook hands and said his goodbyes to his friends, while I pondered what to do next. I decided to leave too.

'It's probably not a bad idea,' said Jay. 'I'll walk you back.'

The next ten minutes passed way too fast, and when we arrived at the hotel I was preparing to say goodnight when Jay followed me inside and headed towards the lift. I panicked.

Oh no! He must think I'm another "hostie" he can sleep with and pay off.

The irony of that thought was not lost on me considering I usually get paid to have sex. I turned to face him as he pushed the elevator button, 'Jay, this is embarrassing. I'm sorry if I've misled you in any way but I can't…' my words trailed off as I looked at his beautiful green eyes, twinkling with mischief.

His face broke into a huge smile, 'Bloody hell Beth, what kind of fella do you think I am?'

Shit.

I was mortified, 'I'm sorry, I didn't mean to imply…'

'Don't look so worried, I'm just playing with you,' he laughed. 'I'm staying here too. In fact, just down the hall from you girls, so you better keep the noise down or I'll know where to come knocking.'

I could feel myself blushing with embarrassment, 'How do you know what room we are in?'

'It's my business to know these things. Gotta look after my girls!'

By the time the elevator reached our floor, you could cut the sexual tension with a knife. We walked in silence down the corridor and when we reached my room we turned to face each other. Jay leant in close to me and his voice sounded husky, 'Beth, I'm glad you agreed to come on this trip. I think we'll have a lot of fun.'

Please kiss me…please kiss me.

He stepped back, 'Goodnight then, sleep tight.'

Don't go!

'Thanks, you too.' I muttered as he turned and walked away.

I took a deep breath as I shut the door behind me. The physical effect Jay had on me was astounding, something I've never experienced in my life. I took a moment to calm myself before going to look for Ruby. I had to talk to her.

I reached Ruby's bedroom door, 'Come on you hunky bastard. Give it to me! Harder, harder, yes, yes, yesssssssss.'

The bloody Italian Stallion is still here!

Frustrated that I couldn't talk to Ruby, I had a shower and then got into bed. I had no idea when I would eventually get to sleep as the shagathon next door was still in full throttle, and just when I thought they'd had enough, it started up again. Finally, between headboard bangs, thumps and screams, I drifted off to sleep thinking about Jay.

The following morning, I left Ruby in bed and went for a walk along the promenade. When I returned, I collided with the Italian Stallion in the doorway as Ruby was pushing him out, 'Si si. Arriva fucking derchi...ciao. Call you later darling,' she said as she pulled me inside and closed the door!

'How are you this morning? You sounded like you had a good night,' I laughed.

'Oh wow! What a night! I think I came about six times.'

'Seven actually, and that was *after* I got back!'

'The fucking Italians! It must be all the pasta they eat over there, carbohydrate overload. I couldn't believe he wanted to go again this morning.'

'I can!' I said smiling.

'Where have you been anyway?'

'Just for a walk.'

'Ah, is little Beth sulking because she spent the night all alone?'

'Actually I...'

'Shit, look at the time!' she interrupted. 'We'd better get a move on or we'll be late. Chop chop!'

'Actually, I had the most amazing evening, thanks for asking, probably one of the best nights of my life! I think I'm in love, yes, you know with arse and abs, barbeque king, lots of white teeth, unbelievable eyes, runs our company, pays our wages.' I mumbled to myself as I walked to the bedroom.

'Beth, what are you mumbling about now? Come on, we haven't got time for this. Like I said, chop chop!'

An hour later, we arrived at the harbour and were escorted onto a luxury yacht.

'Oh super the girls are here...*THE GIRLS ARE HERE,*' shrieked Lulu, our over-excited PR manager. Lulu was like a Duracell bunny, once she started, nothing could stop her.

'Girls, girls, over here sweeties,' she yelled as she gestured us towards her. 'Bonjour, bonjour.' Kiss, kiss. 'I'm sorry,' she mouthed before speaking into her earpiece. 'No, *NO,* absolutely not! Tell him we aren't insured! Never mind that he'll pay up if there's an accident. It's ridiculous! Oh, bloody hell! Leave it with me. I'll report back at 14:00 hours... signing off.' She sighed, 'Oh girls, look at you. You both look divine. Now, your mission for the next 180 minutes is to mingle, mingle, mingle, serve champers and canapés and look beautiful, which of course you do,' she gushed. 'If only I was tall and slim like you girls. Wow! Wouldn't that be something?' she said as she grabbed one of the rolls around her tummy. 'Now girls, what do we say? You are never fully dressed in the aisle without a...?'

'Smile,' we harmonized as Lulu patted our behinds and sent us off on our mission, as she liked to call it.

Ruby was furious, 'Bloody slim, did you hear her? You may be slim but I'm fucking skinny.'

'Oh stop it! She was giving us a compliment, now come on *sweetie* let's mingle.'

Surprisingly the afternoon went really well. I didn't know who we were mingling with, but I concluded that they were all TV executives and media buffs as we were in Cannes for the Annual Advertising Awards. At precisely 150 minutes into our mission, I was opening what seemed like my 100th bottle of champagne when a slightly out of breath, red-faced Lulu, marched up the steps of the boat, 'Excellent, excellent,' she was talking into her earpiece again. *'BETH…hold it right there!'*

I froze.

'Yes, yes, ok got it, 15.30 hours, backstage, RIGHT!'

'Lulu is everything okay, you look a little flustered?' I asked as the champagne cork flew out the bottle and just missed her head. She instinctively ducked for cover, 'Oops sorry Lulu.'

'New mission Beth. Francoise will escort you to the theatre where you'll meet Nadine. She'll explain everything.' She started to usher me down the steps, 'Now don't worry, everything will be just fine. Oh, I almost forgot, swing by your hotel and put on your uniform. OKAY…*GO, GO!*'

I wanted to ask Lulu what she meant by "Don't worry" but by the time I had turned around she was off and running.

Precisely 1200 seconds later, I arrived at the theatre.

'Buon, buon. You av arrived perfectleee,' said a silky French accent, attached to a stunningly beautiful woman.

'Nadine?'

'Oui, oui, and you must be Elizeebeth. You must not be afraid non,' she said as she escorted me backstage. 'Do you like to av fun? Of course, you are young non?' She stopped in front of a huge, angry looking motorbike, 'Ah, voila... ere it is!'

That's not my idea of fun!

I glanced nervously at Nadine, 'I think there's been a mistake, I can't ride a motorbike.'

'Ah, non, ma Cherie, you will not be riding zis, you will be a passengerrr,' she purred.

'I will? Then who's riding it?'

'I believe the answer to that question is moi.'

C.H.A.D!!!

Jay ran his hand slowly over the seat.

Bloody hell, even that is sexual.

'And I have to warn you Beth...the last time I rode a bike was about ten years ago, and it was a lot smaller than this beast.'

'Are you serious? You want me to get on this when you haven't ridden a bike in years? And wearing a skirt, I might add?'

Jay laughed, 'Beth, chill. We're only going about thirty metres.'

'Show me! You go first; I want to see how you handle it.'

'I'm sorree,' interrupted Nadine. 'We don't av zee time for practice, and they need zee stage.'

I looked at Jay.

'Beth, have faith. I mean what is the worst thing that can happen?'

Thirty minutes of nervous tension later, we answered that question. The paparazzi and T.V crew had set up in the orchestra pit at the front of the stage, and there was a huge screen erected above the stage. As the theatre filled up, I could sense that Jay was excited and without warning he started to rev up the bike.

'Wow Beth, do you feel that?'

The only thing I'm feeling is anxious.

VROOM, VROOM.

'Jay, I don't think a skirt is a good idea on this thing.'

VROOM, VROOM.

'Did you say something?' he asked before twisting the throttle again.

VROOM, VROOM, VROOM.

'I DON'T THINK...' I shouted.

Jay tapped his ear with his finger, 'I CAN'T HEAR YOU.'

Turn the bloody thing off!

VROOM, VROOM, VROOOOOOM!

Oh, what the hell.

I placed my scarf discretely between my legs, wrapped my arms around Jay's waist and took a deep breath. Suddenly my head flew backwards as Jay hit the throttle and lunged us forward. In full view of the audience and hundreds of giggling photographers, we stalled!

Jay turned his head towards me, looking more determined than embarrassed, 'Let's try that again shall we Beth. Hold on tight...it's a go!'

I screamed as the bike raced forward at what seemed like 100 miles per hour. The front wheel lifted, and as it came back down and hit the ground, Jay lost control. Both wheels slid underneath us, sending the bike skidding sideways along the floor. The audience gasped as I fell to the ground and when the bike finally came to a stop, Jay stood up and raced towards me. A little disoriented and still lying on the floor, I heard his voice, 'Beth, are you okay? Bloody hell mate, here, let me help you up.'

Snap, snap, snap, snap.

'Great show mate!' shouted a pap.

'Yeah, nice arse love!' yelled another.

I looked at Jay, 'What did he mean by nice arse?'

'Don't worry about that Beth. Are you sure you're okay? No broken bones? I'm so sorry! I thought I'd have a better handle on it than that.'

'What did he mean nice arse love?' I asked again confused.

Jay stepped back as Lulu started pulling at my skirt, 'Oh my sweet, dear, dear, girl, are you all right? Let's get you dressed and out of here.' She turned her attention to Jay, 'Mr. T. You should be ashamed of yourself! I told you it was a stupid stunt. You could have both been seriously hurt, not to mention the lawsuits if that beast had gone off the stage.'

Jay looked embarrassed, 'Yes Lulu, I know. I'm sorry. It won't happen again. I promise!'

'I'll believe *that*, when I see it!' Lulu said angrily as we walked away. 'Yes, yes, I have her...over and out!'

As we neared the side of the stage, I noticed mascara running down Ruby's cheeks.

'Oh Rubes, you big softie. Don't be silly, I'm not hurt,' I said touched.

Ruby wiped her eyes, 'I'm not crying Dora. That was *THE FUNNIEST* thing I've seen in ages...classic! I bet you wish you'd worn knickers now!'

'What do you mean?' I asked horrified.

'Well, if your arse isn't plastered all over the papers to-morrow, it'll be a miracle.'

'That's enough Ruby! Beth's had a little shock and it wasn't …erm…that bad!' Lulu whispered.

'Lulu, get real. Even I could tell you when she had her last wax and I was fifty feet away.'

Horrified at the revelation that I had somehow exposed myself to the paparazzi, I turned to Jay, who had been listening to the whole conversation. He noticed the tears in my eyes.

'Don't worry Beth. I'll sort it out, I promise!'

'Come on Beth, see the funny side of it. You'll be famous tomorrow. Now let's go and get your hairy arse a drink,' laughed Ruby.

'Oh, just FUCK OFF!' I yelled and stormed off.

That evening, despite everyone telling me that the best way to handle a humiliating situation was to face it head on, I couldn't. While everyone went out to dinner, I stayed inside the safe haven of my hotel room. Only it wasn't safe, because despite it hiding me from the outside world, it couldn't hide me from my own mind. As I curled up in bed feeling sorry for myself, I couldn't stop thinking of all the possible outcomes of today's disaster. I was terrified that the story would go global and that one of my clients would recognise me and come forward. The ramifications of that happening shook me to the core, because it wouldn't just be my bum that was being exposed!

'Rise and shine, you sexy minx. Wait 'till you see the papers.'

I pulled the duvet over my head, 'Rubes stop being mean. I want to die.'

'Poor baby! Come on, you'll love it,' she teased.

As Ruby placed a cup of tea on my bedside table, she threw a pile of newspapers on the bed. I took a deep breath and started flicking through them. One...nothing! Two... nothing! Three...nothing!

'I don't understand? Where's my bum?' I asked confused.

Four...nothing! Five...nothing! I screamed with delight.

'*OBVIOUSLY* your arse isn't news darling, so stop sulking and get up. We've got brunch today.'

'I thought we had a free day?'

'Change of plans. A and A is taking us all out. He was really quiet last night, not his usual self. Every time I tried to talk to him, he kept asking how you were. He probably feels guilty that he caused the hairy arse scandal in the first place.'

'STOP saying my bum is hairy, just because I haven't jumped on the Brazilian bandwagon.'

'Don't be so sensitive darling! Anyway, Lulu reckons he had something to do with keeping you out of the papers today.'

'Really? How?'

'Who knows? Maybe *your* arse just isn't news sweetie. Now if it had been *my* arse...well *THAT* would be another story!'

'Here she is, stuntwoman extraordinaire!' cheered Lulu as Ruby and I entered the restaurant, 'Come, come, sit down girls and relax! No missions today, except to enjoy yourself.'

While Lulu wrapped her arms around me and gave me a hug, someone I didn't know said, 'Bravo Elizabeth! Not many people would dare to join this scoundrel on a crazy

PR mission.' He hit Jay rather hard on the back. 'You really ought to take more care young James. One can't be too foolish these days. Next you'll be base-jumping or sky diving all in the name of PR.'

'For heaven's sake Edward, don't give him any more ideas,' scolded Lulu.

'It was only a motorbike Edward, and anyway, no harm done hey?' Jay said as he looked at me apologetically.

Just the way he looked at me caused adrenalin to surge through my body and I had to stop myself from lunging across the table to kiss him.

Why does he have this effect on me? It's intoxicating.

I couldn't take my eyes off Jay's lips as he chatted to Edward.

'Hey, earth calling Dora...I'm talking to you. Hello, is anybody home?'

'Sorry Rubes, I was just...'

'Yeah, I know what you were *just* doing. What's going on? Arse and Abs keeps looking at you and you're acting extra dizzy. Is there something you're not telling me Elizabeth Saunders?'

'No! Absolutely not! I'm still a bit dazed from the fall that's all. Jay is probably just feeling a bit guilty like you said.'

'Right! Well, snap out of it! It's *boring.* Anyway, I heard his girlfriend arrives this afternoon leaving us free to do what we like...so tonight...we partaaaaay!'

I suddenly felt ill. There it was, that horrible word I'd conveniently forgotten all about...girlfriend! Of course, he had a girlfriend; he's been with her since high school.

I wonder why he hasn't married her.

Just thinking about a possible confrontation with the "other woman" made me feel anxious and I realised that I could never meet her. I was in love with her man and I wasn't sure if I could act my way out of that one. My thoughts were interrupted by the soft Australian accent that I was beginning to love, 'Beth, how are you mate?'

Much better now.

'I'm fine thanks. I'm sorry about getting upset yesterday, I was just so worried that my bum...'

'There's no need to explain. I'm the one who should apologise for putting you in that situation in the first place. I hope you can forgive me. It won't happen again.'

'WHY?' I said a little too loudly.

Jay laughed.

I tried to redeem myself, 'I mean... it can! I don't mind really. Apart from the fall, it was quite good fun.'

'Seriously? You'd be up for another mindless PR stunt, as Edward so gracefully put it?'

'Definitely! So long as my "you know what" doesn't get in the papers, I'm game,' I smiled.

'I'll keep that in mind. Anyway, I've got some other business to take care of now, you girls enjoy the rest of your trip. I'll see you soon okay?'

Before I could stop myself the words just flew out, 'Your girlfriend?'

'Pardon?' he turned and looked at me.

'The other business... I hear that your girlfriend is arriving.'

'Oh that?' he smiled. 'Well, actually, yes, she is arriving tonight. However, right now I do have some important *airline* business to attend to.'

I was embarrassed by my lack of maturity and obvious lack of tact, 'Sorry I....'

'No worries Beth, catch you later.' He winked and once again he was gone.

'Bloody hell, what's really going on between you two?' whispered Ruby. 'I could feel the sparks from twenty feet away. I hope you're not planning on boffing the boss Elizabeth Saunders. You know the rule...don't shit in your own back yard.'

'What? Don't be crazy. Nothing's going on. He was just apologising for yesterday.'

And I was acting like a jealous teenager.

'Yeah, you keep telling yourself that darling. Now let's get out of here, we've got some serious drinking to do!'

8

PROFILE PORNOGRAPHY

Two flights and two sexual encounters later, I was sitting at home thinking about my gran when my phone rang.

'Darling, how often do you masturbate?'

'Hi Gran,' I said smiling.

'Never mind... can you come over, I need your expert opinion on something?'

'Well actually Gran, I'm just about to...'

'Oh darling, this is so important. Your dear old grandmother needs you,' she pleaded.

'Okay, I'll be right...' and before I had time to finish my sentence she hung up.

When I reached Gran's house, she quickly pulled me inside, 'Darling, thank goodness you're here. I'm going out of my mind with this blasted contraption,' she whispered pointing to a sparkling new laptop on her writing desk.

'Gran, you don't have to whisper! It can't hear you.' I laughed. 'So you've finally decided to catch up with the times and gone ultra-modern.'

'I know darling, can you believe it?' she said proudly.

'It's very nice; it must have cost a fortune.'

'Oh dear, it is rather spectacular looking but I'm afraid I may have broken it. The nice young chap who installed the net thingy tried to help me, but to be honest, it was all gibberish mumbo jumbo to me darling.'

'What made you change your mind, I thought you hated computers?'

'I do, but I've discovered the most amazing thing (she paused for effect) ...*Internet dating*! Mable Hawthorne has been doing it for years, and apparently she's having an absolute ball: holidays, gifts, romantic dinners. Of course, she hasn't found the right man yet, but she says the sex is incredible. She's having orgasm after orgasm.'

'Do I need a drink for this?'

'Don't be silly and stop looking at me like that. We may be mature on the outside but inside we are sexually adventurous vixens,' she laughed. 'I'm thinking of putting that on my profile page. What do you think?'

'I think we need to find you a man...and quick!'

Once I got Gran's computer up and running, I helped her to upload her profile on the "Young at Heart" dating site, and before I left, I made her promise to let me help her to vet her dates. Somehow, I felt that my lecture on "stranger danger" fell on deaf ears as she engrossed herself in profile after profile.

Later that evening she called me, 'Darling I want to thank you for helping me this morning. Can you come over tomorrow? I've found another site I want to show you.'

'Gran, have you been at it all day?'

'Yes, and it's amazing what you find when you use that net thingy. I typed in "hot males looking for lust" and you wouldn't believe what I found. I'm so worked up that I've decided to have an early night with Victor.'

'Victor? Who's he?'

'Oh Darling,' she sniggered. 'Not who, but what? I forgot to tell you that I bought a fantastic vibrator. It's very cute, with little rabbit ears. I've called it Victor!'

Once I got the image of Gran and Victor out of my mind, I thought about my last two encounters in New York. I had called Julia to let her know I was coming, and she had arranged for another threesome with one of her regulars. It was a welcome change from "Repulsive Roger" as this client was easy. Having a penchant for masturbation while watching "girl on girl," Julia took control of the situation, and once again, all I had to do was lie back and enjoy it. Just watching us both set him off and it was all over in twenty minutes!

The second night was a bit more work and a little frightening. I had initiated a conversation with a seemingly shy man called Peter who was a broker from San Francisco, and after a swift negotiation we headed upstairs. The session started fine, however as we neared the hour he changed tempo, 'Take that you Bitch,' he said as he slapped me hard on my bum. 'No one has ever fucked me like you...SAY IT!'

I did as he asked and for the next five minutes a shower of verbal expletives continued to rain on me while I silently prayed that he would not hurt me.

'Who's the fucking boss now Bitch?' he yelled, pushing inside me as far as he possibly could. I wasn't sure what he would do next, or whether I should yell, 'You're the boss Peter... you're the boss,' when thankfully he shuddered and came. Trembling slightly, I stayed on my knees and waited in silence until he moved.

When he picked up his clothes, he turned and looked at me sheepishly, 'Sorry about the language. I get a bit carried away; it's just that I'm not allowed to swear at home, so I guess I was letting off a bit of steam. I hope I didn't offend you.'

Terrify me would have been a better word for it.

Feeling relieved that I only received a verbal battering I lied, 'Oh...no. I've heard worse.'

As he snuck out of the room, I caught sight of myself in the mirror where he had slapped me.

Yep, that's going to be one hell of a six-hundred-dollar bruise.

9

RIDING MISS DAISY

'Hi Elizabeth. It's Jill here from the promotions department. Can we take you off your flight tomorrow? We need you for an event in London.'

I'll have to call Julia and cancel.

'Yes, of course. When and where?'

'Earls Court. 9 am sharp. No need for a uniform. Are you a size ten?'

'Actually I'm a little bigger, more like...'

'Ten it is then! Oh, and by the way, can you ride a horse?'

Bloody hell!

The following morning as I made my way to London, I wondered what I would be doing on a horse.

'Ah, Beth, here you are.' Kiss, kiss. 'Marvellous, yes, yes, she's here... okay... now? Practice? Yes, absolutely,' Lulu said into her mouthpiece as she took my hand and led me into a room filled with wedding dresses.

It was the UK's annual Wedding Exhibition and as our company had sponsored a local designer, we were putting on a fashion show.

'Here try these four on, we have to be quick, they want you on the horse A.S.A.P.'

Giving Lulu a quick fashion show of my own, we decided on a dress before going to meet Daisy, a beautiful, white horse with a pink ribbon in her mane. My mind wandered back to the last time I rode. I was twelve years old and fell off so many times that I instantly declared myself a "non-horsey type" and avoided horses ever since.

'All right luv. My name's Tone, short for Tony! Now don't worry, she's bin sedated. It shouldn't wear off for a couple of hours at least.'

Sedated?

'Don't look so worried luv, come on, up you get.' Tone said, as he unsuccessfully attempted to help me mount Daisy.

'Am I riding her alone?'

'Don't think so. I believe the Gaffer's on his way.'

My heart skipped a beat, 'So we'll both be on Daisy?'

'Yep, the ole girl is big enough for the two of you.'

'Maybe it's best if I wait then,' I said nervously.

'Nah, you'll be right luv. Come on, we need to see how much room there is, what with all that fancy frilly stuff you're wearin'.'

I finally managed to climb onto Daisy with the help of Lulu and Tone, and as we walked slowly around the room, I began to feel more confident.

'Bravo, bravo Beth,' yelled an excited Lulu. 'Yes, yes, she's on the horse now. Perfect! Perfect, absolutely splendid. When? Okay...will do.' Clap, clap. 'That's enough Beth, we have to get you to hair and makeup, tick tock, tick tock.'

When I was finished with hair and makeup, I wandered to the side of the stage and watched hundreds of hopeful, brides-to-be staring adoringly at the models parading the dresses. My mind turned to Jay and I wondered if he had arrived yet.

Lulu interrupted my thoughts, 'Beth, change of plan! We are putting you on last at 12:00 hours. We'll check hair and makeup at precisely 11:30 hours. Hang tight, don't wander too far and *please* don't eat or drink anything! I don't know what I'd do if we spoiled that dress.'

I can hardly breathe in this dress, never mind eat.

Her phone rang, 'Righty ho! Yes...C.O.P....He's running late. Confirmed 12:00 hours!' and off she hopped.

With an hour to amuse myself, I decided to get more acquainted with Daisy.

'Bloody 'ell, they're cuttin' it fine! Twelve o' bleedin'clock? It'll 'ave worn off by then. I'm not bleedin' givin' 'er anymore. Sod off! They'll 'av to take a chance!' Tone started yelling into his phone. 'Not my bleedin' problem now is it? Should've bleedin' thought of that before. She's my 'orse and I'm not givin' 'er any more pills. Understand?'

When Tone had finished his phone call, I tentatively approached, 'Excuse me Tony...sorry...Tone! I couldn't help overhearing you. Is everything alright with Daisy?'

'Sure luv, don't you worry your pretty little 'ed. Daisy'll be okay, she's quite a mild 'orse anyways and the Gaffer will be able to 'andle 'er.'

Not quite as reassured, as I would like to be, considering how the "Gaffer" handled a motorbike, I decided to stay with Daisy and try to bond a little. I had heard that blowing up a horse's nostrils created a special closeness, but all it did was make her shake her head and grunt.

As I was stroking Daisy's mane, I heard someone whistle. I turned to see Jay walking towards me with a huge grin on his face, 'Wow mate, look at you! Beautiful!'

I could feel myself blushing, 'Hi. I wasn't sure if you were going to make it.'

'Are you kidding? I wouldn't want to miss the chance to ride a horse with my favourite sidekick,' he winked. 'Look at your face! Stop worrying! Riding a horse is like riding a bike, once you've done it, you never forget,' he said after two failed attempts to mount Daisy.

Stop looking at his bum!

'I certainly won't forget how you ride a bike.'

Jay laughed, 'Now now, be nice!'

With the help of Tone, Jay finally mounted Daisy. Now it was my turn!

'Young lady on the back please,' ordered Tone.

'What?' Jay and I said in unison.

'You 'eard me. That dress is far too big for you to sit at the front. Don't worry, Miss Daisy 'as a big enough arse for you to sit on. You won't 'urt 'er. Just 'old on tight to the Gaffer,' he chuckled.

Jay took my hand while Tone pushed up my feet and surprisingly, we did it on the first attempt. I hated to ask the next question, but I had to, 'Jay, when *exactly* did you last ride a horse?'

'If my memory serves me correctly, I believe I was twelve.'

Bloody hell!

Daisy was obviously as nervous about this as I was and decided at that moment to rear up. Her front legs rising into the air as I slid off backwards, landing in a crumpled mess on the floor.

'Crikey Beth, are you okay? Did you hurt anything?' asked Jay as he tried to control Daisy.

Tone picked me up and brushed me down, 'Bleedin' 'ell luv, I told you to 'old on tight to the Gaffer! Daisy's not used to 'avin someone sittin' on 'er arse, but she'll be okay in a mo. Let's try that again shall we?'

A little dazed, I climbed back onto Daisy.

'Right Gaffer, don't forget, if Daisy takes off, pull on both reigns and yell, 'Whoooaaaa Daisy girl.'

'Right, will do!' Jay said enthusiastically. 'Isn't this fun Beth?'

Bloody hysterical!

He turned his head and whispered, 'Hold on tight.'

Standing at the top of a huge "T" formation runway and looking out to a sea of faces, I wanted to close my eyes but knew that I couldn't. Hundreds of paparazzi and excited women were clicking away with their cameras. As Daisy slowly plodded along, I kept a smile on my face and waved to the crowds. When we reached the end of the runway, I felt myself relax. All Jay had to do was steer Daisy to the left, turn around and come back up the middle.

Halfway home.

Letting my focus drift from Daisy to Jay, I leant in closer so I could breathe in his smell. I felt Jay's heart rate increase as I pushed my chest into his back and wrapped my arms tightly around his waist. I closed my eyes.

I love y…

Before I could finish the sentence in my head, I was jolted back to reality by the sound of a loud horn echoing around the arena, followed by jeering and yelling. Startled by the noise and the commotion, Daisy neighed, bucked, and reared up, kicking her front feet high into the air.

'Hold on Beth,' yelled Jay. 'WHOOOOAAAAA DAISY.'

As Jay attempted to regain control of Daisy, she bolted towards the other end of the runway. I clung to Jay as tightly as I could and for some unknown reason, all I could hear in my mind was the theme tune to the TV show, "Champion the Wonder Horse."

Oh my God, this is it! I'm dead!

I started screaming, 'LOOK OUT! MOVE!'

'WHOOOOAAA DAISY, WHOOOAAAA!' Jay yelled in vain.

I momentarily closed my eyes and when I opened them again, it was just in time to see Daisy a couple of feet away from the end of the stage. Pandemonium ensued with girls screaming, laughing and falling over one another in a desperate attempt to avoid being trampled on. I braced myself for the big jump, but instead of going off the stage Daisy came to an abrupt stop... and I was suddenly flying!

If I were watching someone else I would have thought it was spectacular, a huge white angel wearing toile and lace, floating above the crowds. In reality, I remember screaming, falling and waking up to a sea of faces peering down at me. Jay was holding my hand, yelling at people to stay back, and Lulu was crossing herself and snivelling into a tissue.

'She's not dead,' yelled Tone. 'Bloody 'ell, I thought she was a gonna!' he said to Lulu who started to cry even more.

'She's alive! She's alive!' echoed through the arena, as everyone started clapping and cheering.

I tried to get up and Jay put his hand on my shoulder, 'You're going to be okay Beth, but try not to move until the ambulance arrives.'

Apparently, I had been very lucky. I had miraculously landed on a pile of boxes filled with "Honeymoon Lingerie" and only been unconscious for a few minutes. Once the ambulance men had removed the bras and panties that had somehow got caught in my hair, I was taken off to the hospital for a check-up. Jay insisted on coming in the ambulance with me.

I looked at Jay who was in deep thought, 'How's Daisy?'

'Daisy's fine. I think coming out of the sedative state and the loud horn gave her the willies. I'm more concerned about you, I'm just hoping you haven't hurt yourself.' He tenderly moved some hair from my eyes, 'Now I can't promise I can keep this one out of tomorrow's papers, but I'll do my best.'

We both laughed and after a couple of minutes of silence, Jay surprised me by taking hold of my hand. He looked serious, 'Beth, there is just one thing I've been wanting to ask you.'

'Yes?'

He leant in towards me, his voice hoarse and sexy, 'Are you wearing knickers?'

'YES...YES,' I laughed. 'Thank God I bloody well am!'

10

LAS VEGAS: ONE WEDDING AND A FUNERAL

A month had passed since the wedding dress fiasco and as Jay predicted the press had a field day with the photos and the "Driving Miss Daisy" headlines. Yet, despite being the object of ridicule for weeks, I still maintain that the photo of me flying through the air is spectacular. Even Gran has a framed copy hanging on her toilet wall.

As for my secret life, I decided to take a break. My last three flights were just like the old days: shopping, sightseeing and partying with the crew. I didn't want to think about men, or sex, or sex with one man in particular. I just wanted to have fun and getting back to the "old me" seemed like the perfect way to take my mind off everything.

So, when I received a call from Lulu, asking me to go to Las Vegas for four days, I was genuinely shocked. I was convinced that my days as Jay's sidekick were well and truly over, since every time we were together something ridiculous happened.

Once Lulu confirmed that the event did not include vehicles or animals, I agreed to go and immediately called Ruby, 'Rubes, are you coming to Vegas?'

'What are you talking about?'

'Lulu just called.'

'Nobody's called me! Why hasn't anyone fucking called me? I'll call you back'…clunk!

Five minutes later my phone rang, and when I picked up Ruby was fuming. Her voice seemed to have risen another octave, 'They didn't even have me on the list of crew! Can you fucking believe *that*? How long have I been the number one girl Beth? Tell me, is there anyone as good as me on the team?'

I moved the phone away from my ear and could still hear Ruby ranting, 'No! Well I told them to do something about it as I wasn't *fucking* happy.'

'So are you coming?'

'They're calling me back. There's the other line.'

Clunk!

Twenty-four hours later, Ruby and I arrived in Vegas and our hotel was out of this world. We were sharing a suite again and this time I suggested she take the master bedroom.

'That's kind of you darling, but let's face it, I am the one who's going to need the bigger bed.'

'Planning a repeat of Cannes?'

'One can only hope,' she laughed. 'I do need a bloody good shag. The last two were useless.'

Must remember to get my earplugs out.

An hour later we were in our uniforms and back in the hotel lobby where Ruby and I introduced ourselves to Becky and Claire, who had flown up from LA to join the team. After we were each given a copy of the itinerary Ruby turned to me,

'Beth, have you seen this? It's madness. How are we going to fit all those parties *and* a wedding into four days?'

I looked at my itinerary, '*And* we have to be bridesmaids. I wouldn't want complete strangers being my bridesmaids, would you?'

'Never mind "complete strangers," I hope she's not bloody insecure. Can you imagine if she's easily intimidated, she'll die when she sees us?'

'I can't imagine she is. If she is willing to have Jay as her best man, I doubt a few pretty girls will ruffle her feathers.'

'Pretty? Speak for yourself! I'm fucking stunning darling!'

We all headed to the first party where Lulu met us at the door, 'Excellent, my girlies have arrived! Looking beautiful I might add. Beth and Claire, you are on the door. Make sure everyone has an invitation and then send them inside to Ruby and Becky. You girls will be handing out the name tags and VIP bracelets. At 21:00 hours all come inside and mingle. No need to serve champers tonight girlies, we've got special "Showgirls" for that.'

We applied the last touch of lipstick and headed to our respective positions. As the guests poured in I was getting increasingly excited about seeing Jay, but by nine o'clock there was still no sign of him.

'Girls, girls,' said a breathless Lulu. 'This party is going to go on *all* night. Why don't you go back to the hotel and change into something a little more razzle dazzle?'

'Really?' I asked surprised, prompting Ruby to elbow me in the ribs.

'Yes, yes, it's okay. His highness has given the all clear.'

I followed Lulu's finger and that's when I saw him smiling in our direction.

He's been inside the whole time!

'Now off you go, take one of these VIP bracelets so you won't have trouble coming back in.'

'Bloody hell, did you see the hunks in there tonight?' said Ruby. 'I bet you'll even get laid Beth. How long's it been since you had a good shag?'

The temptation to shut Ruby up by telling her about my secret life was overwhelming, but somehow I managed to keep quiet. The truth was, I had not noticed any of the men who came in tonight, all I could think about was seeing Jay and I was eager to get back to the party to find him.

After slipping into a slinky, little, backless number and silver heels, I ventured into the party with the girls. It was so crowded that an hour passed before I found Jay, who was sitting in a private booth surrounded by adoring women. I was about to turn away when he noticed me and jumped out of his seat, 'Beth! Over here mate.'

I motioned to Becky and Claire to follow me and smiled to myself as I watched Jay make space next to him, 'Wow, you look amazing!' he said handing me a glass of champagne, 'I'll have to have you out of your uniform more often.'

His comment made me laugh and Jay realised what he had said, 'Oh I didn't mean it like that, I meant...'

I couldn't help but flirt and whispered in his ear, 'Your turn to chill Mr. Thorsen. Although you "having me out of my uniform more often" sounds like a nice idea, I understood what you meant.'

For a moment we sat with our eyes locked on each other's until Jay was interrupted by one of the women. As I watched Jay chat to her, I couldn't believe how I found everything about him sexy, from the way his lips moved when he talked, to the way he sat with his hand resting on his lap. He really was intoxicating, and I couldn't seem to control the internal sexual volcano that was erupting inside me. I was starting to feel dizzy.

I looked around to see if I could see Ruby and saw her chatting to a guy dressed as a Gladiator. I laughed as I watched her touch his biceps and run her hand down his washboard abs towards his groin. Within minutes she was dragging him away by the hand in the direction of the toilets.

Jay turned to me, 'Right Beth, pick three people.'

'Why?'

'Do you always ask questions?'

'Yes,' I smiled. 'That's easy…Ruby, Becky and Claire.'

'Perfect,' he said as he took my hand and told Becky and Claire to follow us. On our way out we ran straight into Ruby in a tongue lock with Gladiator, 'Excuse me there fella, but I'm afraid I'm paying for her tonight so she's coming with me,' Jay said as he took Ruby's hand and pulled her out of the door.

'Bloody hell, he's going to think I'm a prostitute. What did you say that for?' she yelled, before realising *who* she was yelling at.

'Well, it's true isn't it? Not the prostitute part of course, but the fact that I *am* paying you tonight; now get your skinny little arse in there.' Jay said as he pointed towards a waiting helicopter.

Ruby saluted him with a smile, 'Yes Sir, skinny arse at your command.'

The following twenty minutes could only be described as a dream and a nightmare rolled into one, as our pilot thought it was hilarious to engage in some hair-raising, aerial acrobatics. As we dived in and out of buildings, screaming with every dip and whooping with every climb, it felt exhilarating and terrifying at the same time. As fear gripped me, the only consolation I had was that every time I screamed Jay placed his hand on my thigh.

'What's going on?' mouthed Rubes.

'Nothing,' I mouthed back.

Instantly, Ruby's eyes fell on Jay's hand, which was still resting on my thigh. I quickly moved my leg and shrugged my shoulders at her.

'I'll speak to you later young lady,' she said as she gave me one of her "mother knows best" stares.

Jay, who was watching our exchange, seemed amused by the commotion he was causing and wickedly winked at me as a slow smile crossed his face.

Back on terra ferma I prepared myself for Ruby's onslaught but was saved by Gladiator who whisked her away as soon as she walked through the door. Jay also disappeared, so I joined Becky and Claire on the dance floor and lost myself in the music. As I moved slowly to the rhythm, I caught sight of Jay staring at me intently. I met his gaze and while I continued to dance, his eyes never left mine. We were lost in the song together, our souls connecting. Almost in a trance, I watched as Jay stood up and excused himself, only to be pulled back by Lulu who introduced him to a group of people. I could see the disappointment register on his face as his attention was diverted back to the group. I didn't see him again for the rest of the evening.

At two am, when I couldn't dance anymore, I decided to call it a night and go back to the hotel. I dragged my exhausted body into bed and drifted off to the grunts and moans of the Gladiator battle next door.

'Bethhhh...answer the fucking phone!' screamed nightshade.

I'm sleeping!

'Bethhhh!'

I opened my eyes and looked at the clock. It was four am!

'Okay, okay,' I shouted, reaching for the phone.

Why do I have to answer the bloody phone?

'Hello, Beth speaking,' I said sleepily.

Silence.

'Hello?'

Silence.

Great!

I hung up, unplugged the phone and fell back asleep.

It was wedding day and I was excited. A couple had won a competition in their local newspaper to get married in Vegas and they could choose a celebrity to "give them away." Being big fans of the airline, they chose Jay and thought it would be fun to have "Hosties" as bridesmaids.

When the limousine pulled up, Claire, Becky and Ruby jumped in. Lulu grabbed my arm, 'Beth, you come with us. We can only have three in that one.'

I stepped inside the second limousine to find Jay pouring champagne into three glasses. His face lit up when he saw me, 'Well hello, this is a nice little surprise! I'm going to need another glass.' Jay handed everyone a drink, 'Come on ladies, it's not every day you get to be a part of a wedding, let's celebrate.'

Something was off. Lulu looked at Debbie who looked at me, and then we all looked at Jay.

'Mr. T are you okay?' Lulu asked suspiciously.

He laughed and spilled his champagne, 'Absolutely!'

She handed him a napkin, 'You're not acting okay.'

'Lulu, I'm fine. Just a bit tired from last night; it was such a *huge* night.'

Lulu continued with her interrogation, 'What time did you get back exactly?'

'Well, actually, I'll tell you a little secret,' Jay put his finger up to his lips, which I thought was cute but Lulu and Debbie were definitely not amused, 'I didn't exactly "G*et back*." The owner of the club kept giving me drinks, one thing led to another and suddenly we are all eating breakfast somewhere!'

Lulu looked horrified, 'You mean to tell me, you are most likely *over the limit* right now?'

'That depends on what *the limit* is,' he laughed.

I started to giggle but abruptly stopped when I noticed Lulu's face turn red with anger.

'Mr. T! This is *totally* unacceptable! There will be press everywhere today, not to mention that it's a very important occasion for our young couple. How could you be so inconsiderate?'

Poor Lulu! She was obviously very distressed, and Jay only made the situation worse by insisting that she, 'drink some champagne to lighten up.'

'Right!' said Lulu, grabbing the champagne away from Jay, 'you listen to me! The minute this ceremony is over, you are going back to your hotel. You will have a shower *and* a sleep, and you will be ready for exactly 17:45 for the evening reception.' She turned to me, anger still flickering in her eyes, 'Beth, I trust you to ensure that he arrives at the "Hotel Monte Carlo" at 18:00 precisely. Understood?'

I could feel Jay's eyes burning through me, 'Yes. 18:00…
Hotel Monte Carlo.'

Lulu looked expectantly at Jay, 'Well?'

'Okay, message received and understood! Now come on
Lulu, be a sport mate and give me back my champagne so we
can all celebrate. I'll be a good boy. I promise!'

Jay kept his word and the wedding ceremony was beautiful. Standing next to the bride, I couldn't help but steal
glances over at Jay, once again imagining what life would be
like with him. I was jostled out of my daydream by Ruby's
elbow, 'Take the flowers,' she hissed.

The bride and groom were staring at me. 'Sorry!' I
mouthed as the bride handed me the flowers.

'One bloody thing Beth! The only thing you had to remember…I'm seriously getting worried about you Dora!'

I ignored Ruby and glanced over at Jay who was quietly
smiling at me. He looked so gorgeous…tired, but gorgeous.

Once the ceremony was over, Lulu insisted that we keep
to the plan and asked me to escort Jay back to the hotel. When
we got into the car, Jay started to laugh, 'You sound cute when
you're sleepy.'

'That was you? The phone call this morning?'

He smiled.

'Why didn't you speak to me?'

'I don't know. I felt guilty I guess for waking you up, and
I was *really, really,* drunk. I'm sorry!'

'That's okay, apology accepted,' I smiled. 'What did you
want anyway?'

He paused before answering and fixed me with his eyes,
'That's the thing…I don't really know.'

I stared into his eyes until the sexual tension was so unbearable that I had to force myself to look away.

'Beth...why aren't you married?'

Because the man I'm in love with isn't available.

I forced myself to look at him again, 'I don't know. I guess I haven't met the right man yet,' I lied.

His eyes tore into my soul, and just as he opened his mouth to say something the car pulled up outside the hotel.

Jay sighed and looked at his watch, 'You can report back to Lulu that "the eagle has landed" and will be ready at *precisely* 17:45 hours. Now, don't forget, you have to chaperone,' he smiled. 'I'll be waiting...Suite 405. Come early if you like and we can have a "pre- party" drink.'

The driver closed the door and as we drove back to the wedding venue, unlike the driver who was taking his time, my mind was racing. I wasn't sure I could trust myself alone with Jay in his room.

The next couple of hours dragged on, and despite knowing that I was playing with fire, I could not stop myself from going to Jay's suite. At five o'clock, I tentatively knocked on his door.

Jay answered with only his trousers on and a huge smile, 'Come in and grab a drink. I won't be a minute.'

Bloody hell, Ruby was on the ball with the "Arse and Abs" nickname.

Jay's abs were incredibly toned, and his bum looked amazing in his trousers. I tried not to imagine what the rest of him looked like as I poured myself a glass of champagne and gulped it down. A couple of minutes later, I felt Jay place his hand on the small of my back as he reached for the bottle, 'Easy tiger, we can't have you drunk before we get there. Lulu will have a fit.'

Electricity shot up my spine.

'Now let's have a toast! To the most beautiful bridesmaid I've ever seen...actually, to the most beautiful "flying bride" I've ever seen. And to me...the man constantly putting her in compromising positions.'

'I'll drink to that,' I said as we clinked glasses.

'Correct me if I'm wrong Beth, but there seems to be a theme happening around us. Do you think someone's trying to tell us something?' he glanced at me with a mischievous look in his eyes.

My whole body started tingling.

Shit, I knew this was a bad idea!

'We do seem to get into some pretty ridiculous situations,' I said stepping away from his intoxicating gaze.

Jay followed me to the sofa, and thankfully the mood lightened as we talked more about life outside of work. I was impressed that he had remembered so much from our conversations in LA and Cannes, especially the stories about my gran. I glanced at my watch and after sharing Gran's latest, hilarious, adventures of internet dating, we reluctantly left for the party.

In the car we shared a comfortable silence and when Jay let his knee rest against mine, I let it stay there.

When Lulu saw Jay and I enter the hotel lobby, she rushed over, 'Ah Beth, you are both here! Perfect, thank you, you are an angel. The seating plan is over by the door, go and take a look and we will see you soon. James, I want a word with you!'

I left Jay and Lulu and wandered into the reception room. It had been staged as a "Winter Wonderland" and it was the most beautiful setting I had ever seen. A frozen forest of trees, fake snow and fairy lights surrounded two huge, silver thrones, while the ceiling sparkled like a night's sky full of stars. The groomsman and bridesmaids were placed on either side of the thrones, and the remaining guests, who consisted of family members and media staff, sat on circular tables set in a heart formation.

I took my seat and smiled to myself that I had been placed next to Jay.

'You look happy,' said Ruby when I sat down.

'I am. Weddings have that effect on me.'

Jay took his seat.

'Hmm, just weddings?' Ruby whispered.

'Well mate, seems like we've been "throne" together again,' Jay said giving me a sexy wink.

I handed him a glass of champagne, 'It seems so...mate!'

'How nice is this setting?' he said looking up at the stars.

'It's beautiful. A real Winter Wonderland.'

Jay's eyes lit up, 'So you like the snow?'

'Saying I like the snow would be an understatement. I *love* the snow, although I can't say the same for ice. We don't get along so well.'

He smiled, and I could virtually see his mind ticking away. I was just about to ask him why when we were told to stand for the Bride and Groom.

The next couple of hours flew by and after the Bride and Groom had shared their first dance, "Someone Like You" by Van Morrison started playing. Jay jumped up out of his chair, 'Beth, will you dance with me? I love this song.'

Ignoring Ruby's disapproving look, I followed Jay onto the dance floor and as he held me close I noticed something hard pressing against me. Either he *really* loved this song, or he was actually very attracted to me and wasn't afraid to show it. I tried to slightly shift my hips away.

Jay held me tighter and whispered in my ear, 'Easy tiger... just relax.'

OMG... I'm in sooo much trouble.

The song finished and I was actually relieved when Lulu whisked Jay off for press photographs. I needed to calm my nerves. I had never wanted anyone so badly in my life and I wasn't sure if I could control myself around him anymore.

When the party ended, I decided to go back to the hotel and catch up on sleep. Claire and Becky were joining the wedding guests at a local nightclub, and Ruby told me not to wait up as she had met a banker from New York, who she later labelled, "The wanker from New York."

Sometime later, the distant ringing of the telephone woke me.

I hope it's him.

'Hello?'

'Hey, how's my favourite bridesmaid doing?'

'Hey back, how's my favourite troublemaker?'

Jay laughed, and I waited for what was coming next, 'So Beth...did you have fun tonight?'

'Yes, did you?'

'I did...but,' there was a moments silence, 'I was wondering if you would like to make it an even better night?'

'What do you mean?'

'Well, I was thinking that maybe there was something else I could do for you, to make it even more special.'

I laughed at his cheesy line.

'Okay, okay, I'll get to the point.'

I stayed silent, but I was sure that Jay could hear my heart beating loud and fast on the other end of the line.

His voice turned husky, 'Would you like to come to my room?'

Shit! Say no Beth.

'What do you have in mind?'

'Well, we could finish off the bottle of Champagne we started earlier. Maybe we could dance some more, or (pause) we could just see what happens.'

My heart wanted me to run like Usain Bolt to his suite, but my mind was screaming NOOOOOOO. It took every ounce of willpower for me to say, 'Jay I don't think it's a good idea.'

'Then don't think about it Beth...just come,' he said seductively.

You have no idea how much I want to.

'I can't Jay. I'm sorry.'

'Are you sure?'

No.

'Yes.'

'Okay,' he sighed. 'As Lulu would say, message received and understood. Good night Beth.'

I said goodnight and after I hung up I wanted to punch myself.

How can I sleep with random men, yet when the one man I have fallen in love with offers me sex on a silver platter, I turn him down?

Lying in bed, I thought about it and realised that the men I had sex with were strangers. They may be married or have girlfriends, but I don't know them, so it's easy to pretend I'm not hurting anyone. Jay was different. I knew him, I knew he had a partner, someone he had been with for a very long time and it just didn't feel right to cheat on her. Besides, I didn't want to settle for an affair. I knew that if I ever had Jay, I wanted all of him.

The following morning, I didn't have time to think about my conversation with Jay as the girls and I were ushered between a hectic schedule of press conferences and meetings. When Lulu gave us a few hours free in the afternoon, I joined Ruby at the hotel pool for a bit of sunbathing.

Ruby removed the cold towel from her eyes and looked at me, 'Beth, are you going to tell me what's going on?'

'What do you mean?'

'You know exactly what I mean. Arse and fucking abs?'

I placed my cold towel over my eyes so Ruby couldn't see them, 'Rubes drop it. I just get on well with him, that's all. We are friends.'

'Bollocks! No such fucking thing. He wants to get into your pants.'

'He does not! He's never been anything but a gentleman to me.'

'You better not be lying to me Elizabeth Saunders. You don't want to be another fucking notch on his bedpost. Capeesh?'

'That's not going to happen.'

'Yes, well, make sure it doesn't. Because *I'm* going to be the one picking up the pieces when he moves on to the next bit of fluff and leaves little miss "I don't shag for fun" in a crumpled mess on the floor.'

Once again, the temptation to shut Ruby up and tell her the truth about my secret life was overwhelming but I knew I couldn't. Instead, I thought about Jay. Maybe Ruby was right about him and maybe I would get my heart broken. However, that wasn't my only concern...Jay was famous. If we became a couple it would be all over the media, and it would only take one man to recognise me and come forward, for my life to be over. My secret life would be exposed; my family would be devastated, I'd lose my job, my friends, and my relationship with Jay.

The thought of that happening terrified me to the core, and despite the ache in my heart, I knew exactly what I had to do. I had to put an end to all the flirting and forget about any romance with my boss.

At seven pm, sun tanned and feeling good, Ruby and I made our way to the next party. We were working at a fashion show being held in the old part of Vegas, and my job for the night was to escort the VIP guests to their seats and offer them a welcome drink. After the show, we had to serve champagne at an exclusive party full of beautiful people, movie stars and pop artists.

Four hours into the party, Lulu ran up to me, 'Beth, I need you. Mr. T has gone *crazy*. I don't know what his problem is at the moment but he's...let's say, a little...no...*a lot* worse for wear.' She leaned in and whispered, 'He's been drinking again...*a lot*!'

'I doubt he's going to listen to me,' I whispered back.

'Sweetie, I know he trusts you, and I know I can trust you to be discreet. I need you to take him back to his hotel and make sure he gets *inside* his room. I can't have him wandering around Las Vegas like a drunken lout, not with all the press around. We better do it quick before he makes a complete fool out of himself. You get him, and I'll get the car, go, go, go.'

Lulu ran off and I looked for Jay. I found him surrounded by a group of men who were all staring at him as if he was mad, 'Australia kicks your Pommie arses every time. There is no competition mate! Face it...the Aussie boys are all over you.'

I pushed my way through the group, 'Excuse me gentlemen, I'm sorry to interrupt, but I must speak with Mr Thorsen.'

Jay's face lit up when he saw me, 'Ah, here she is! The most beautiful...'

Before he could finish, I grabbed his arm, 'Jay, come on, I'm getting you out of here.'

'Nice one! So, you're going to take me up on my offer? I knew you'd come around my beautiful Beth,' he slurred.

Shit, it's worse than I thought!

'Jay, please be quiet! People are staring at us. Come with me, I'm getting you out of here before you do any serious damage.'

As I pushed him into the waiting car, Lulu gave me a hug, 'Well done Beth, you are a trooper!'

On the ride to the hotel, Jay was intolerable. I found it physically hard to push him away as he attempted to kiss me. When I had finally had enough battling, I yelled at him, 'Jay STOP! I said NO!'

He looked at me horrified, and then he looked angry, 'You're just a bloody tease aren't you Beth? All this time, flirting, giving me the come on, and now you don't want anything to do with me. What's your story? Is this a big game to you? Wind men in, get them to fall for you and then turn them away?' he said viciously.

'Jay stop it! You're drunk...*again*...and I know you'll be phoning me tomorrow apologising. I haven't led you on. I do like you...a lot, but you're *supposedly* in a relationship and I don't want any part of that!'

Jay looked furious, 'Well, you could've bloody well made that clear before you hooked me in. Get out of the car! I don't need a babysitter. Go on, get out!' he yelled as he moved over to the other side of the car. 'Driver, stop the car! Little miss tease is getting out.'

It was my turn to be furious, 'I am NOT getting out of the car in the middle of the night...in the middle of Las Vegas. How dare you speak to me like that! I'm taking you back to the hotel because Lulu asked me to. And as for *us*, face it Jay, you're practically married! I'm not going to be someone you just sleep with and toss aside. I deserve better than that!'

The driver looked at me in the rear-view mirror and kept driving. When we reached the hotel, Jay got out of the car quickly and started marching towards the front door. I asked the driver to wait for me and ran after Jay, 'Jay, wait!'

By the time I got inside the lobby, Jay was standing by the elevator. He turned and saw me coming towards him, 'Elizabeth, hold it right there! I don't need you to take me to my room. I'm a big boy. Go back to the party and find some other bloke who isn't *practically married* and tease him!'

I stared at Jay, as tears pricked my eyes. I wanted to tell him that he was wrong and that I loved him, but the words wouldn't come out. I stood in front of the elevator and watched the doors close.

'You're wrong,' I whispered as tears fell down my cheeks.

In the car I couldn't stop crying. I felt so hurt and angry at the things Jay had said to me. I couldn't believe how cold and cruel he had been. The driver looked at me in the rear-view mirror, 'If you don't mind me saying Miss, you are a really good friend. Mr T doesn't know it, but you probably saved his ass tonight. Not many girls would've stood their ground like you did. Well done Kid.'

For a moment I was worried that he may talk about the incident, but he patted his nose with his finger and winked at me. This was all I needed to know that our secret was safe. When the car pulled up in front of the party venue, I knew that I was too upset to go back inside and judging by the concerned look on the driver's face, so did he. He swiftly turned the car around and headed back to the hotel.

'Beth, Beth, wake up. What a fucking awesome party. Where did you go darling? I was looking all over for you. I met the most *delicious* guy, *and* he has a friend...for you!'

'That's great Rubes,' I said with all the enthusiasm I could muster.

'Too fucking right it is. We are meeting them tonight. Apparently, we only have to work at lunchtime and then we are free. Look on the bright side darling... you may *finally* get laid!'

I managed to pull myself out of bed and checked my phone. There was no message from Jay.

That's not a good sign.

The luncheon was even worse than I expected. Jay didn't even look at me, and when the press photographs were taken, he requested Claire and Ruby to be in all the shots. Lulu asked me if everything went smoothly the previous night, and thanked me for, 'being a trooper.' If only she knew what really went on. I didn't even know if Jay did go to his hotel room. All I did know was that he looked awful too.

When it was time to leave I glanced quickly at Jay who was deep in conversation with a lady sat next to him. Ruby noticed and reminded me that we have some serious partying to do. She was so determined that we spend our last night in Vegas, 'getting drunk and getting laid,' that for once I didn't argue with her.

After a couple of hours relaxing at the pool, we got ready to meet our dates. Ruby had set me up with Josh, who turned out to be very cute and very funny, and for the first time in what seemed like months, I was attracted to someone else.

The evening was so much fun and at one am the four of us stumbled into our hotel lobby. Ruby kissed me on the cheek, 'Beth, the room is all yours darling. I'm going with "fuck me features" to his hotel...enjoy!'

I suddenly felt nervous until Josh turned me around and planted a luscious, soft, slow kiss on my lips. I wasn't sure where my passion came from, maybe it was all the pent-up sexual tension I'd been feeling for Jay, but I was really turned on.

Inside the elevator, Josh's gentle kiss turned more urgent as his hand wandered up my skirt. Within seconds I was panting for more and wanted him to take me right there. Our make out session was really heating up when we were interrupted by the sound of the elevator bell. As the doors opened so did my eyes! I gasped when I saw Jay standing there. He looked at me, and then he looked at Josh who still had his hand up my skirt. Josh continued to try to kiss me, oblivious to the fact that we had company.

'Jay!' I blurted awkwardly, as I tried to release myself from Josh's wandering hands. 'This is Josh. Josh, this is my *boss*... Mr Thorsen.'

'Hi,' said Josh as he wrapped his arms around my waist and snuggled his face into my neck.

I wanted the elevator to suddenly drop, taking me with it. Jay said nothing, but his steely expression and blazing eyes told a different story as he stepped into the elevator and stood next to me. When the doors opened at my floor, I attempted to salvage the situation and murmured goodbye to Jay, but he ignored me.

'Oops, someone's in trouble with the boss man,' Josh whispered like a naughty schoolboy. 'Now come on sexy, let's finish what we started. I want you...*now!*'

Inside the hotel room, my confusion over Jay was temporarily forgotten. Josh wasted no time taking my dress off and within minutes I was laying naked on the bed with his head between my legs. The sex was incredible. After the second time I called "time out" and fell asleep, only to be woken a few hours later by a very aroused Josh.

Oh well, third time's a charm!

11

LA: RISKY BUSINESS

It had been three weeks since my disastrous confrontation with Jay in Las Vegas and I was still hurt, angry and disappointed in him. He hadn't sent me his usual apology text or even attempted to call, so I decided to take a break from working on promotional events to prevent running into him.

Feeling the need to confide in someone, I decided to speak to Gran. Omitting a few of the details I told her a brief summary of what happened in Vegas. Her theory in situations like these was to give each other space and either one of two things would happen; over time I would realise that I was merely infatuated with my boss and forget about him, or we would both realise that we can't live without each other. Simple!

Despite Gran's wisdom and my pent-up frustration at Jay, I was missing him. It didn't help that every time I looked at social media or turned on the TV, he seemed to be smiling straight at me. It was driving me crazy, so I decided that I needed to do something to take my mind off him. I implemented a self-imposed social media ban, took some leave from work and flew to Los Angeles, where I was going to have a holiday and focus on my "other business."

Julia from New York had given me the number of a lady called Jade, who was the "woman in the know" on the West Coast. After a quick phone chat, she agreed to meet with me at a coffee bar in Malibu, 'Darling, I'm hosting an incredible party tonight at a home in Bel Air. Why don't you come? I have an amazing calibre of gentlemen attending and it will be a wonderful opportunity to introduce you to my girls.'

I wasn't sure why, but I felt nervous, 'It sounds amazing. Can I think about it?'

'What on earth is there to think about darling? You will not be disappointed; I can assure you. The financial reward is fantastic, *and* I only invite the best of the best.'

After Jade explained the rules and told me what I could potentially earn, I accepted her invitation.

When I arrived in Bel Air, I was still feeling extremely nervous and I couldn't understand why. I asked the driver if he could wait and took a moment to compose myself before getting out of the cab. Standing in front of an enormous mansion, I took a deep breath, pulled my shoulders back and climbed the steps to the front door.

'Kat darling, you made it! Do come inside and make yourself at home,' Jade said, air kissing and hugging me as though we had been friends for years. 'Do take a look around and if you fancy a swim there are plenty of swimsuits in the master suite. Most of the girls are in there now if you want to go upstairs and introduce yourself.'

I thanked Jade and made my way up to the next floor. A stunning, Spanish looking girl floated past me wearing a tiny bikini. I followed the sound of chatting and laughter until I saw two, huge, double doors slightly ajar. I looked inside the room to see at least thirty naked or semi naked girls, running around trying on bikinis. I closed the door, turned around and headed back downstairs.

Relieved to see a waiter, I took a glass of champagne from his tray and walked outside to the pool area.

My nerves were getting stronger and I had no idea why. Something just didn't feel right. In a bid to calm myself down, I introduced myself to a few of the girls and finally started to relax.

I picked up from a sweet girl called Savannah, that the men liked to chat with as many girls as possible before they approached someone, and if I didn't want to go to a room with a particular man it was okay to say no. I just had to tell him that I already had a commitment.

'What if no one picks me?'

Savannah touched my hand, 'Sweetie, trust me, you will have more than enough men interested. You are beautiful... and that accent!'

By ten pm four men had invited me to their room, but I had declined all of them. I didn't know what I was looking for, but I found it about half an hour later. He was standing with his back to me, leaning against a tree and looking out to the city. His physique reminded me of Jay. Although he looked a little thinner, he was tall, and his hair had the same little curls at the ends. I decided to make a move.

Four steps in; I stopped dead in my tracks. My "man without a face" turned and smiled at another man walking towards him. For a moment, I was petrified, paralysed by fear. There was no mistaking those teeth and those eyes!

Bloody fuck!

Suddenly my whole body was screaming for me to run. I quickly turned and headed for the house, knocking over a waiter in the panic.

Please don't let him see me; please don't let him see me.

I raced up the stairs into one of the rooms on the first floor, locked the door and fell to the ground.

'Jade, did you see the girl who came running in here a moment ago...red dress...brown hair?'

'As a matter of fact, I did. I do apologise James; I don't know what got into her. I hope she hasn't caused you any trouble...more than I can say for the poor waiter.'

'No trouble at all. Do you happen to know where she is? I would like to speak with her.'

'Sorry darling, but I think Kat is busy...if you know what I mean!'

'Kat?' he sounded confused.

'Yes darling. A beautiful feline, *very* popular tonight!'

Silence.

'You look disappointed James. Maybe next time we can arrange something?'

'Oh, no thanks. I must have made a mistake, no worries.'

As I fell onto the bed wondering how on earth I was going to get out of this one, there was a knock on the door.

'Kat, open up...it's me, Jade.'

I unlocked the door and let Jade in.

'I'm so sorry Jade. I didn't know what to do. You see, I know him, and he doesn't know....'

'It's okay darling, I understand. These things happen, but next time try not to make it so obvious. The poor waiter didn't know what hit him,' she laughed. 'Why don't you compose yourself in here for a while and I'll send someone up in about twenty minutes? I think I have just the right man for you.'

After Jade was gone, I stepped out onto the balcony. I desperately needed to calm my nerves, so I sat down and opened the bottle of champagne that was chilling on ice. I couldn't believe Jay was here. I knew why I was here, but I didn't think that he was someone who *paid* for sex! I was beginning to wonder if I knew him at all! As I tried to silence my mind, I heard voices below me.

'How's it going tonight Jay?'

You've got to be kidding.

'Well, there are better things I can be doing,' he laughed. 'I only agreed to come to keep Charles company. If Tanya caught me here, I'd be dead meat.'

'How are you and Tan mate? You don't talk about her much these days. Is everything okay?'

'To tell you the truth Marcus...it's not.'

'Come on, It can't be that bad.'

'I'm afraid it is!'

'Nah, you've been through some turbo times before, I'm sure it'll pass. Maybe you should hook up with one of the chicks here. Offload a bit of that stress.'

'It's not that simple!'

'Of course it is...look at the pussy here. I've got myself a real beauty lined up. Live a little man, it's about time you dipped your pen in some new ink.'

'Marcus cut it out. Like I said, it's not that simple!' Jay sighed, 'There's someone else.'

'Bloody hell Jay! You dark horse! Who is this chick?'

'It doesn't matter, it's no one you know.'

The following few minutes of silence was excruciating. I wanted to pop my head over the balcony and yell, 'Is it me?' but instead, I sat waiting and hoping that Jay would start talking again.

'It's a bloody nightmare. Every time I'm around this woman something absolutely ridiculous happens, and it makes me want her more. She has no idea how beautiful she is, or how sexy.'

'How is the sex?'

Silence.

Marcus laughed, 'You haven't even hooked up yet have you?'

'No. That's what makes this whole thing absurd. Nothing's happened romantically, and to be honest, the way I behaved the last time we were together, I doubt anything will *ever* happen. I think I really pissed her off mate.'

'Wow, I can't believe it Jay. You've never had eyes for anyone but Tan. You seriously haven't slept with her yet?'

'Never! Not even a kiss.'

'Whoa, she must be something special if you're feeling like this.'

'She is Marcus. I think I'm in...'

'Jay darling, there you are!' interrupted Jade. 'Your car is here. Now don't worry, I promise I'll look after Charles. In fact, the girl I have in mind is purrrrfect,' she laughed. 'Now off you go.'

Jade's timing was disastrous, and I wanted to scream, but I had an even bigger problem. I had a horrible feeling that she was bringing Charles up to see me. I ran to the door and as I reached for the handle, I realised it was too late; I could hear her voice at the bottom of the stairs. I dived under the bed just as the door opened.

'That's very strange. I'm sorry Charles but Kat must have gone off with somebody else. Never mind dear, I'll get you Kimberley.'

As soon as I heard Jade's voice trailing off, I popped my head out of the door and saw her enter a room down the corridor. As quickly as I could, I ran down the stairs, grabbed my coat and flew out of the front door. I knew there was a slight chance of bumping into Jay, so I pulled up my hood, put my head down and stepped into a waiting cab.

After an early morning stroll along Santa Monica beach, I picked up breakfast and headed back to my hotel. I had to call Jade to apologise for my abrupt exit from her party the previous night.

'Darling, it's perfectly understandable,' she said. 'You do appreciate that I won't be able to pay you for last night. However, I am having a party tomorrow night in Malibu if you would like to give it another go.'

I politely declined. I got shivers down my spine at the thought of running into Jay again, or even worse, sleeping with Charles or Marcus. As soon as I hung up from Jade my phone rang. It was Ruby, 'Where the bloody hell are you? Why aren't you staying at the crew hotel?'

'I fancied a change. When did you get in?'

'Yesterday, and you're not going to believe who was on our flight.'

I think I will.

'Fucking arse and abs darling! We thought he'd take the crew out to dinner last night, but he had a private function. Anyway, too bad for you but he's gone now. Apparently, he had some "urgent personal business" to take care of back home.'

'Rubes, how do you get all of this information?'

'You know me darling...I have my sources. So, are you coming over to stay with me or what?'

'Yep, give me thirty minutes.'

I joined Ruby and the crew for dinner and had more fun than I have had in a long time. Partly because I was getting bored being in LA on my own, but mostly because Jay was interested in "someone else" and I was willing to bet that the "someone else" was me.

12

HONG KONG FOOK ME

I was so excited to be taking Gran on a "Frip" (fun trip) to
Australia. We had planned to meet Ruby on our stopover
in Hong Kong and then Gran and I were continuing on to
Sydney.

'Gran, please leave Victor at home.'

'Oh darling, don't be such a prudey pants.'

'Well, I'd rather not hear that thing buzzing away while
I'm trying to sleep.'

Gran laughed, 'Okay darling. If it makes you feel better
I'll leave him here. I suppose on the bright side, it will encour-
age me to have some real fun.'

When Gran and I boarded the plane, we were surprised
to discover that Ruby had organised an upgrade into first class
for us both, which made Gran scream with delight. For the
next twelve hours we were spoiled rotten, and when we finally
landed into Hong Kong, Gran was so inebriated that the crew
organised a wheelchair for her and made her promise not to
speak until she got through customs.

That evening while Gran slept off the alcohol, I joined
the crew for dinner and drinks at a local bar. After a couple
of hours, I said my goodbye's and headed back to my hotel. I

was walking through the foyer when I heard the unmistakable Irish twang.

'Bloody hell, if it isn't the delectable Kitty Kat!'

This can't be happening. Not Jay in LA and now Baileys in Hong Kong!

I turned to see Baileys smiling at me, 'John! What a small world!'

'So ye remember me do ye?'

'Of course.'

'Then how come I haven't heard from ye gorgeous arse? Did my failin' to show up put ye off callin'?'

How about the fact that you are married?

I lowered my voice, 'Actually, I don't do *that* anymore.'

'Ah come on. Sure ye do. Why would ye waste a talent like that?' He stepped closer. Mesmerising me with his ridiculously beautiful eyes he ran his finger down the side of my face and across my breast, 'What are ye up to right now?'

Why are you so bloody sexy?

'I have to go.'

'Come on; don't pretend ye have somethin' better to do. I just made a killin' on the horses; I'll make it worth your while?'

As well as being turned on, I thought about the extra spending money, 'How much?'

'Fifteen K. What's that, about nine hundred quid?'

Wow, he must have won big on the races.

I smiled and Baileys took this as a yes. He grabbed my hand and led me to a waiting cab. I recognised where he was taking me, and when we stepped inside the lobby I was happy that Bitchzilla wasn't working at the reception desk. Baileys organised the room while I tried to forget the fact that he had a wife and children. The money was just too good to give up, and after all, I did want him…he was hot!

As Baileys explored my body with his tongue and hands, I let myself escape and feel every intense sensation without guilt. I wasn't going to let him leave this time without feeling him inside me, so I pulled him up to face me, looked into his deep pools of blue and told him to, 'Fuck me.'

He liked my assertiveness, but he was not ready to give me what I wanted just yet. He continued to tease me, entering me slightly then pulling away, driving me crazy! Eventually, I could not stand it any longer, 'Put the fucking thing in or I'm going to die,' I yelled.

Baileys laughed and finally gave me what I wanted. As he pushed deep inside me, a surge of passion rose throughout my body.

Our session lasted for quite a long time because Baileys was determined to not let me down. I could sense him pulling away every time he thought he was about to come, which in this scenario I did not mind a bit. Finally, he had his release but not before I had two of what Gran refers to as, "earth shattering, curl your hair orgasms."

After we both caught our breath, Baileys turned to face me, 'Wow! That was bloody fantastic. When can we do it again?'

On a post-coital high, the words flew out of my mouth, 'Tomorrow night?'

He leant in and kissed me slowly. It was delicious.

Luckily, Gran was tired and wanted an early night, so I put on some new, sexy, red lingerie and headed back out to meet Baileys. When I arrived at the apartment building, I came face to face with Bitchzilla. She handed me a key and told me to go straight up to the room. I opened the door to see a trail of red rose petals, candles and soft lighting.

'John?'

'Follow the path.'

I did as he asked and followed the petals which led to the bathroom. The spa bath was full of bubbles, champagne was on ice and a very sexy, naked Baileys, who was obviously happy to see me, was sitting on the edge of the spa.

'This is very nice,' I said surprised by his thoughtfulness.

He stood up and pulled me to him, and as his tongue traced the outline of my lips his hand moved up the inside of my thigh. Pushing my panties to the side, he put his finger inside me and began to thrust into me slowly as he darted his tongue inside my mouth.

'This is nicer,' he said between kisses.

He peeled off my clothes and took his time to kiss every part of my body, before sitting me down on the edge of the bath. Getting down on his knees, he opened my legs and started kissing his way from my feet to my sex. It was unbearable how much I wanted him.

'John please!'

'Shhh,' was all he said as he continued to tease me. His hot breath and butterfly kisses driving me wild. When he finally kissed me between my legs, my body finally gave in to the waves of intense pleasure that rose within me. He stood up and gently kissed me on the mouth.

After we shared a spa together, Baileys led me to the lounge where he had set up a food platter and more champagne. I had no idea that eating fruit could be so sensual and once again we had explosive, passionate sex.

As I watched Baileys dress, I thought about the intense sexual chemistry between us and how nice our conversation had been in the spa. I was really starting to like him, and I knew that meant danger…he was married, and I was in love with someone else. I reminded myself that our relationship was purely a business transaction and that this had to be our last time together!

Baileys looked at me and smiled, 'So when can I see ye again? I have to say, ye kind of blew me mind!'

I smiled, 'I do agree that it was a little mind blowing.'

'Only a little hey?'

'Okay, a lot…but I can't see you again.'

'Yeah ye can…and ye will,' Baileys said smugly.

'Actually, I really can't.'

A look of anger flashed across his face, 'And why is that?'

'It's nothing to do with you personally, it's just…'

'Just what?' he snapped. 'Got what ye wanted did ye and that's it?'

I was taken aback by the aggressiveness of his tone, 'John, what is wrong with you? Why are you getting so upset? You are paying me to have sex with you. This isn't personal!'

His eyes were almost black, 'Sure it's not.'

He was mumbling something under his breath, so I took his arm and told him to look at me, 'John, listen to me, this *isn't* about you. It's about me choosing not to do this with *anyone* anymore. So, whether I like you or not, it's irrelevant.

This..."us"...isn't going anywhere. You have a family. The last two nights were just business and I *won't* be doing it anymore!'

His eyes were blazing with fury as he moved my hand away. I thought he was going to say something but instead, he threw the money on the table and left without saying a word. Shocked and a little confused, I got dressed, took the cash and left.

13

RUBY BLUESDAY

Early the next day Gran and I set out to explore Hong Kong. After a full day of shopping, eating and shopping some more, I persuaded Gran to join me back at the hotel for a little siesta before we headed out for the evening.

Rested and refreshed, I took Gran for dinner at a local Vietnamese restaurant, and then we met Ruby at a beautiful bar in Central called, "The Feather Boa." When we walked through the door, I was very surprised to find that we had stepped back in time to Paris in the 1920s. The ornately decorated ceiling, glowed with the light of the chandeliers and lush, velvet sofas complimented the interior décor that resembled a Parisian boudoir.

Gran couldn't wait to try their famous cocktails, so we made ourselves comfortable and soaked in the atmosphere. As the bar was packed full, it was not long before we were joined by a group of American men.

Gran laughed up a storm with George from Texas, while Ruby was pursued by George's nephew, Chuck.

When Chuck went to get drinks, I turned to Ruby, 'How's it going with Chuckleberry?'

'Jack? He's okay, not really my type, but after a couple more of these babies he may have potential,' she laughed as she held up our two empty glasses.

'I thought his name was Chuck?'

'Oh pleeeease! If he has any chance with me, that name has got to go! There's no way in hell I'll fuck a Chuck.'

After my fourth chocolate and strawberry daiquiri, I decided to call it a night. Gran wanted to stay on with George and even though Ruby had decided that no matter how drunk she was she couldn't bring herself to, 'fuck a Chuck,' she decided to stay out too.

A couple of hours later, somewhere in my drunken sleep, I heard the sound of giggling and breaking glass. I looked at my bedside clock and it was three am.

'It's okay darling, it's only me...sshhh,' Gran called from the lounge. 'Georgie be quiet or she'll hear you...shhhh...now come with me big boy. Do I have a surprise for you?'

Wondering how on earth I was going to sleep with Gran and George doing it next door, I put in my earplugs, placed a pillow around my head and hoped for the best.

In the morning I walked into the kitchen and was confronted with the sight of George, stark naked, bending over to get something out of the fridge. It was only when he turned around that I saw the cause for all the yelling and moaning from Gran.

Good Lord!

George had an incredibly athletic physique for a man his age.

'Hey, how's it hangin'?' he asked as he attempted to cover himself up with a tea towel.

How do I answer that?

Seemingly uncomfortable at my silence...and my staring, George smiled nervously while I mumbled an apology and retreated to my room.

Two minutes later Gran knocked on my door, 'Darling, can I come in?' she whispered, as she entered my room grinning like someone who had a coat hanger stuck in their mouth. 'Now sweetheart, don't be embarrassed about seeing Georgie in the altogether. He forgot you were here.'

'It's okay Gran; I think George may be more embarrassed. I didn't expect...well...you know.'

'Yes darling...*believe me*, I know,' she giggled. 'Now about today, do you mind awfully if I give our shopping a miss? Georgie wants to show me the sights and if it's alright with you, I'd rather enjoy that.'

Doubting that the sights were the only thing big G was going to show Gran I gave her my permission to play hooky for the day, 'Of course. You have fun, it's your holiday too.'

'Oh goody. You are a good girl,' she said clapping her hands like an excited seal. 'Well, I'll see you later darling. Enjoy yourself.'

Lunchtime

'Rubes, where have you been, I've been calling your room all morning?'

'Keep your knickers on...I've been busy.'

Silence.

'Rubes?'

'Oh sorry, I was just thinking about...never mind! What's happening?'

'Well, I thought we could go to the spa this afternoon before we head out tonight.'

'About tonight, I've sort of made plans,' she said in a weird dreamy voice.

'Who with? Not bloody Chuck? What about our plans?' I asked miserably.

Silence.

'And why are you acting so weird? Are you drunk? You are acting very strange!'

More silence.

'Helloooo? Are you seriously standing me up for a shag on our last night together in Hong Kong?'

Finally, Ruby spoke, 'Sort of…well yes actually.'

'Come on Rubes, Gran has gone off with, "hang your hat on this" George and now you! Can't you just arrange to meet whoever it is after dinner?'

'Beth, you don't understand,' she sighed. 'He has the best cock I've *ever* seen, and you know I've seen a few…and his accent just drives me *insane*. He's unbelievable, and I never thought I'd say this, but he may be "The One!"'

My giggling was quickly silenced by Ruby's "The One" statement. She wasn't joking! In all the years I had known her, she had only gone back for a sequel with two men and I had *never* heard her talk about love, never mind "The One." Feeling a little selfish as this was obviously a really big deal for Ruby, I asked her to come out to dinner with me first and then meet Mr Magic Cock later. She reluctantly agreed and we arranged to meet at six for an early dinner.

All through dinner I was mesmerised by Ruby's strange behaviour. I had never seen her act like this before. It was as though she was on another planet. If she wasn't checking her mobile phone every five minutes, she was staring into space. By seven o'clock, I'd had enough, 'Rubes for God's sake, just call him if...'

Before I even had time to finish the sentence, she was out of the restaurant door and back again within two minutes, 'He's coming...he's fucking coming!' she squealed. 'Oh my God, how do I look? He's just around the corner.'

Confused, I looked around for "Merlin," but Ruby yanked my head back and like a woman possessed, screamed into my face with uncontrollable excitement. Her behaviour was getting stranger by the minute and the very fact that she asked me how she looked was even more disturbing, 'Where is my best friend and what have you done with her?'

'Shut up! He's just...I don't know. This is different Beth. It's not just the sex...even though it is fucking *amazing*! He's not like anyone I've ever met before...he's special!'

'But you only met him last night!'

'Well, it's like they say, "When you know, you know!"'

Leaving Ruby in Dreamland, I made my way to the ladies and decided that I would quickly meet the guy who had cast a spell on her, then go back to the hotel. On my way back to my seat my curiosity turned to sick panic as I locked eyes with the stranger who had a "great cock and sexy accent," who was no stranger to me. Unable to move a muscle due to sheer terror and staring into the face of Baileys, I wondered if I could make a quick run for it. But it was too late, Ruby had seen both our reactions and was demanding to know what was going on.

After our last encounter, I wasn't sure what to expect, but it didn't take me long to realise that Baileys wasn't going to play nice as he glared angrily at me. My eyes pleaded with him not to say anything, but a wicked smirk crossed his face, and he took the opening shot, 'Ah, if it isn't the delicious Kitty Kat! It is indeed a small world that we live in. How nice to see you again…and so soon!' He ran his finger across my cheek to my lips. 'So tell me Katie…are ye both in the same business? Do I get two for the price of one?' he said venomously as he moved away from Ruby.

'Who the fuck is Katie?' demanded a confused Ruby. 'And what do you mean…two for one?'

'I think you have me confused with someone else,' I said cutting Ruby off and glaring at him.

'I don't think so darlin'. Delicious or not, I never forget a *slut* when I meet one.'

'Hey,' interjected Ruby, 'just a minute John, you are making a fucking *huge* mistake. This is my best friend Beth, and believe me, if you think she's a slut then you won't be able to find a word for me darling.'

Just as Baileys started to open his mouth to say something, I quickly tried to salvage the situation, 'Look, John, is it? I think we've gotten off on the wrong foot, maybe I just look like this "Katie" girl,' I said holding out my hand, praying he would take it. 'These things happen, no harm done.'

My eyes pleaded with him to drop it and for a tense minute I thought he was going to take me down, but then his eyes softened, he took my hand and started to laugh, 'I had ye that time, didn't I, me girlies? Ruby darlin' ye should've seen ye pretty little face.'

'Not fucking funny John,' said Ruby elbowing him in the ribs. 'For a minute there I thought you were some kind of psycho.'

You're not far off.

I took a deep breath, 'Okay, I'm going to leave you two lovebirds alone and head back to my hotel.'

Baileys smirked, 'Why don't ye stay? I'd like to get to know Ruby's best friend a little better. Besides, after me callin' ye names, it would be rude of me not to buy ye a drink.'

Ruby swooned, 'See, didn't I tell you he was special Beth? Come on stay for a drink. You two can get acquainted while I pop to the ladies.'

When Ruby left to go to the bathroom I stood up to follow her, but Baileys grabbed my elbow, 'So...Beth is it?' he said evilly. 'Do ye think Ruby would be up for a threesome?'

'Stop it,' I said trying to pull my arm free of his grip, 'you're hurting me and she has no idea that....'

'What? That ye are a fuckin' whore?' he sneered.

Tears stung my eyes, '*What* is wrong with you? Why are you so mad at me?'

Baileys stared at me for a minute, but this time I saw something else in his eyes... hurt. I wondered for a moment if he actually did like me and if I had bruised more than his ego.

'Listen John, it was nothing personal the other night. I had already decided that I didn't want to do *that* anymore. You were my last time.' I placed my hand on his, 'I think I'm in love with someone and...'

'Hey hey bitch, hands off my man,' interrupted Ruby. 'I know you've been closed for business for a while Beth, but he's mine.'

The following fifteen minutes were excruciating watching Ruby get sucked into Bailey's every word, knowing that he was going to break her heart. I could not bear to watch anymore so I decided to leave. I said goodbye and hoped for Ruby's sake that this was just a shag. I would not have the heart to tell her that he was married with kids, partly because I did not want to hurt her, but also because selfishly, I did not want to expose my secret life.

In the cab back to the hotel I started to cry. I was not sure if they were tears of relief for not getting caught or tears of frustration for allowing myself to get into this mess in the first place. One thing I was happy about was that I was leaving Hong Kong the following morning and would hopefully never see Baileys again!

14

WALTZING MATILDA

The events of the past couple of days had shaken me to the core and I was still feeling anxious when Gran and I were on our way to the airport to fly to Sydney. I managed to avoid Ruby, who had already left three aggressive messages on my phone demanding that I speak with her immediately. I knew I wouldn't see her for at least two weeks, and I hoped that by then she would have forgotten what was so urgent and our lives could go back to normal.

When our plane landed into Australia, I was still feeling anxious.

Gran touched my hand, 'Darling, what is the matter? You have been quiet the whole flight. I know you well enough to know when you are unhappy, now tell me what happened last night. Did you have a squabble with your friend?'

'It's nothing Gran, I'm just a little tired,' I lied and then tried to change the subject, 'anyway, did you have fun with George?'

Gran was too smart, 'I know what you are doing darling. Now come on, tell me what happened.'

For the next hour I opened up a little, we talked about men and love. I told Gran about my feelings getting stronger for my boss, the huge fight we had in Las Vegas, his girlfriend, and the fact that we could never be together. She accepted this as my reason for being subdued and didn't ask me anymore questions; instead, she kissed my cheek and held my hand while I cried, 'Things have a way of working out the way they are supposed to darling. The more you fight the longer it takes to get what you want. I've learnt over the years to just let things go and it has worked for me. I know it's difficult but try to forget about your boss and see what happens. If you are meant to be with this fellow it will happen despite any barriers. Believe me, the Universe is truly powerful darling... have faith.'

Australia

Sydney exceeded all my expectations. Beautiful landmarks littered the waterfront, and the city was a vibrant mix of cultures. Gran and I hit the tourist spots hard on our first day; even climbing the Sydney Harbour Bridge was no challenge for Gran. I think the fact that she was attached to a man she described as a, "Six-foot God looking Aussie" motivated her to keep going to the top! By three o'clock I was exhausted and needed a rest.

'You sleep darling, I'm going to do some more exploring,' Gran said closing the door behind her.

I crawled into bed and as soon as I closed my eyes I fell into a deep sleep. Sometime later, in the darkest depths of my mind I could hear a strange sucking noise, accompanied by blows to my head, 'Darling! Wakey wakey. You simply *must* wake up or you won't sleep tonight.'

I slowly opened my eyes to find a five-foot kangaroo staring at me, held up by a five-foot lunatic wearing a hat with corks dangling from it!

Bloody hell, it's a female Crocodile Dundee.

Gran was overly excited about something as she buzzed around the room picking out clothes for me to wear to dinner. I was literally pushed into the bath by Skippy and told in no uncertain terms to, 'make an effort.'

'Gran, what's going on? What are you scheming?'

'Well darling, it's our first night in Sydney so I'm treating you to a very special dinner, and I think we should dress up… that's all.'

Eying her suspiciously I wasn't totally convinced of her explanation. I knew Gran well enough to know when she was up to no good, 'You've set us both up on a double date haven't you?'

'No! Don't be so silly! Although, it's not entirely a bad idea,' she chuckled as she tried to escape the bathroom.

Stopping her in her tracks I told Mrs Dundee to, 'fess up.'

'Oh darling, if you insist! I did meet someone but it's not what you think.'

'Gran! What about George?'

'Like I said beautiful granddaughter, it's not what you think. I met a charming *young* man today who's kindly invited us both out to dinner.'

I started to protest but she cut me off, grabbed Skippy and began twirling around the room singing, 'Que sera, sera, whatever will be will be.'

I give up!

Within an hour Gran's enthusiasm for life was rubbing off on me and we arrived at the restaurant feeling happy and relaxed.

My happiness soon dissipated when we were greeted by a rather, snooty hostess at the front desk, 'It's members only night. You'll have to go somewhere else.'

Feeling a little disappointed I turned to leave, but Gran had other ideas. She whispered something to the hostess who instantly blushed. Suddenly, she was falling over herself to help us, escorting Gran and I to a beautiful table out by the pool. Gran winked at me and as we took our seats in the land of the beautiful and I wondered what kind of evening we had in store.

Two glasses of champagne and three hundred strawberries later, I was beginning to think we had been stood up, 'Gran, do you think he's coming?'

'Of course darling, in fact he's already here. You hoo,' she yelled like an excited Beatles fan.

Turning to me with raised eyebrows and a look that said, 'Don't I know how to pick them,' I stared in disbelief at the man walking towards us. His hair was a little longer and lighter, but it was definitely him!

What the...?

He headed straight for Gran, 'Good evening Matilda.'

I watched in shock as he leant down and kissed Gran on both cheeks, before turning to me, 'And *you* must be the delightful granddaughter I have heard so much about?'

As he brushed my cheeks with his lips, I inhaled the familiar smell of his aftershave and felt like I had been hit by lightning. I looked over at Gran who was doing her favourite impression of a clapping seal, 'Beth darling, this is James. We had the most delightful time together this afternoon.'

'I'm sorry I'm late, but I had an important call to attend to,' Jay said smiling his crooked smile at me.

Still unable to utter a word Gran stepped in, 'Beth, what's gotten into you? I didn't realise you were the shy type. Anyway, there I was about to buy a surfboard, when this dashing young man appeared.'

'Surfboard?' I stammered.

'*Anyway...* we got talking and when James told me who he works for...finally!' she said waving a finger at him, 'I almost fainted. What an amazing coincidence. You both work for the *same* company!'

Jay was smiling and as I suddenly realised what was happening, I couldn't help but smile too. Gran had no idea who he was!

Later at dinner Jay excused himself from the table and Gran grabbed my arm, 'Isn't he a dish? Now you can forget all about that silly boss of yours. *This* man is gorgeous. If I were a bit younger, you'd have a fight on your hands. Lord, knows how he can afford a membership at this establishment on his salary. Anyhow, that's not important. Have you seen his teeth? Good Lord he could do a toothpaste commercial, and check out his package, it's....'

'Ladies,' Jay interrupted, and sat down next to Gran whose eyes immediately shot to his crotch area.

'Stop it!' I mouthed, but Gran just giggled and kept looking.

Thankfully our waiter arrived with the bill and Jay took out his credit card.

'Good heavens, you can't be expected to pay for our dinner James. It'll cost a small fortune and let's be honest, we all know how much you get paid for your job. Seriously, for the work that you flight attendants do, one would expect...'

Jay was finding it hard to hide his smile, 'Matilda, please allow me. After all, I invited you to dinner and I wouldn't dream of letting you pay. Besides, my boss is a nice guy and he's just given me a raise,' he said giving me a sexy wink.

I laughed, however Gran did not see the funny side and insisted that we all go out again the following evening so that she could return the favour.

'I would love to Matilda, but sadly I'm flying to the Sunshine Coast tomorrow morning.'

Gran was clearly disappointed, 'Oh dear, that is a shame.'

Jay looked at me and then turned to Gran, 'Why don't we go out for a nightcap now? And Matilda, I insist that you pay.'

Gran's face lit up, 'What a splendid idea, but James I must insist that you call me Tilly.'

Oh my god, is she flirting?

In the nightclub, I was feeling a little left out. Despite Gran trying to set me up with Jay, she wasn't doing a good job of leaving us alone. They had already danced to four songs and although I enjoyed watching them, my mind kept going back to the last time Jay and I saw each other. I couldn't forget the look of hurt and disgust on Jay's face when he caught Josh with his hand up my skirt in Las Vegas. Not to mention, the unbelievably close call in LA. Thank goodness he had not caught me at the mansion, and who knows what would have happened if I had slept with his friend Charles!

Finally, Gran relieved Jay from the dance floor and insisted that we dance together. As Jay held me close, I felt the familiar feeling of belonging as I melted into his chest.

'Beth, I've wanted to talk to you for a while,' he whispered, 'I just...'

'It's okay,' I said looking into his beautiful green eyes. 'There's no need to explain. I never intended to lead you on, and I don't blame you for what you said.'

'No. My behaviour was unforgivable. I was angry and extremely confused. I'm truly sorry for what I said to you in Vegas. You didn't deserve it.'

I placed my finger on his soft lips and nuzzled my head back into his chest as he held me, because I did not want to ruin this moment. We stayed that way for two more songs and sadly we were brought back to reality by the buzz of his mobile phone.

'I'm sorry Beth; I have to take this.'

I sat back down with Gran, who was beside herself believing that she had introduced me to a sex God, 'I just knew that the two of you would get along darling. The minute I met him I thought that he was the one for you. Call it intuition, but didn't I tell you that the Universe works in very mysterious ways?'

Apparently so!

'Who cares if he's a flight attendant,' she whispered as if it was a bad word, 'he's a spunk.'

I decided it was time to take Gran back to the hotel and as I helped her to put on her jacket Jay re-joined us, 'Beth, what are your plans over the next few days. I really need to discuss something with you?'

Gran tried to elbow me and missed. Luckily, I caught her from falling flat on her face, 'We were thinking of going to Brisbane for a couple of days.'

'Really?' he sounded excited, 'I'm going to be up in Noosa all next week. It's a couple of hours north but I'd love it if you can both come.' He handed me his business card, 'My Australian number is on the back.'

I slipped the card into my purse, helped Gran into the cab and turned to Jay, 'I don't know if...'

This time Jay put his finger on my lips and looked directly into my eyes, 'Beth,' he whispered, 'I've left her!'

With impeccable timing Gran popped her head out of the door, 'Darling, I really must go, I'm feeling a bit squiffy. James sweetheart, thank you for a delightful evening but I must steal my granddaughter from you. Will we see you again?' she asked hopefully.

Jay looked at me expectantly, 'I hope so.'

That night I could not sleep. My mind was still digesting his words, 'I've left her.' I was excited and terrified at the same time wondering what it meant for us, but deep down I already knew the answer. I had a chance of love with Jay Thorsen and I was not going to blow it!

15

THE NAKED TRUTH

'Gran, I don't think you understand, but my boss, the man I'm in love with is....'

'Oh darling, forget about him,' She interrupted. 'James is adorable, he's handsome, charming and he has an *amazing* physique. Just imagine your children, they would be...'

'Gran, stop please! I'm trying to tell you that James *is* my boss! He's the one I've been telling you about.'

Gran looked confused, 'My James is your James?'

'Yes!'

'And he's your boss?'

'Yes.'

Suddenly she stopped in her tracks and turned to me with a look of dismay, 'Oh dear, didn't you mention that he has a girlfriend?'

'Not anymore...Apparently!'

'Oh darling, he's going to think I'm awful.'

'Why on earth would he think that?'

'I insinuated that he has no money and assumed that he was a flight attendant.'

'Don't be so silly Gran! Jay loves you, and so do I,' I smiled as I kissed her cheek.

With newfound enthusiasm, Gran started organising our trip to Noosa with the precision of an F.B.I. agent, 'We are mixing with the big leagues now darling...time to step it up!'

Once all the bookings were finalised, I sent Jay a message on his phone with our flight and hotel details. I was pleasantly surprised when we arrived at the Sunshine Coast Airport to find that Jay had arranged for a car to take us to our hotel. On arrival we were upgraded to a suite, and Jay had ordered champagne and chocolates to be delivered to our room, with an invitation to dinner. Gran was beside herself with excitement and wasted no time in pouring us both a glass of champagne.

At seven o'clock I was ready to meet Jay for dinner. Expecting Gran to be waiting for me on the lounge, I was surprised to find her in bed.

'Oh, do forgive me darling. I fear I've had a little too much of the "Devil's tipple." I have the most dreadful headache and I'm afraid I simply can't join you both for dinner.'

'Gran! I can't go alone!'

'Now now, you're a big girl. Stop worrying! You don't need me to hold your hand. Now off you go and enjoy yourself. You deserve it!' she winked.

Knowing full well that she was faking a headache, but loving her for it all the same, I met Jay as planned.

When Jay saw that I was alone, he couldn't hide his joy and wasted no time in holding my hand. Walking along Hastings Street with him felt magical; the tree-lined avenue was illuminated with fairy lights and laughter rang out from the numerous restaurants and bars.

As we turned the corner at the end of the street, the breeze from the ocean swept over me, 'Where are we going?' I asked.

Answering with a smile, Jay guided me up some stairs and led me through a doorway into a beautiful restaurant located at the edge of the beach. The ambience was heavenly, as the candlelight created a soft glow over the cream-coloured marquee and the moon glistened over the softly breaking waves.

Our conversation during dinner flowed effortlessly. Jay opened up about ending his relationship with Tanya and how he had been longing to contact me, but still felt embarrassed about his behaviour in Vegas. We laughed about Josh, and Jay confessed that he was so jealous, he got ridiculously drunk and missed his flight back to the UK the following morning.

'Lulu was livid and threatened to resign if I didn't get my act together.'

I imagined Lulu's fury, 'Poor Lulu. You do seem to rattle her nerves.'

'Yes, I suppose I do,' Jay smiled. 'Or rather I did. I decided to be a good boy after that little episode, and you'll be pleased to know that I'm back in her good books.'

'For how long?' I teased.

Jay gave me a devilish look, 'I'm afraid I can't answer that.'

I studied Jay's face, 'What brought you to Australia?'

Jay played with his napkin before answering, 'You.'

I was taken aback, 'Me?'

'Yes.'

Is he blushing?

'I was about to jump on a plane back to the UK after finalising a deal in Hong Kong, and I couldn't believe it when I saw Ruby at the airport.'

'You spoke to Ruby?'

'I did. Admittedly, it took some persuasion for her to tell me you were on holiday in Sydney and where I could find you.'

'How was she?'

'I have to tell you; she seemed a little angry with you and wants you to call her back.'

Shit, this has to be about Baileys.

I could feel myself tensing up, but I let it go. I did not want anything to spoil this evening, not even Ruby. I smiled at Jay, 'She'll get over it.'

After dinner, as we strolled along the boardwalk, Jay put his arm around me, and a surge of energy ran through my soul.

We found a spot on the beach, sat down on the sand and watched the moon shimmer over the gentle waves that were breaking softly towards the shore. I looked up at Jay and as he met my gaze a slow smile spread across his face, he leant down and finally embraced me with his kiss. It was as sensuous and delicious as I had imagined, and as his tongue gently darted inside my mouth, I melted into his arms.

'Beth, maybe I should take you back to your apartment,' he said breathlessly.

I kissed him again, this time with more passion and urgency, 'I want to be with you tonight,' I whispered.

His eyes bore into my soul, then he held me tightly and kissed me with such passion that I wanted to rip off my clothes and give myself to him right there on the beach.

'Let's go,' said Jay pulling me up off the sand.

When we reached Jay's apartment neither of us talked. In the hallway Jay turned me to face him, and with just the sound of our breathing, he started to undress me. As I stood in my underwear, he gently kissed me on the mouth, trailing his kisses down my neck, to my chest, as he teasingly peeled off my bra. Just his touch set my skin on fire. When his lips reached my breasts, he circled my nipples with his tongue as his hands wandered down to my thighs. Seductively tracing his fingers up the inside of my legs and around my panties until finally he found me, teasing me, until his lips caught up.

After wanting Jay for so long, my body responded with urgency as wave after wave of delicious feelings rose within me. He seemed to know instinctively what to do, as if he had done it a million times before, and within minutes I was crying out in ecstasy.

Jay picked me up and took me to the bedroom. When he placed me down on the bed, I desperately wanted to please him, but he wouldn't let me and raised my arms above my head.

Jay kissed me softly before moving to the bottom of the bed, 'I've waited a long time for this Beth.'

As Jay caressed his way back up my body from my toes, I had another rush of consuming pleasure sweep over me. When his lips reached my face, he looked into my eyes, and I could see into the depths of his soul. I held his face in my hands and kissed him as he slowly entered me. Finally, after all this time of longing for each other, we both felt the full force of our emotions exploding as our bodies seemed to magically mould together in a mind-blowing fusion of ecstasy and passion.

With every thrust came a wave of pleasure that was so exquisite, sounds escaped me that I had never heard before, and eventually we screamed in unison as we both reached the point of no return.

Both spent and speechless at the intensity of our love making, we held each other tightly, lost in our own thoughts. I could feel Jay's hot breath on my cheek, and I knew that words were not necessary. Our fate had been sealed. I belonged to Jay now…and he belonged to me.

The week we spent in Noosa was wonderful. Gran gave Jay and I a lot of time alone while she amused herself getting to know the locals, having surfing lessons and shopping.

On our last night Jay invited me to join him in his roof-top pool. As he stood looking up at the stars, I dropped my robe and slipped into the water. I silently made my way towards him and wrapped my arms around his broad shoulders. Pressing my breasts against his back, I could feel his heart rate increase as I held him. So far, our lovemaking had been gentle, tender and intimate, as opposed to wild, and I wanted to change that tonight. I planned to do something to Jay that I had learnt from a client in New York. It had driven me wild with anticipation and I was hoping it would have the same effect on Jay.

Jay turned and looked at my exposed breasts before our eyes met, 'Do you have any idea how beautiful you are Beth?'

I could feel myself blushing.

Jay continued, 'And you have the most incredible soul.' He ran his hands down my chest, 'Your body is perfect…and those lips,' he said as he leant in to kiss me.

I wrapped my legs around his waist. Swiftly, he lowered me onto him and as we kissed slowly and deliberately, we moved rhythmically together in the moonlight.

Before our lovemaking came to a climax, I removed myself from Jay. When he protested, I placed my finger softly on his mouth, 'Come with me.'

I lead Jay into the bedroom, and he noticed the two silk scarves that were dangling from each side of the bedhead. A slow grin spread across his face.

I pulled him to me, 'Do you trust me?'

'Completely,' he grinned.

'Lie down!'

I sat astride Jay and softly secured his wrists to the sides of the headboard with the scarves, 'One more,' I said as I took another scarf and covered his eyes.

I kissed him on the lips and whispered, 'Give me your tongue.'

Jay moaned when I began to simulate oral sex with his tongue. After a couple of minutes, I reached for a cold carton of yogurt and a spoon out of the ice bucket; I traced the outline of Jay's lips with yogurt and licked it off slowly. After we kissed, I ran the spoon down the centre of his body until I reached his groin. Putting a spoonful of cold yogurt in my mouth, I gave him oral sex. He was now beside himself and was begging me to sit on him.

'Not yet,' I teased.

I was really enjoying his reaction, so I retraced my steps. This time with a piece of ice in my mouth, I made my way up his body, while simultaneously stroking his inner thighs with my hands.

'Bloody hell Beth, this is too much. Please, let me take you!'

'No…it's my turn,' I said smiling to myself.

Finally, when I could tell Jay couldn't take any more, I removed the blindfold so he could see all of me. I held the top of the headboard and positioned myself so I was directly above Jay's mouth. He knew what I wanted, and he didn't hesitate. As he probed, kissed, and explored between my legs, I felt the surge of arousal consume me. My moan turning into a scream as my body shuddered above him.

'Beth, please...?' Jay was desperate now.

I placed myself on top of his hips and as I teased him slowly inside me, I finally gave him what he was begging for. But when I sensed that he was about to come, I moved off him again.

'For the love of God Beth! Put it back in!'

I turned around so Jay could see my behind, and I lowered myself onto him again. I knew that this view drove him wild, so I moved on top of him, slowly at first, and then increasing the pace. It didn't take long for Jay to climax.

When I finally untied Jay, he gave me a look that I hadn't seen before. I smiled, 'You like?'

'I love!'

With a huge grin on my face, I snuggled into Jay's arms and fell asleep. It seemed like we had only been sleeping for a short time when I was woken by Jay trailing one of the scarves down the middle of my body. He had a wicked glint in his eyes, 'My turn!'

I didn't protest...instead, I let Jay tie me up, tease me, love me and give me the best orgasms of my life.

Afterwards, as I lay exhausted in his arms, I couldn't believe how lucky I was to have him.

A week longer than planned, Gran and I reluctantly packed to leave Sydney. She had been acting strange since we left Byron Bay and was constantly giggling. I noticed that she had a box that I had not seen before.

'Gran, what's that?' I said pointing to the box.

'Oh that's nothing darling, just some pretty little cakes that nice, hipster fellow, Storm gave me. They are quite delicious, I had one this morning.'

'I knew it! You've been acting strange ever since we left Byron. Gran, he's given you cakes laced with Marijuana...you can't eat these, they are illegal!'

Gran looked at me as though I had taken Victor off her, and then burst out laughing, 'Oh darling, how absolutely wonderful. Let's finish them off before we leave. It'll be such a shame to waste them,' she said, attempting to stuff another one in her mouth.

I wrestled them off her and threw the box in the bin, 'Do not touch them again!'

Gran pulled a face, 'Spoilsport.'

A short time later I heard Gran calling from her bedroom, 'Darling, come here I've got something to tell you.'

'Got some other illegal possessions that you would like to confess?' I laughed.

'Oh stop being so silly. I actually had something pierced yesterday. As far as I know, it's completely legal.'

I realised it could only be one of two places and winced.

'Oh darling, don't be such an old Fuddy Duddy. It's quite safe. I was reading on the Internet that having one's "you know what" pierced enhances sexual stimulation and can even result in better orgasms.'

I covered my ears with my hands and closed my eyes, 'I'm not listening.'

'I think Georgie will be very pleased. It really is quite extraordinary how it changes the appearance of my...'

'Gran!' I finally snapped, 'I'd rather just take your word for it. I'm sure it is beautiful; however, I do not want to discuss your "you know what" if you don't mind!'

'Oh darling! For someone so worldly, you are funny sometimes. Now where did I put Victor?' she said as she disappeared into the kitchen.

I was about to question Gran on the fact that she promised she was leaving Victor at home, but I decided to let it go. It was only when Gran was stopped at airport customs that I told her off. She had placed Victor in her carry-on bag and had to explain herself when the customs official found it. I was mortified, however Gran insisted on giving the Customs official the website address for the products, and told him in no uncertain terms, 'You simply *must* buy one for your wife dear; it will improve your sex life considerably!'

16

THERE'S A WHOLE LOT OF LOVIN' GOING ON

The following two weeks after Gran and I arrived home were wonderful. Ruby was away on a promotional tour of the UK and although she had left several aggressive messages on my phone, I had not returned her calls.

My relationship with Jay was also moving very fast. He had secretly managed to find me every night while I was away on trips. Surprising me in New York and France, it did not seem to matter where I was, he said that I was like his own little drug and he wanted to spend as much time with me as possible.

It was not all rosy though, there were times when Jay answered difficult calls from Tanya and even though he was visibly upset, he would not discuss it with me, and I did not push him; I felt that he would open up when he was ready.

'Beth, there's something I have to tell you,' he whispered as he ran his fingers down the side of my body. 'I don't want there to be any secrets between us.'

The way he said it made me feel uneasy.

'I think we need to be very honest with each other, don't you?'

I froze.

He moved his lips close to my ear and I could feel his breath on my neck, 'Beth…I know!'

I felt nervous energy rise within me, 'You know?'

'Yes, I know!'

Fear engulfed me and I felt sick. Questions flooded my consciousness, and images raced through my mind trying to decipher how he could know.

Who told him? Did he see me in LA? Was it Ruby? Was it a client? Why is he still in my bed if he knows who I really am?

After a few minutes of silence Jay spoke, 'It's okay Beth. I think we can both handle it.'

I could hardly hear him. I felt dizzy and my mind continued to race.

How can we have a future together when he knows that I've slept with men for money? What must he think of me?

Jay turned my head to face him, and he could see that I was crying, 'Beth, please don't cry. I knew the truth after I first met you.'

Between the tears, I found the words. 'You did? Then why didn't you tell me before…before we…?'

'I'm telling you now,' he smiled.

Why is he smiling?

'Beth,' he said as he wiped the tears from my cheeks, 'I know that I love you!'

My body collapsed in his arms, relief replacing the adrenalin that was coursing through my veins. Jay did not know about my secret life as Kat. All Jay knew was that he loved me!

'Beth?' he laughed. 'Are you okay mate? You look a little...
shocked!'

'I'm fine, it's just...'

'Shh, you don't have to respond. I know I'm moving a
little fast here, but I had to tell you. You take your time, it's
all good.'

I wanted to tell him that I loved him too, but I could not
bring myself to say the words, so I showed him in a different
way, the only way I seemed to know how. I crawled under the
sheets and made my way down his body.

The following morning while I was packing for my trip
to Los Angeles, Jay came into the bedroom and wrapped
his arms around my waist, 'Beth how would you like to stop
doing that?'

'Jay, I don't have time. You'll just have to wait.'

'Actually, I wasn't talking about *that*, but now that you
mention it.' His hands slipped under my skirt. I pulled away
and he turned me to face him, 'Beth, how would you like to
come away with me this week? I've got business meetings in
Italy and I would love you to come. We can make a holiday
of it?'

Italy! It sounded ideal. Since I became involved with Jay
I had cancelled all my clients, ignored repeated calls from
Julia and managed to keep Ruby at bay. I could switch off
my phone, forget about everyone, and just be Beth Saunders
on holiday with the man she loves. It seemed like the perfect
solution to my problems.

I doubt I'm going to be able to get off work at such short notice.

As if Jay read my mind, 'There's no problem getting you
off work Beth, in fact the wheels are already in motion, all
you have to do is say yes!'

I smiled, 'One of the perks of sleeping with the boss I guess. Well in that case...yes, yes, yes!'

While Jay disappeared to make the call, I sent an email to Gran to let her know where I was going. Her reply was instant...*Have fun darling...you lucky girl!*

'But darling, there's no need to be intimidated. Victor will never replace you. Now stop being a baby and take your pants off.'

George looked at his new love with a twinkle in his eye. 'Matilda Worthington, you are a very, very naughty gal!'

Matilda was in heaven. She never thought that she would find love again and thanks to Beth, she had met George. Not only was he handsome, athletic, and incredibly kind-hearted, he made her feel like the most loved woman in the world.

When Matilda returned to the UK after her holiday with Beth, there was an envelope from George waiting for her. It contained a first-class ticket to Texas and she literally re-packed her suitcase and jumped on a plane. That was six weeks ago, and every day she emailed Beth detailing where they had been, what they were planning to do, and how many orgasms she had!

'Say honey, do you like Texas?' asked George as he helped Matilda down from her horse.

'Why of course darling. It's simply fantastic.'

George smiled. 'What d'ya say we make this holiday a little more...how shall I put this...permanent?'

'Well, darling, I don't have any immediate plans, but I will have to go home eventually. My business won't run itself you know, and one has to make a living.'

George smiled and as Matilda led her horse into the stable, she noticed that he had walked away in the opposite direction towards a huge oak tree. Matilda put her horse away and walked back towards where George was sitting.

'Darling is everything all right?' she asked concerned by the serious look on his face. 'Whatever is the matter?'

George sighed, 'Well Tilly…it's you!'

'Me?' she asked slightly worried.

'I've worked hard ma whole darn life, and I thought I had everything that I needed just here with ma horses and ma family. I thought I was happy. Then I met you…and none of that stuff seems important anymore.'

Matilda went to speak but George silenced her with his hand. 'I can't remember when I felt like this about any one person in my whole darn life. I keep thinkin' that it's just a sexual thing, but I know it's not. Matilda Worthington you've changed me, and I like how it feels,' he smiled. 'I've waited ma whole life to meet someone like you.'

George dropped down on one knee and pulled out a beautiful, antique, diamond ring from his pocket, 'Call me an 'ole fool, but Matilda Worthington, I would be honoured if you would make me the happiest man alive and agree to be ma wife?'

Matilda was blinded by tears. She knew in her heart that she would be happy with George and that she already loved him, so she nodded her head yes and allowed George to place the ring on her trembling finger.

George wrapped her in his arms and looked into her teary eyes. 'I love you Tilly and I promise to look after you for the rest of ma life. You won't have to worry about anythin' ever again. Do you hear me?'

Matilda was overwhelmed with emotion, but she shook her head, and kissed him softly, 'I love you too Georgie.'

'Ye are the sexiest piece of ass I have ever had the pleasure to fuck!'

Ruby looked at Baileys and smiled, 'You're not so bad yourself handsome. Now where shall we go today? Do you fancy a drive into London? I can show you around a little and then we can have some lunch in a pub.'

'Get ye ass back here first, I'm still horny and we've got some catchin' up to do before we go anywhere. Now put ye mouth to good use and suck me cock before I put it some-where very dangerous!'

Their lovemaking went on for hours and instead of going out, they ordered dinner and snuggled up on the sofa. Ruby was in love and she could not believe it. For years she had ad-amantly protected her heart. With a preference for one-night stands, she was happy to "love them and leave them," because she did not want to get hurt. Now, for reasons that she could not fathom, she had let down her barriers with John and was so serious about their relationship that she was considering moving to Hong Kong. The only thing upsetting her was Beth. After Beth left the bar in Hong Kong, Baileys admitted to Ruby that he did know her. He had attempted to explain to Ruby what had happened between them, but she always stopped him. Ruby did not want the details; she felt she could handle it better if she did not know all the facts. Ruby's only wish was for Beth to get over her problem with John, so they could all get along. She did not know how she would cope if the two people she loved could not be in a room together.

Beth had not returned any of Ruby's calls and despite John telling Ruby to forget about her, she could never do that. Ruby and Beth were like sisters, and Ruby firmly believed that whatever had happened between Beth and John was not worth losing their friendship over.

Baileys interrupted Ruby's thoughts, 'Hey, what are ye thinkin' about me gorgeous girlie? You look sad. Come here and let me put a smile on ye face.'

Baileys kissed Ruby passionately while his skilful fingers explored her body. He could sense her excitement by the pounding of her heart and the rosiness of her cheeks, so he didn't stop until she screamed his name.

The week Baileys and Ruby spent together flew by, and Ruby was getting anxious because she did not know when they would see each other again. There was no question in her mind that he was the man she wanted to spend the rest of her life with and she wanted to talk to him about their future. On Baileys last night she broached the subject of living together and was surprised when he agreed, 'Ye can have anythin' ye want gorgeous, but remember, I travel a lot so ye won't see much of me.'

That was good enough for Ruby. She knew with her flight schedule and John's work travel that time together would be a challenge, but she would take what she could get…she was in love!

I really loved our week in Italy. Jay had booked a villa overlooking Lake Como, and despite making love at every given opportunity, we did manage to do a little sightseeing. We toured the lake on a private yacht and took a helicopter to Nice in France. For the whole time, I felt like I was living in a dream, and although I never would have believed it possible, I had fallen more in love with Jay with each passing day.

'Do we really have to leave? I love it here,' I moaned as Jay packed his case.

Jay laughed, 'Beth, we can come back. It's not that far from London you know! Now stop sulking, we have the whole day to enjoy before we head home. I just have one important thing to do this afternoon, but the rest of the day belongs to you...I promise!'

Blessed with a beautiful morning of sunshine, we took a train to the top of a mountain and ate breakfast overlooking the town of Como. After a short ferry ride, we reached a small village on the other side of the lake called Cernobbio, where we ate gelato on a park bench overlooking the lake.

Jay looked at his watch, 'Come on Beth, we have to leave.'

'Where are we going?'

He smiled, 'You'll see,'

We got into a waiting car and drove over the Swiss border. For over an hour, we drove through the most beautiful countryside I had ever seen. Snow-capped mountains surrounded small villages, and swizz chalets were dotted between ancient churches and stone buildings. The contrast of green grass against the mountainous backdrop took my breath away, and when the car finally came to a stop, I realised that we had reached the top of a mountain. As I stepped out of the car, the freezing cold wind brushed my face.

'Here, put this on,' Jay said as he handed me a thick coat. 'Come on, we are going for a walk.'

Absorbing the picturesque scenery around me, I followed Jay along a snowy path. When he stopped at a clearing over-looking a small town, he asked me to sit down on a rock.

'Wow, this view is amazing Jay. How did you find this place?'

Jay joined me on the rock and nestled me into his arms, 'My parents brought me here on my very first holiday to Europe. It has a special significance in our family, and I wanted you to see it.'

'It's the most beautiful place I have ever been to.' I looked up into his beautiful, green eyes. 'Thank you for bringing me here.'

His eyes danced with happiness, 'I'm glad you like it.'

We sat in silence for a while, both lost in our thoughts. I was looking out onto the snow-capped mountains when I could sense Jay staring at me, 'Beth, do you want to know *why* this place is so important to my family?'

'Oh sorry! Yes, of course I do.'

'It's actually the exact spot where my grandfather proposed to my grandmother. Thirty years later my father brought my mother here, and well, you can imagine what happened.'

'Oh!' I suddenly felt uneasy. 'Did you propose to Tanya here too?'

Jay laughed, 'No! Absolutely not!' He pulled me closer, 'Actually, that was one of the reasons we never got engaged. I didn't want to bring Tanya here.'

I turned my head to face him.

'Beth, that in itself told me something, because all I could think about from the moment we met was bringing you here and sharing it with you.'

I could feel tears stinging my eyes as Jay leant in and kissed me slowly. When we finally pulled away from each other Jay took my hands and asked me to stand up.

'Do we have to leave now; I'd love to stay a little longer?'

Jay smiled and pulled me to my feet so I was facing him, 'Yes, we can stay a little longer.'

I was about to sit back down but Jay kept hold of my hands. He took a deep breath and looked into my eyes, 'Elizabeth Saunders, despite being the most accident-prone person that I have ever met, you are so much more,' he smiled. 'You are beautiful, kind, funny, incredibly sexy,' he cleared his throat, 'and…I would like to know if you will do me the honour of becoming my wife?'

Is this really happening? Did he just ask me to…

'Beth?'

His voice brought me back to the present with a startle. Dazed, I stepped back and lost my footing and within seconds I was flat on my back in the snow. Jay fell to his knees beside me, 'Beth, are you okay?'

As I lay in the snow, all I could do was laugh. Suddenly I felt Jay pulling me up into his arms, 'Beth, will you please say yes and marry me, so I can take care of you and at least stop you from hurting yourself?'

I rubbed my cold nose on his and yelled, 'Yes, yes, yes, yes, yes!'

As the sound of my voice echoed around the mountain Jay placed the most beautiful ring I had ever seen on my finger.

'It was my grandmothers.'

I looked at the stunning, antique, diamond ring, sparkling against the light of the snow and tears spilled down my cheeks. Jay took my face in his hands and after kissing my tears, he placed his salty lips on mine. In that one moment, nothing else mattered, except that I was going to be Jay's wife.

17

SECRETS AND LIES

'Ruby, about next week, I've just realised that I'm not goin' to be in Hong Kong after all. I have to go to Manila,' Baileys lied.

'Oh well, that's okay, maybe I can fly to you for a couple of nights.'

'Actually, that won't be possible. I'll be with business colleagues and I won't have time to spend with ye.'

Ruby smiled, 'I don't mind. I'll just wait for you in bed. After all, that's really all I want you for.'

Baileys looked agitated, 'I said NO! All right!'

Ruby was stunned by his outburst and attempted to make light of the situation, 'Keep your knickers on. No need to yell.'

The air instantly turned tense and as Baileys got out of bed he turned to look at Ruby. He thought about apologising but changed his mind.

They drove to the airport in silence and as they walked towards the check-in desk the tension was palpable. Baileys turned to Ruby, 'Look Ruby; I'm sorry that I yelled at ye. It's just that I have a very serious job and I'm not used to havin' to share me time with anyone. I'll try to make it up to ye okay?

What do ye say if I fly back here the following week? We can look at ye roster and work it out.'

Ruby's sadness instantly turned to joy, 'That will work. I'll call you tomorrow and we can make pla…' Ruby stopped in her tracks and looked like she had seen a ghost, 'Oh my fucking god!'

'What's wrong?'

'Over there! Bloody stupid cow! What the hell is she doing?'

Baileys followed Ruby's eyes and a slow, sly, smile crossed his lips, 'Well, well, well, what has kitty Kat snagged now?'

Ruby grabbed Bailey's arm, 'We have to leave. NOW!'

Baileys released his arm from Ruby's grip, 'No way girlie, this is too good to miss.'

He had instantly recognised who Beth was with, after reading a recent article about the world's most eligible bachelors. He was not about to let this opportunity pass and Ruby had no choice but to follow him.

'Well well, if it isn't the delectable kitty Kat!'

Jay and I were walking towards the exit when I heard his voice. I turned around and was confronted by the last two faces I ever expected to see.

Fuck!

Ruby glared at me, 'Beth…Mr Thorsen.'

Jay looked at me, but I was frozen with fear and rendered speechless, so he stepped in, 'Hello Ruby, what a coincidence meeting you here. Sorry,' he said holding his hand out to Baileys, 'how rude of me not to introduce myself. I'm…'

Baileys cut him off, 'Mr James Thorsen! No introduction needed,' he smirked, looking directly at me. 'In fact I've just been readin' about ye. I'm John Davenport, a friend of Ruby's and a *very* close friend of Beth's.'

His evil smile made me feel sick.

'Oh,' Jay looked confused, 'Beth never mentioned you. Maybe she can fill me in later,' he said innocently.

Ruby was staring at my left hand and Baileys followed her gaze, 'Well, well, what have we here' he said grabbing my hand, 'is there somethin' ye haven't told us Beth?'

I shivered.

Baileys was almost salivating, 'That ring must be worth a small fortune. Ruby look what ye little girlie Beth has gone and done. Got herself a nice, *rich,* fiancée.'

Jay seemed a little uncomfortable, 'Ruby, I'm sure Beth was going to tell you the minute she got home. We only got engaged yesterday, and if you don't mind we would like to keep it a little quiet for now. As you can imagine, it may cause a few complications on the work front for Beth.'

I could almost see the smoke coming from Ruby's nostrils and Baileys looked like he had just struck gold. I had to get out of there and fast, 'Well, it was great seeing you both,' I lied. 'Jay we had better go.'

'Oh, little Beth, there's no need to rush,' Baileys put his arm out to stop me. 'I want to ask Mr Thorsen somethin', if ye don't mind?' he looked at Jay. 'Do ye have a business card? I have a little venture that I wouldn't mind someone like yerself givin' me a second opinion on.'

Lying bastard!

'Of course,' said Jay as he passed a card to Baileys. 'Send me an email and we can have a chat. Any friend of Beth's is a friend of mine.'

Baileys took the card, looked at me and winked, 'Oh and another thing…Beth, I seem to have misplaced ye mobile number. Silly me. Any chance ye can write it here on this card? Ye never know, I may need a chat…for old time's sake.'

I took the card and reluctantly wrote down my number. I considered giving him a false one but knew that all he would do was call Jay and that was the last thing I wanted.

'Well,' said Jay, 'I guess we'd better get going. Ruby, John, nice to see you both.'

Ruby was still glaring at me and I had to look away. My mind was reeling.

Why does that snake Baileys want Jay's number? What is he up to and why is he here in London with Ruby?

'Seems like a nice enough bloke,' said Jay, 'although he seemed a little pissed with you for some reason.'

I didn't respond and kept walking as fast as I could.

'Not an ex-boyfriend that you haven't told me about is he? Do I have some competition?'

'NO!' I said a little too aggressively, 'Not at all. He's with Ruby.'

'Maybe we should invite them to dinner. Celebrate our engagement.'

I didn't answer.

Back at the airport, Ruby was saying goodbye to Baileys, 'I don't know what's gotten into Beth; she used to tell me everything. I knew something was going on between those two, but I didn't realise it was so serious. And what the hell was all that about, "Seems like she's got herself a rich fiancé…Beth, can I have your mobile number?" I was mortified.'

Baileys shrugged his shoulders.

'John, I'm serious,' continued Ruby, 'I think it's time I actually heard what happened between you two because I don't have time to waste on someone who's in love with my best friend!'

Baileys looked at Ruby for a moment, 'Are ye sure ye want to know because it's not pretty?'

'Yes,' Ruby said defiantly. 'I want to know *everything*!'

For the next hour, Baileys told Ruby how he had first met Beth, and how she told him that her name was Kat. He didn't go into detail about the sex, but he did tell Ruby about the last time he and Beth got together, the night before he met Ruby.

When Baileys had finished, Ruby didn't know whether to believe him. She knew Beth more than anyone, or at least she thought she did! But then again Beth hadn't told her the truth about Jay, and Ruby questioned why John would lie about such a thing, what did he have to gain?

Ruby sat in silence for a while trying to digest what Baileys had told her, and her mind flashed back to the first time she introduced Beth to John in the bar in Hong Kong. She remembered how strange both of them had behaved and recalled the look on both of their faces when they saw each other; John calling Beth a whore and another name. Then she thought about their interaction when she returned from the bathroom and it all made sense. If Beth was getting paid to have sex, it certainly explained all the extra money she seemed to have lately.

Ruby felt sick. She didn't want to believe it, but she knew that Baileys was telling the truth. What she didn't know was how she was going to deal with it.

Ruby could feel the tears welling in her eyes and the last thing she wanted was for the man she loved to see her cry, 'I have to go. I'll call you in a few days.'

Baileys watched Ruby walk away, and even though he knew she was upset, he couldn't stop smiling at how events had unfolded.

On the flight to Hong Kong, Baileys could not sleep. Instead, he was planning how he was going to get his revenge on, "the little, money-grabbing whore." He still could not believe his luck at bumping into Beth and her *extremely wealthy* fiancée at the airport, and he knew exactly what he was going to do.

Turned on by his own thoughts, he beckoned the stewardess who had been giving him the eye since he boarded, 'Hi gorgeous, are ye up for some fun?' he winked.

She smiled, 'What do you have in mind sir?'

'Well, I'm about to become very, very, rich, and the only thing that turns me on more than money is a hot, blonde, flight attendant.' He beckoned her closer, 'I was wonderin' if ye can help me out with a little problem. I seem to have somethin' wrong with me?'

The flight attendant followed Bailey's eyes to his crotch, and it was obvious what his problem was, 'Is that somethin' ye can help me with?'

'Oh dear, that is a problem. I think you ought to follow me sir.'

As the pretty, blonde, flight attendant walked towards the toilets at the rear of the plane. Baileys rose from his seat and followed her.

Back in Hong Kong, Bailey's wife and children were excitedly waiting for him to return home from his business trip in Europe. It was their tenth wedding anniversary and his wife had arranged a surprise party for him. She was also waiting to tell him her little secret…she was four months pregnant!

18

WHAT GOES AROUND...

One week after bumping into Ruby and Baileys at the airport, I got the call, 'Check your email kitty Kat!'

Feeling nervous, I turned on my computer and opened up my email. On the screen was a mock newspaper article with my photo and the headline:

"Billionaire Bachelor To Marry Whore"

I quickly read through the article and by the time I had finished, my whole body was shaking with rage and my eyes were locked on the threatening words that he had written at the bottom of the page...

This can all go away kitty Kat! I want all the money back that I paid you in Hong Kong and an extra US $100,000 by the end of the month.

You know the drill:
Tell anyone and I go to the media.
Don't pay up and I go to the media

Transfixed by the words in front of me, I was brought back to the present by the ringing of my mobile. I thought about ignoring it, but I knew it would be Baileys and I wanted to give him a piece of my mind, 'You sick bastard! Where do you think I'm going to get that kind of money from in two weeks?' I yelled.

'Now now Kitty Kat, there's no need to be hysterical. I'm sure the future Mrs James Thorsen can figure that out. It'll be like small change for you soon.' He laughed and then his tone turned threatening, 'You have imagination Beth…use it!'

You evil, fucking bastard!

With shaking hands, I put down my phone and collapsed on the floor. This time my whole body gave in as I cried. I felt like I had nothing left. I could not tell Jay and I certainly did not have the money to pay off Baileys. He had given me no alternative but to end my relationship.

It seemed like hours had passed when I heard Jay's voice, 'Beth, what's the matter? What happened?' He picked me up and scooped me into his arms. 'Why are you lying on the floor? Have you been crying?' He moved some hair from my face, 'Tell me what's happened so I can fix it!'

I could not speak, but I knew in my mind that this was one thing that Jay could not fix. I let him hold me while I tried to gain the strength to tell him that our relationship was over.

Jay was concerned, 'Beth, I can't help you if you don't talk. Now please tell me why you are so upset.'

I had no idea where the words came from, but before I could stop myself I was telling Jay that I owed someone a lot of money. Jay asked me how much, and when I told him the amount he laughed!

'It's not funny. It's a ridiculous amount of money and I don't have it,' I cried.

'Beth, look at me,' he said sympathetically, 'please don't take this the wrong way, but to me, that's not a lot of money. Now, dry your eyes and stop worrying because I'll give it to you. I can't stand to see you this upset.' He kissed me gently as he wiped the tears from my cheeks, 'Once we pay off your debt, we can have one of my accountants help you to budget so it doesn't happen again, okay?'

'But...' I started to talk and Jay cut me off with another kiss. I felt immensely relieved, however, I hated the fact that I was giving in to Bailey's demands. He was evil and bitter, and I knew deep down that he was never going to stop. Blackmailers never did!

Four weeks had passed since I transferred the money to Baileys, and I was finally starting to relax. Despite feeling complete panic every time I opened my emails, I had not heard from him and had convinced myself that it was over. I sat down at my computer and feeling confident, I opened my inbox. As I looked at the screen I felt adrenalin rushing through my body... there it was: **"New message from JD69."** With trembling hands, I clicked on the message.

To: BS
Subject: COP
From: JD69

Things have changed. Fucking stupid wife got pregnant again! I need more money... $200K. You have 8 weeks!

I stared in disbelief at what I was reading.

Is he bloody serious?

Shock turned into rage, I dialled his number on my mobile, not caring about the time difference or the consequences. His voicemail came on and I decided against leaving a message in case he used it against me in the future.

For the next hour I thought about what I was going to do and concluded that besides hiring a hit man, there was only one option and I did not like it…I had to speak to Ruby!

Walking towards Ruby's front door, I felt extremely nervous. I had no idea if she was home, but I had to take a chance. I knocked on the door and waited.

Ruby opened the door and glared at me, 'What do *you* want?'

'Can I come inside? I need to speak to you about something.'

Her eyes were blazing, 'So, you've finally decided to fess up to being a hooker?'

Ruby's words hit hard, and I was shocked that Baileys had told her. I took a deep breath, 'Please can I come in?'

After a minute's pause, Ruby turned her back and walked over to the sofa. I closed the door and followed, 'Ruby, I know this is difficult, but you are my best friend and I miss you. I don't know what Bail… John has told you, but I didn't mean to hurt you.'

Ruby refused to give me eye contact and stared straight ahead. With pure disgust registering on her face she finally spoke, 'I want to hear everything! I want to know the truth Beth… or whatever the fuck name you are calling yourself now. I want to know about John…about Jay. You have lied to me for a very long time and I'm not fucking happy!'

For the next hour I told Ruby most of the truth. I felt like I had nothing to lose. I could not pay Baileys the money and I knew that he would go to the media eventually. No matter how painful the conversation was going to be, I thought it would be best for Ruby to hear it from me, just as it was going to be best for Jay later. When I got to the part about Baileys blackmailing me, Ruby looked at me for the first time. Her eyes were brimming with tears, and instead of anger I saw disappointment. I did not know who Ruby was crying for, but I figured it was probably the fact that her best friend and the man she loved had both lied and deceived her.

Finally, Ruby spoke, 'I'll speak to John about the money. I'll get him to stop.'

'Are you sure? I don't know if it's going to be that easy.'

'He'll stop,' she muttered.

We sat in silence together for a long time and as Ruby's disappointment filled the air, I felt shame and guilt overwhelm me.

Ruby noticed that I was crying too, 'How long did you do it for?'

'A few months,' I lied.

'Have you stopped?'

'Yes. I stopped when I became involved with Jay.'

'Fuck Beth, what were you thinking? What about Jay? He's not just someone off the street, he's famous! What will happen to him if someone comes forward when you get married? What if someone else tries to blackmail you? Have you thought of the consequences?'

'Yes, and I don't know.'

'Fuck! Of all the people in the world, I never would have thought you would spread your legs for money!'

I looked away, embarrassed.

Ruby shook her head, 'I'm a fucking idiot. Here I was this whole time thinking that I was the slut, meanwhile my best friend is shagging her way around the world and getting paid for it!'

I looked down, desperate to change the subject, 'I'm thinking of ending it with Jay.'

'Well hello for fucking Fredo! I don't think you have an option.'

Even though I didn't want to hear it, I knew Ruby was right.

'What will you tell him?'

'I don't know. I'll have to lie.'

'Well, you're good at that!' she said bitterly.

I looked at Ruby knowing that I fully deserved that. She looked away, 'I'm going to fly to Hong Kong to sort this out. This isn't the kind of thing you do over the phone. I want to see him anyway; it's been over two weeks.'

I wondered then if she knew that he was married, 'Rubes, can I ask you a question?'

'What?' she barked.

'How much do you know about John?'

'I know that he slept with you and paid you for it! I also know that I'm in love with him and that I'm moving to Hong Kong to be with him as soon as I can get a visa. Anything else?'

I was shocked. Either Baileys had left his family, or not told Ruby about them. I was willing to bet it was the last one. The next words to come out of my mouth were the hardest that I have ever had to deliver, 'Rubes, I don't think that John is being honest with you.'

'That's rich coming from you.'

'Rubes please…' I took a deep breath, 'I think he's married.'

'You *think* he's married? How the fuck would you know? Anyway, I *know* you are wrong.'

I could see that Ruby was upset but I had to tell her what I knew. I told her about the letter that I got from Baileys the first time that I met him, and the recent email saying that his wife was pregnant.

'That doesn't mean anything. He could have just been saying that to extort more money from you,' she said defiantly.

Ruby had a point, but I knew that she was wrong, 'What are you going to do?' I asked.

Ruby sat down at her desk and opened her laptop, 'I'm going over there. I need to see him!'

Despite acting tough, I could see her hands shaking and I knew this was my cue to leave. I walked to the door and looked back at the woman I loved like a sister, 'Rubes, are we going to be okay?'

She looked up from her computer, 'I don't know Beth,' she said sadly. 'I don't know who you are anymore.'

I felt a pain in my heart, 'I'm still me. I just made a mistake!'

Ruby looked down, 'Like I said, I don't know.'

I closed the door feeling empty and hurt. I thought Ruby and I were so close that nothing could come between us. I could not face the fact that I had possibly lost her…and was about to lose Jay too.

19

LIAR LIAR

Hong Kong

Ruby touched down in Hong Kong feeling more excited than upset. On the flight she had been thinking about her relationship with John and she did not believe for one minute that he was married. She was going to prove Beth wrong.

Riding in the cab to Discovery Bay Island, Ruby started to imagine what her life would be like when she finally lived in Hong Kong. Passing beautiful buildings and pristine lawns, Ruby could easily see herself enjoying the lifestyle, and she was delighted when the cab stopped outside a huge villa.

As Ruby walked up the path towards Bailey's door, she started to feel a mixture of excitement and anxiety. She suddenly wondered if she had done the right thing by just showing up, after all, John travelled so much, and he may not even be home.

Oh well, it's a bit late now!

Putting her nerves aside, Ruby knocked on the door and actually felt a little relieved when there was no answer. Then the reality hit her that her journey may have in fact been wasted, and she wasn't sure what she should do.

Ruby decided to take a walk and found a nice little bar close to the shops. Making herself comfortable on the terrace, she watched the locals and expats playing with their children on the grass. Her eyes were drawn to a pretty, petit, pregnant woman with three small children, who were playing happily in the sand pit. Ruby had never really thought about having kids, but since she had met John that had changed, and for the first time in her life she considered becoming a mother.

After two glasses of wine, Ruby decided to try John's home again, only this time when she knocked on the door, she could hear voices coming from inside. The door opened and Ruby was shocked to see the same pregnant woman that she had noticed earlier, standing in front of her.

'Hi, can I help you?' asked the pretty, pregnant, blonde.

'Sorry! I must have the wrong number. I'm looking for number fifty-six.'

Looking confused, the pretty, pregnant, blonde nodded her head just as a small boy grabbed her legs, 'Mummy, what time is Daddy coming home?'

'Very soon darling. Now Mummy's helping this nice young lady, so go and sit with your brother and sister and I'll be with you in a minute.' She smiled at Ruby who was mesmerised by the little boy hiding behind his mummy's skirt, 'I'm sorry who are you looking for? Maybe I will know them. It's a very small place here.'

Ruby did not need her help. She knew by looking into the eyes of the little boy that this was the correct address and that Beth had been right all along. John was married and he didn't just have a family, he had a beautiful family!

Fighting back the tears, Ruby managed to say, 'Actually, it's okay; I think I know what's happened. Sorry to have bothered you.'

Ruby quickly turned her head to the side so that Bailey's wife could not see her tears, at the same time she heard a car door slam behind her. Ruby closed her eyes; she could smell his aftershave a mile off.

Could this get any fucking worse?

When Ruby turned around, she was face to face with Baileys. She noticed the horrified look on his face, put her head down and pushed passed him.

'John darling, maybe you'll know who that lady is looking for, why don't you help her?' said his wife.

Ruby prayed that he didn't come after her, but Baileys was at her side in seconds, 'Ruby, what are ye doin' here?' he whispered.

'I came to surprise you…but fuck! What the hell? When were you going to tell me about your fucking pregnant wife and kids?' she hissed.

'I wasn't!' he said arrogantly.

Ruby reeled back in shock. Her heart felt like it shattered right then and there, 'You were *never* going to tell me? How was that going to work John?' His look told her everything she needed to know, but she wanted more answers, 'Don't you even care? What about *us*? What about our future?'

She was bordering on hysterics.

'Keep ye voice down! There is no us! Fuck Ruby; I have a pregnant wife and three kids. Ye are a fantastic piece of ass but I'd never give them up for ye!'

Ruby felt the sudden urge to punch him, but was conscious that his wife was still standing in the doorway, 'What was all that talk about us moving in together? Why would you say something like that if you had no intention of following through?'

'*You* talked about it, not me! Let's face it Ruby, ye are just a flight attendant. It was never goin' to work!'

Ruby was livid now, '*Just* a flight attendant? What the fuck does that mean? I guess she's a scientific genius is she?' Ruby said looking over at his wife.

'Will ye keep ye fuckin' voice down? Ye know what I mean. Most men want to fuck a hostie. It's a fantasy and it's over, so let's move on.'

Ruby felt tears sting her eyes, 'You bastard! I thought...'

He cut her off, 'Yeah well, ye thought wrong!'

Ruby was shaking with anger, 'I feel sorry for your wife!'

'Whatever!' he said indignantly. 'If ye have finished, I suggest ye leave...NOW!'

John was acting so out of character, it left Ruby wondering how she had gotten it so wrong. She decided to deliver the final blow, 'Actually, I'm not quite finished,' she glared at him. 'I've heard all about your little blackmailing scheme with Beth and it's not going to work this time. You're going to have to find some other way to support your family!'

'Is that so?' he smirked. 'If that stupid bitch doesn't pay up, she's goin' to regret the day she met me.'

Ruby took a step closer to his face, 'She already does,' she said venomously. 'I suggest you leave Beth alone...or else!'

'Or else, what?' he said defiantly.

'Or I'll tell your pretty little wife about our plans and see where that leaves you.'

'She won't believe ye. She loves me. Anyway, I'll just tell her that ye are a stalker hostie that's been hasslin' me since ye served me on my flight to Europe.'

'Will she believe Beth? Or would it be better if she introduces herself as Kat?' Ruby let her comment sink in, 'How will little wifey feel when she reads the letter you gave to Beth cancelling your seedy little sex session? I imagine you spending the family money fucking hookers isn't going to go down too well is it?'

Baileys glared at Ruby with pure hatred.

'And how do you think she'll feel when she knows that instead of going away on a business trip, you were in bed having a fuck fest with another woman? Think she'll still love you then?' Ruby was on a roll, 'I wonder how she'll explain to your kids why their daddy doesn't live with them anymore!'

Baileys stood there for a moment, anger boiling up inside, but he softened his tone, 'Ruby, why would ye want to do somethin' like that?'

'Oh, I don't know! Maybe it's because you are a lying, narcissistic, whore fucking, blackmailing, bastard!'

They glared at each other.

'I mean it. Back off Beth! So help me God, if I hear that you contact her one more time, or anything gets in the papers, I'll personally make sure your life is hell! Get it!'

'I dare ye,' goaded Baileys.

Ruby stood her ground, 'I wouldn't be daring me. You have no fucking idea who you are dealing with.'

'Ye bitch! Ye don't have the balls to do somethin' like that!'

Ruby was fierce, 'Try me!'

Baileys opened his mouth to say something, but Ruby silenced him with her hand. She did not want to hear anything else that he had to say. Ruby just wanted to get away quickly before the man who had shattered her heart and stolen her dreams saw her cry. As she walked away, Ruby could hear his wife, 'Thank you darling, that poor woman looked lost, you're so kind.'

For the next couple of hours, Ruby walked aimlessly around the island. Eventually, she sat down on a bench overlooking the ocean and oblivious to the stares of strangers, she let the tears continue to fall.

The feeling Ruby was experiencing was nothing new; it felt as raw as it did when she was a young child. The void she felt in her stomach and the urge to throw up overwhelmed her, but she knew that she had to ride it out. She reminded herself that this heartbreak was exactly why she had never allowed herself to fall in love. The last time it happened, it took years for each little piece of shattered heart to fit back together.

As the sun set over the ocean an old man sat down next to Ruby and asked her if she was all right. Too emotional to speak, she turned to look at him and when he looked into her eyes, the pain he saw there told its own story.

The kind, old man decided to sit with the beautiful, sad girl and placed his hand on one of hers. Ruby did not fight it, she could not fight it, and instead she let the stranger comfort her while she continued to sob.

Three days later, I still hadn't heard from Ruby and I was getting worried. I was contemplating jumping on a plane to Hong Kong when I received her text.

"Coming home on flight 2nte. Pick me up?"

The following day, I anxiously waited at the arrivals gate for Ruby and when she finally emerged, I was taken aback by her frail appearance. Her pain was so evident by her body language, and even though she wore dark glasses I had no doubt what they were hiding.

In the car, my fears were confirmed when Ruby removed her glasses briefly. The dark black circles underneath overshadowed her red-rimmed eyes and she looked so miserable that it was heartbreaking. We drove home in silence until Ruby finally spoke, 'It's over.'

There was no doubt in my mind that she was talking about her relationship with Baileys and not the blackmail, but that seemed irrelevant right now. Seeing Ruby in so much pain made me feel guilty for telling her, 'I'm so sorry Rubes.'

She looked out of the window, 'So am I!'

When we arrived at Ruby's place, she dropped her luggage on the floor and sat down on the sofa. I made us both a cup of tea and then sat down next to her. I could see that Ruby was heartbroken, and all I wanted to do was to hold her and tell her that she would be okay. Tentatively, I put my arm around Ruby and was surprised when she leaned into me and allowed me to comfort her. As Ruby cried freely, I let my silent tears fall down my cheeks and wondered how it had all gone so drastically wrong!

20

TILL DEATH DO WE PART

I was about to open the door to Gran's bedroom when I heard her talking to someone inside. I put my ear to the door, and I could hear muffled sobs, so I decided to investigate and found Gran slumped over her dressing table, 'Gran, is everything okay? Why are you crying?' I looked around the empty room, 'and who were you just talking to?'

She dabbed her eyes with a handkerchief, 'Oh darling, it's nothing.'

I walked towards her and saw the reason for Gran's tears. On the dressing table was a photo of Grandad. When Gran realised that I had seen it, she looked at me as though she was committing a crime.

'Gran, you can't feel bad about marrying George. Grandad would want you to be happy.'

'Oh I know darling. I keep telling myself that, but I feel as though I am betraying his memory. I really love Georgie, but your grandfather was… well, he was the love of my life. I feel like I'm cheating on him!'

'Gran, that's silly! George loves you and you love him. You both deserve to be happy! No one will ever replace Grandad and he knows that. In fact, I wouldn't be surprised if he had something to do with you meeting George in the first place!'

Gran looked at me, confused.

'You know, watching out for you from the "other side." I could see she wasn't convinced, 'Gran, look at me! You have found a wonderful, sweet man, who adores you and wants to take care of you. Some people fail to find love once in their lifetime; you've found it twice! You deserve this.'

'Oh darling, you are such a sweet girl. I know that you're right. I do love Georgie, and I do deserve to be happy. If you don't mind, I just need another minute with your grandfather, and then I will be right out. I promise!'

True to her word, Gran appeared a few minutes later. My father took her arm and kissed her on the cheek, 'Are you ready Tilly?'

With a huge intake of breath and a nervous smile she nodded, and then took her first step towards a new life.

When George heard the music begin to play, he turned around to watch Gran walking towards him. The look of love on his face should have left Gran with no question that she was doing the right thing. When my father handed Gran over to the new man in her life, I stepped to the side and watched her become, 'Mrs Matilda Worthington Stanthorpe Hewson.'

George had spared no expense for the reception and after party, and I was ecstatic to see Gran so happy. I glanced over at Ruby (who still wasn't really speaking to me and had initially been reluctant to come) laughing with Chuck as he dragged her onto the dance floor. I had not seen her smile in months, and it warmed my heart to see her enjoying herself again.

Since Ruby confronted Baileys a few months ago, I had not received any emails or phone calls from him, so I made the decision not to end my relationship with Jay. Ruby was not happy that I had gone back on my word and was very quick to tell me, 'I hope for your sake and everyone else's that no other snakes come out of the grass. If they do Beth, you are on your own!'

After the wedding Gran and George left for their cruise around the Caribbean, so Jay and I decided to spend a few days in New York before returning to London. We invited my parents to join us and they were thrilled, especially my mother, who seemed to have fallen in love with Jay herself!

Shockingly, on our second day we received the awful news that George had suffered a massive heart attack and had been airlifted to a hospital in Miami. My parents decided to fly home to London and Jay wasted no time organising a private jet to fly us both to Miami to be with Gran.

'Oh darling, what if he dies? I'll never forgive myself!' she said snivelling into her handkerchief.

I put my arms around her, 'Gran, stop being hard on yourself, it's not your fault.'

'But darling…it is!' she said sheepishly. 'I encouraged Georgie to try something new that I found on the Internet… you know…to enhance his stimulation,' she whispered. 'I believe *that* is what caused the heart attack. He was going at it like a mad man, quite extraordinary really, but it was too much for his heart to take.'

I wanted to interrupt Gran to ask her to spare me the details, but she kept talking, 'I had the most incredible orgasm and I thought that he was too, but quite the opposite! The poor man was convulsing and screaming in pain!'

'Gran, it doesn't matter. You can't blame yourself! George is a grown man and he made the decision to take a stimulant.

Anyway, the Doctor said that George will make a full recovery, you just have to ease back on your bedroom activities!'

Gran looked bereft, 'Oh darling, I know,' she nodded. 'It is so unfortunate; I'm getting quite addicted to orgasms. But I suppose if all else fails, I still have Victor.'

'And…you still have George,' I reminded her.

She smiled at me lovingly, 'Oh darling, how selfish of me. Of course, I still have my beautiful Georgie.'

21

YOU CAN RUN... BUT
YOU CAN'T HIDE

"Can all remaining passengers for Flight VS001 to New York please make their way to the Gate Eighty-Nine."

Baileys drank down the last of his Gin and Tonic, put away the magazine that he had been reading in the Virgin Atlantic Upper-Class lounge and made his way to the aircraft. He was slightly drunk and very angry.

Ever since that fuckin' whore came into me life, I've had nothin' but bad luck. Bloody stupid wife gettin' pregnant again. Two disastrous business decisions and the bitch messin' up me affair with Ruby. Fuck ye Kat, or Beth, or whatever the fuck ye name is. I'll get ye bitch!

Baileys had been digging around for information about Beth ever since she had told Ruby about his family and refused to give him any more money. He wanted to bury her.

As he made himself comfortable in his seat, he smiled at how lucky he had been on a recent flight to London when he showed one of the flight attendants a photo of Beth. When Amanda told him that they were really good friends, Baileys invited the cute little blonde to dinner, flirted, and the rest was history.

Not only had Baileys found Beth's phone number in Amanda's phone while she was sleeping, but he had also managed to prize some very valuable information from his unsuspecting date about the venues the crew frequented in each city. During their little chat, Bailey's interest peaked when Amanda told him about a club in New York that offered "rooms for rent." Amanda thought it was disgusting, but Baileys knew in his gut that if he went there, he would be sure to strike gold.

As the aircraft taxied on the runway in New York, Baileys took Beth's photo out of his pocket and an evil smile spread across his face.

Ye can run bitch, but ye can't fuckin' hide.

After checking into his hotel, Baileys wasted no time jumping into a cab and going to the club. He was feeling excited, but two hours later his enthusiasm had turned to frustration. He had been flashing Beth's photo around hoping that someone would recognise her, but no one seemed to know who she was.

Just before leaving, Bailey's thought he'd try one more thing and made his way upstairs to the actual rooms. Two huge bouncers stood at the bottom of the stairs, for a moment Baileys thought about turning around but he had a gut instinct to try his luck with the men…BINGO!

'Yeah man, how could we forget that one,' laughed one of the bouncers as his sidekick snatched the photo.

Baileys watched on confused as the two men started yelling and hooting like they were at a football game, 'Gentlemen, sorry to interrupt ye private joke, but do ye know this girl or not?'

The bouncer didn't like Bailey's tone, 'Well sure, but we aint about to disclose any information to you. That goes against our confidentiality clause and all.'

Baileys let out a frustrated sigh, 'I don't want to know about the girl, I already know who she is. I just want to speak to her regular clients.'

'You a cop?' asked the second bouncer.

Baileys handed them a business card, 'No, certainly not, but I will make it worth ye while if ye call me when one of her regulars comes in. I'm in New York for another two days.'

As the bouncers looked over his card, Baileys took out a wad of cash from his pocket and handed it to one of the men, 'Here's a down payment for ye trouble.'

The two men looked at each other, nodded in agreement and split the cash.

The following evening Bailey's phone rang. He pulled himself off the Asian prostitute he had booked for the night and took the call. When he came back into the bedroom his excitement was obvious, 'Let's finish this off Ting. Then get dressed. Somethin's come up.'

Baileys sat staring at the little, fat, ugly man opposite him and he couldn't help but wonder how on earth Beth had slept with this pathetic excuse for a man. He certainly liked to brag, and the disgusting little squirt wouldn't shut up about how "tight" she was. Roger was going into great detail about his, 'amazing one-time fuck' and Baileys was starting to get irritated. After fifteen minutes Baileys couldn't listen to him anymore and he cut Roger off mid-sentence, 'Give me ye business card and I'll be in touch if I need anythin' else.'

Roger looked confused but handed Baileys his card. He couldn't put his finger on it, but he knew this was a man that you didn't say no to. Baileys took the card, turned his back and without another word to Roger, he walked away, 'Fuckin' imbecile, I'll have to do better than that pathetic runt if I want me plan to work,' he said under his breath.

22

THE LUCK OF THE IRISH

On his last night in New York Baileys decided to go back to the club. He wasn't necessarily looking to get information about Beth; he was feeling horny and liked the vibe of the place. Sitting down on one of the red sofas, he caught the eye of a cute girl standing by the bar. He couldn't help but notice the size of her huge breasts and he was instantly turned on.

Julia looked at the handsome stranger and couldn't believe how beautiful he was. She gave him her best smile, and when he winked at her that was all the encouragement she needed to walk over, 'Wow, aren't you a handsome devil?' she said as she sat down next to Baileys. 'Jeez I could get lost in those eyes.'

'I could get lost in those tits.'

Julia moved in closer, 'And cocky too I see.'

Baileys smirked at the thought of his erection, which was clearly visible through his trousers, 'Ye got that right!'

Julia looked at his crotch and smiled, 'Gosh, I'd even do you for free, but a girl needs to pay her rent, so it will cost you.'

Baileys stood up. She was exactly what he needed, and he didn't care about the cost. Upstairs they wasted no time getting down to business and Baileys loved that Julia certainly knew her way around the bedroom. She was up for anything and had given Baileys the best blowjob of his life. When they had finished, Baileys stood up and walked towards the sofa. As he picked up his trousers, Beth's photo fell onto the floor.

Julia froze when she saw the face looking back at her, 'Hey, you're not a cop are you?'

Why does everyone keep asking me that?

'No, definitely not!'

'Well, what are you doing with that photo?'

Baileys saw Beth's photo on the ground, 'It's nothing. She's just a friend of mine,' he lied, and continued to dress.

'You know Kat?'

I must be the luckiest bastard alive.

Baileys stopped getting dressed, turned around and gave Julia his best smile, 'How much did ye say ye needed for tuition this year?'

For the next hour, Julia gave Baileys all the details of her encounters with Kat. She left nothing to the imagination on how they first met, the threesome with the sexy Latino and how she introduced Kat to Jade in LA. As Julia was talking, Baileys sneakily glanced down to check that his mobile phone was still recording the conversation.

It gets better... lesbian sex, three ways and fuckin' whore houses!

When Julia finished talking, Baileys could hardly contain his excitement. He put her details into his phone and promised to take care of her, that was after he took her one last time.

Baileys sat on the plane heading back to Hong Kong and even though he didn't consider himself a religious man, he was thanking God for his good fortune in meeting Julia. He couldn't remember ever feeling this happy, and he felt no remorse about what he was about to do, 'That silly little bitch deserves everythin' that's comin' to her.'

'Excuse me sir, did you say something?' asked the pretty, brunette flight attendant. 'Is there anything I can help you with?'

'Well, yes, actually there is…'

Baileys removed the blanket from his lap so the flight attendant could see the extent of his excitement. Her beautiful warm smile turned cold as she leant into Baileys and whispered, *'That* is very inappropriate Sir. If it happens again, I'll have you escorted off this aircraft and arrested for indecent behaviour.'

Baileys scoffed as she walked away, 'Your loss sweetheart!'

23

REALITY BITES

I can't believe that I'm back in Noosa and about to marry the man of my dreams. I feel so incredibly blessed as I watch the sun hitting the surface of the crystal-clear ocean and reflecting like a thousand fairy lights. I take a moment to look at our closest friends and family who are here to share our special moment, and then I look at Jay's face which is so full of love and hope. My thoughts are interrupted by the words of our celebrant, 'Do you James Robert Thorsen take...'

Suddenly, something catches my eye as I shift my gaze from Jay. I notice a group of men approaching from the left and panic rips through my body. I recognise Baileys with an evil smirk on his face, leading the charge; Repulsive Roger and Latino are also in the group, running like a pack of hungry wolves ready to slaughter the lamb. I quickly glance over at Ruby and she looks paralysed with fear. In an instant they are upon me, my eyes are momentarily blinded by the flash bulbs that appear from nowhere, and an orchestra of voices echo, 'Whore...Gold digger...Slut...Money grabber.'

I turn to Jay; his expression is one of anguish, confusion and hurt, as I am dragged away from him by the pack. His face becomes distorted until I can no longer see him, as the chanting gets louder. I place my hands on my ears to silence the noise. I close my eyes in protection from the flashbulbs, and I hear myself screaming as I am engulfed by the pack!

I shot up in bed, covered in sweat, as uncontrollable sobs escaped my throat.

Jay is already awake, 'Darling…same nightmare again?'

I nodded yes, as I gasped for breath.

'Come here, you're shaking,' he said as he lovingly wrapped me in his arms. 'Maybe you should reconsider talking to a specialist darling. You've been having this same nightmare for months now. Are you ready to tell me what it is, maybe I can help you?'

Still unable to speak, I shook my head to say no. Jay nodded his understanding and held me tighter as he whispered how much he loved me. I could do nothing except surrender to his embrace and collapse into his arms.

Later, as I watched Jay sleep peacefully next to me, I wondered what to do. I knew that a therapist couldn't help me, and I agreed with Jay that I had to do something to stop the nightmares. The only person I could confide in was Ruby and we were barely on speaking terms. She still hadn't completely forgiven me for lying to her and in her words, 'Spreading my legs for money.' However, I needed a soundboard to help me to make a decision and although I wasn't sure if she would even speak to me…I needed Ruby!

24

CROSSING THE VOID

Ruby opened the door, 'So what do you want?' she asked as if my being there was a huge inconvenience.

'Can we talk?' I said sheepishly. 'Please?'

'I don't think there's anything to discuss Beth. I told you, I'm not sure how, or if I can forgive you.'

Tears stung my eyes and my heart felt like it was breaking into tiny pieces. I loved Ruby like she was my own flesh and blood and I desperately wanted her back in my life. I wanted her to love me again, 'Rubes, please! I love you; I miss you… and I need you.' I was sobbing now, 'I can't change the past, but I can change the future. Please hear me out.'

She looked at me without moving from the doorway, 'I'm listening!'

I took a deep breath, 'I'm going to end it with Jay.'

She scoffed, 'Sure you are. You've said that before.'

'This time is different.'

Ruby rolled her eyes, 'Well, go on then!'

'Rubes you are right. You have always been right. I can't live this lie, it's not who I am. Staying with Jay makes the risk of exposure way too big. I'd hurt so many people if the truth came out and I can't live with that.'

'Well, hooray for fucking Freddo,' she said sarcastically. 'It took you long enough to figure that out. Beth, I love your parents like they are my own, what do you think this will do to them?' Her voice sounded slightly hysterical, 'I am shattered by your deceit and I'm not even blood!'

'As good as,' I blurted just before a sob escaped my throat.

Ruby looked like she was going to say something but stopped herself, and then suddenly her whole demeanour softened as she looked at me, 'Bloody hell Beth, stop crying and come here.'

As she wrapped her arms around me the floodgates opened. I don't know how long we stood holding each other and crying, but I knew that we had crossed the void. Gaining Ruby's trust and her friendship back was going to be a long road, but I was happy that she had given me a small piece of her back today. That was all I needed right now.

Eventually we let go of each other and Ruby allowed me to come inside. I confided in Ruby about my ongoing nightmare and the strange phone calls that I had been receiving for the past two weeks. Every time I answered the phone, I could hear faint laughter and then the line would go dead. The laughter was different every time, sometimes a woman, sometimes a man, and it had really started to freak me out. The calls were increasing too; I'd already had three in the past week and they were getting stranger every time. We both wondered if it was Baileys, but I wasn't convinced as passive intimidation wasn't his usual style.

When Ruby broached the subject of how to tell Jay that it was over, I felt sick to my stomach. I couldn't bear the thought of lying to him again, which is exactly what I would have to do. I knew with every cell in my body that Jay truly loved me, and that I was about to break both of our hearts. I was also aware that the alternative was much worse. To lose Jay's heart was one thing, but to lose his respect and for him to think of me as a whore, was a completely different ball game. No matter what amount of pain I was about to inflict on both of us, I knew that it was time for me to do the right thing. I had created this mess, and I had to accept that what I was about to do was the only way forward for everyone's sake. I hated myself for it, but I knew that I would hate myself more if the press exposed the truth about my secret life, and I lost everyone and everything that I loved.

25

TANYA'S TEARS

Tanya sat at the coffee shop and stared out of the window. She wasn't sure why she had finally agreed to come here, but he had been so persistent in meeting her, that eventually she gave in.

As she gazed at a couple kissing in the street, her mind wandered back to when she first met Jay. It was the start of the summer holidays and Tanya was sitting on the grass with some friends. A group of boys were playing football close by and the sun was shining. When the football landed between the girls, one of the boys came over to retrieve it. As the tall, skinny boy picked up the ball, Tanya couldn't help but notice that he had the most beautiful face she had ever seen. He had huge, almond shaped, green eyes, and large full lips. When the boy noticed Tanya looking, he smiled at her, revealing his metal braces. Tanya giggled and wiped the smile right off his face. The boy looked away embarrassed, muttered his apologies and ran off, leaving Tanya feeling awful.

Although usually quite shy, Tanya walked over to where the boys were playing, 'Excuse me,' she said directly to the boy with the braces, 'can you come here?'

He walked over sheepishly.

'I'm so sorry. I didn't mean to laugh at you,' she said sincerely.

Tanya remembered how he was staring at her, taking in every part of her face, making her feel self-conscious, 'Anyway, I just wanted to apologise. Sorry!' she said before turning to walk away.

'Wait!' said the boy. 'What's your name?'

Tanya turned to look at him, 'Tanya.'

'You're pretty.'

Tanya blushed.

'I'm Jay.'

They both smiled. They were fourteen years old.

'Are you okay Miss?' asked the waitress.

Tanya didn't even realise that she was crying. She nodded her head and wiped her eyes with a tissue.

When will this end?

As she sipped her tea, her mind drifted off again. Her relationship with Jay took off from that day, and except for Jay playing his sport, they did everything together and became instant best friends. When it came time to go to University, despite both sets of parents encouraging them to have a little distance from each other, they enrolled in the same University and moved into an apartment together. Neither of them felt that they were missing out on anything because they were very much in love.

Even though Tanya and Jay were very different people, their relationship worked because they complimented each other. Jay was sociable and extroverted, while Tanya was quiet and reserved. Tanya supported Jay through his sporting events and stayed in the background when he started appearing in the media. She was so confident in their love and she trusted

Jay so much that she never worried about other women. As the years went on, Jay became increasingly famous as a Triathlete and Tanya concentrated on her growing Interior Design business, becoming very successful in her own right.

Life wasn't perfect though, despite having a beautiful home and both having successful careers, Tanya always hoped that one day Jay would propose to her. She desperately wanted a family, but whenever she broached the subject with Jay, he always said the same thing, 'Tan mate, why spoil a good thing? We've got years ahead of us. I'm sure we'll have a baby one day.'

Tanya felt disheartened every time he said it, and as each year passed, as another friend got engaged, married or pregnant, she would feel more and more yearning. So, the day after her thirtieth birthday and still no proposal from Jay, Tanya confronted him, 'But James, we've been together for sixteen years! I want to get married and have a family.'

Jay put his arms around her waist, 'Tan, we're happy aren't we? Why mess with a good thing?'

'Because I am ready!'

Jay looked sad, 'I'm not.'

Jay's comment had triggered something in Tanya, and she knew that their relationship was at a major turning point. The reality hit her...if Jay wasn't ready after sixteen years, would he ever be ready? Tanya knew that she had to make a decision.

Do I leave James now while I'm young enough to find a man who wants to start a family with me, or do I accept that this is all we will ever be and take whatever I can get from James?

The thought broke Tanya's heart and terrified her at the same time. Jay was the only man she had ever been with; he was all she knew. And one fact remained; she was still hopelessly in love with him. She decided to stay!

Tanya glanced at her watch, she still had thirty minutes before she was meeting him, and she couldn't help but wonder what was so important. It had been almost a year since Jay had spoken the words that shattered her heart, 'Tan, I'm sorry… but I've met someone else.'

She remembered it like it was yesterday. She had noticed an instant change in James' behaviour when he returned from a trip to Los Angeles a few months earlier. It was as if the spark had gone from his eyes when he looked at her, and he seemed distracted. At first she thought that it must be something to do with work, but their sex life had reduced dramatically, and he was becoming more distant and disconnected. On the day that James said that he needed to talk, Tanya felt relieved. They had ups and downs like any couple, but it was usually very short lived and very quickly forgotten, so she felt confident that whatever James was going through, they could get over it together.

When Jay told her that this time was different and that he wanted to separate, Tanya just stared at him like he was talking in another language. She couldn't actually comprehend what he was saying to her. Tanya tried everything to convince him that he was making a mistake, she pleaded with him to reconsider, she begged him to go to therapy, and she tried to seduce him with sex, but all her attempts where futile.

For a couple of weeks, Jay held Tanya while she cried, he calmed her down when she got mad, and eventually he gave in to her pleading to make love one last time. Tanya thought being intimate with Jay would make him realise their bond, however, she had regretted it as soon as it was over. She did all she could to please Jay, but he couldn't even look at her, and it was obvious that he was just going through the motions.

Tanya had to face the fact that Jay was emotionally unavailable to her now, and the whole experience had left her feeling worthless and embarrassed at her lack of self-respect. The day after they had sex, Tanya moved into the spare bedroom and thought she would die from the sense of loss she was feeling. It was like her heart had shattered into thousands of tiny pieces and she did not have the energy or willpower to put them back together.

Tanya took a sip of tea and shivered at the memories of the pain. She recalled how she didn't want to eat, barely slept and stopped working. All she wanted to do was curl up in the foetal position and cry. She spent hour after hour reliving memories of their life together, like a movie playing in her head, trying to figure out where it went wrong and what she had done to make him fall in love with someone else.

Every morning when Jay left for work, she would go to the window and watch him walk away. It was like she was taking photos of every bit of him to add to the filing cabinet in her mind; his hair, his neck, his shoulders, the way he walked. And every morning the same panic rose through her at the realisation that he was no longer hers. The man she had given the last twenty-one years to, the man she had dreamed would one day ask her to marry him, the man whose children she wanted to bare, all she had ever loved, and still loved, was gone.

This constant cycle went on for four weeks. When Jay returned home, Tanya would pull the covers over her head and pretend to be asleep. She knew that he was checking in on her to make sure she was okay, because that was the kind of man he was. When Jay quietly called her name or leant over her to see if she was still breathing, she wanted to grab him, pull him into her and never let go.

Every day as she lay drowning in her tears, she tortured herself wondering who it was that had stolen Jay's heart. She convinced herself that it was someone famous, most likely a model involved in humanitarian work, someone much more accomplished than herself. Tanya knew that whoever it was would be beautiful, because some incredibly beautiful women had propositioned Jay in the past, and he was far too good for "ordinary."

She had tried to hate him, in fact she wished she could. It would have made the whole experience easier, however despite how much Jay's decision was crippling her, she couldn't bear to think ill of him. Jay was decent and loving and she knew that if he had decided to walk away, it would be for a very good reason.

Tanya looked at her watch, fifteen minutes. She drank some more tea and allowed herself to remember. She woke up one night, it was late, and Jay was on his phone. Tanya put her ear to the door.

'Marcus. Yes. Mate, it's killing me. I never thought I'd be responsible for causing her so much pain.'

Tanya strained to listen.

'No, I can't leave her yet. I don't know if she can handle it, she looks awful. Seriously mate, I can't bare to look at what this is doing to her, and I'm really worried for her wellbeing. I'd never forgive myself if Tan…'

Tanya had heard enough; she fell to the floor and any piece of her heart that was still in place exploded in her chest. She tried to calm her breathing but the pain in her chest was unbearable, and as she lay in the foetal position uncontrollably sobbing, she wished that she was dead.

Tanya had no idea how she got to bed. Did Jay take her? Did she crawl herself? She didn't care, but she woke up the following morning with a new resilience. Something had shifted for her yesterday, and she now had a degree of clarity about what she had to do. Hearing Jay on the phone had hurt her deeply, and she now understood that she was never getting him back; she knew that she had to finally let him go.

Tanya took a deep breath and wiped her eyes. She wasn't sure why she was reliving the memories that she had tried so hard to lock away. She looked at her watch...ten minutes!

She closed her eyes and remembered how she walked into the kitchen where Jay was eating breakfast, and her presence startled him. As if it was possible, the past four weeks had aged her considerably, but she had somehow managed to get herself up and into the shower, fix her hair, put on some make up and get dressed. The hollow of her eyes were masked by foundation and powder but the red rims from crying could not be disguised. Jay had noticed how skinny she was getting, and Tanya knew by the look on his face that he felt immense guilt and sadness.

'Tan...' he started to talk but she cut him off.

'I want you to leave!' she said, keeping her eyes fixed on the kitchen table.

Jay looked at Tanya with true sorrow in his eyes, 'Tan, please look at me, I...'

'Stop!' She couldn't say his name, 'I want you to leave *today*. I'll have my solicitor Simon chat to Giles to sort out the finances.'

Jay tried again, 'Tan, let's talk ...'

Tanya cut him off again, 'Please! I know you want to go, so just go.'

Finally, she lifted up her head and looked directly at Jay. What he saw broke his heart, 'Tan…'

Tanya held up her hand to silence him, 'I don't know if I'll ever understand your decision…I thought we were forever.' She took one last look at Jay, 'Twenty-one years…I just hope she is worth it.'

When Jay started to cry, Tanya couldn't handle it and ran out of the room.

'Miss, I'm sorry but are you sure that you are okay?' asked the waitress again.

'Yes, I'm fine. Thank you,' replied Tanya.

Tanya looked at her watch. She had two minutes. She took out a compact from her bag and applied some face powder and lipstick. She could see that she looked awful, but she didn't care.

'Hello Tanya,' he smiled and his eyes lit up, 'thank ye so much for meeting me. I know this must be difficult for ye.'

Tanya stared into the most beautiful eyes she had ever seen, 'Hi, John is it?'

'Yes, that's right.' He held out his hand, 'John Davenport.'

26

LET THE GAMES BEGIN

Baileys looked at the sad woman sitting in front of him. He could see that she was pretty once, not stunningly beautiful or sexy, but just "girl next door" kind of pretty. She had definitely lost a lot of weight since he last saw her in the newspaper, and it showed in her face. Her eyes were puffy and red, and he knew that she had been crying because he had been watching her for the past thirty minutes.

'I can see ye are upset, would ye like to do this another time?'

Tanya wiped her eyes, 'No, I'm fine, sorry! My emotions just take over sometimes. You think you are over something and all of a sudden, one trigger and you realise that you have been fooling yourself.'

Baileys looked at her sympathetically and placed his hand on top of hers, 'I hope ye don't mind. I don't want to make ye feel uncomfortable, it's just that I hate to see a beautiful woman so upset.'

Tanya smiled, 'It's fine. It's nice of you to care.'

'I know what ye are goin' through. Well, I'm assumin' ye are still upset about yer breakup with James.'

Tanya looked away.

'Forgive me if I'm steppin' out of line.'

Tanya looked into his beautiful eyes, 'It's stupid I know, it's been so long now. I'm being quite pathetic.'

'Tanya look at me. Please never call yerself pathetic. A heart takes time to heal and it's okay to get sad and even angry. I know ye story, ye have every right to be upset. Ye gave up years of ye life to someone, and it was taken from ye. It's more than okay to cry, especially in front of me.'

Tanya lowered her head. Baileys placed a finger under her chin, 'Tanya look at me.' She raised her head and Baileys wiped her tear-stained cheeks, 'Ye are a beautiful woman. Ye can get anyone ye want, someone who'll love ye and cherish ye. Trust me, in time everythin' will be okay.'

'Will it?' she replied sadly.

'I promise ye,' said Baileys convincingly.

Tanya couldn't believe that someone so beautiful could also be so compassionate and kind to a stranger, 'Forgive me for my bluntness, but why are you here? You have been pretty persistent in meeting me; however, I have no idea what you want.'

'I do want to discuss somethin' with ye, but let's get to know each other a little first hey? There's plenty of time to discuss other business.'

Tanya agreed, partly because she was curious to hear what he wanted, but mostly because he was not only beautiful but also very kind.

For the next hour, Baileys charmed Tanya. He wanted to make her to feel special, he wanted her to feel a connection, and he wanted her to be vulnerable with him. It was working! Baileys told Tanya that he too had recently experienced heartbreak and thought he would never get over it. His story was so convincing that this time Tanya placed her hand on top of his.

Baileys knew it was time to make his move, 'Tanya, I know we've only just met and this may seem a bit forward, but will ye let me take ye out for dinner tonight?' He let his question linger for a moment before continuing, 'It's been really nice gettin' to know ye. I feel like we have a connection, and I think we've got much more in common than ye realise.'

Tanya wasn't sure and hesitated. She looked at the handsome, dark-haired man, with the insanely piercing, blue eyes, who had somehow stirred something up inside of her that she didn't even realise was still possible.

Gosh, he's really beautiful.

'Well?' asked Baileys, giving her his sexiest smile.

Tanya still wasn't sure, but she nodded, 'Yes.'

When they left the café, Tanya felt a new level of excitement, and so did Baileys, but for a completely different reason, 'That was so fuckin' easy,' laughed Baileys as he got into his car. 'Women, so bloody predictable…pathetic!'

27

THE PLAYER

Tanya was waiting for Baileys outside her apartment at seven pm as planned. She was feeling a lot of mixed emotions and still didn't know what he wanted from her. One thing was certain; he was the only man that she had ever met besides Jay that stirred up feelings inside her, and for the first time in a long time Tanya was thinking about sex. She hadn't made love to any other man besides Jay and she wondered if given the opportunity, whether she had the confidence to actually go through with it.

Baileys was whistling as he stopped his car outside Tanya's apartment. He knew he was going to have sex with her tonight, so he had reserved a table for dinner at a romantic restaurant and stocked his hotel room with Champagne and condoms.

Dinner flew by. Baileys found it easy to make Tanya laugh and Tanya couldn't remember the last time she had felt so relaxed and happy. She had no idea that Baileys was playing her. He was serving the right amount of sympathy, comedy and flirting, and Tanya was eating it up. By the time the waiter brought the bill, Baileys knew he had Tanya exactly where he wanted her.

'How long are you in town for?' asked Tanya.

'A couple of nights.'

Tanya dropped her head, 'Oh.'

That was the signal Baileys was waiting for. He took her hand, 'Come on, let's get out of here.'

On the drive home they were both silent, but the air was thick with intense, sexual energy. Baileys parked the car outside Tanya's apartment, and they looked at each other for the first time since leaving the restaurant. Baileys had been with enough women to know that Tanya wanted him, so he leant over and kissed her. It was slow, deliberate and sensual. Tanya moaned as Baileys glided his hand over her breasts, down her stomach and along her thighs. When he reached the bottom of her skirt, he moved his hand up inside. Tanya was overwhelmed by her desire for him and she opened her legs. Baileys traced his fingers around the edge of her panties, driving her wild with anticipation. When he could sense that Tanya was desperate for his touch, he moved her panties to the side. As his fingers moved expertly inside her, he darted his tongue in and out of her mouth. The more he teased, the more she moaned and within minutes her whole body was quivering as she gave into the orgasm that consumed her.

'Does that feel better?' he whispered.

Tanya caught her breath, 'Yes.'

Baileys kissed her neck, 'Let's do this again tomorrow.'

Tanya looked at him and said something she never would have dreamt about saying a day ago, 'Let's do it now!'

28

WHAT GOES UP
MUST COME DOWN

Their clothes were off before they made it through Tanya's hallway, and as Baileys pushed her up against the wall Tanya let all her inhibitions fall to the floor with her clothes. Baileys tugged at her bra to expose her breasts; softly circling her nipple with his tongue as he pushed his finger deep inside her. Tanya thought she was going to faint.

Slowly and deliberately, Baileys teased his way down her body with his lips, and when he opened her legs slightly and kissed Tanya between her legs, she could hardly contain herself.

It has been years since she and Jay had enjoyed oral sex, it just wasn't something they did. Tanya pushed the thought of Jay out of her mind and ran her fingers through Bailey's hair, fully immersing herself in the feelings of ecstasy that were now engulfing every part of her.

'GOD!' she screamed.

'I'll take that as a compliment,' Baileys said, picking her up and taking her to the bedroom.

Once they were on the bed, Baileys knew that he would have to direct Tanya, so he took her hand, 'Touch me.'

Tanya surprised him by pushing him down on the bed and sitting on top of him. This time she let her tongue explore his whole body until she reached his penis. It didn't take long for Tanya to find her rhythm and when Baileys was about to come, he asked her to stop. Rolling Tanya over onto her stomach, Baileys placed his body on top of hers, and cupping her breasts, he slowly entered her from behind. With small thrusts of his hips, he teased his way inside her, gently pushing deeper and deeper until she could feel the full length of him. As Baileys gained momentum, he could feel the surge inside rising until he couldn't hold off anymore and finally came.

Tanya felt the full force of his weight when Baileys collapsed on top of her, his hot breath tickling her neck and his heart beating fast against her back.

Baileys rolled to the side and let out a sigh, 'Wow, that was fuckin' amazin'.'

Tanya smiled to herself, and as Baileys snuggled in behind her, she drifted off to sleep.

The following morning Tanya woke to Baileys running his fingers up the inside of her thigh. She rolled onto her back and closed her eyes as Baileys caressed her whole body with his lips.

I can't believe he wants to do this again!

Baileys parted her legs and entered her swiftly. Taking control, he put Tanya in positions she didn't even know existed and she found it very erotic. Tanya had never made love like this with Jay, it was always nice, but it was never passionate or adventurous and she very rarely had an orgasm.

When they had finished, Baileys pulled Tanya in close to his body and kissed her slowly on the lips. As he studied her face he brushed some hair from her eyes, 'Ye are a beautiful woman. I can't believe that stupid bastard would let someone like ye go... for a whore!'

As Baileys let his words fill the air, he could feel Tanya's body stiffen, 'What do you mean...a whore?'

Baileys pretended to be shocked, 'Ye don't know do ye?'

Adrenalin rushed through Tanya's body, 'Know what?'

'Ye don't know who it is that James left ye for?'

Tanya pushed Baileys away and rolled over so he couldn't see her face, 'I never asked.'

Her feelings of elation had suddenly turned to anguish, as she desperately tried to dismiss the image of Jay with another woman from her mind. Baileys snuggled in behind her and started to slowly rub her bottom, 'Don't be sad! I didn't mean to upset ye,' he whispered as he kissed her shoulder. 'It's not important anyway. Now just forget about that bastard and his whore and let me show ye what a real man is.'

Baileys forced himself inside her, with no resistance from Tanya. He knew that she was crying, and it turned him on even more.

29

LET ME ENTERTAIN YOU

Once Baileys had finished with Tanya, she got out of bed and went to take a shower. She felt like she had been punched in the stomach. She hadn't asked Baileys who he was referring to when he said James had left her for a whore, but she knew she was going to find out, and something told her she wasn't going to like what he had to say.

Baileys smiled to himself. The way Tanya had reacted to his comment gave him confidence that his plan was going to work. He didn't even understand himself why he hated Beth so much, but every time he thought about her and especially since she had gotten engaged to a billionaire, he got angry and fired up. He wanted her to suffer and he knew exactly how he was going to do it.

When Tanya came out of the bathroom Baileys turned on the charm and asked her if she wanted to go out to lunch. Tanya declined and said she had business to attend to, so Baileys asked her to dinner…she hesitated.

Baileys walked over to her, 'Come on Tanya. I know I up-set ye earlier, but I think we have somethin' here.' He touched her cheek then let his hand graze over her breast, 'Don't we?'

Tanya sighed; she was already turned on by his touch. Baileys saw his opportunity and slowly started to unbutton her blouse.

'John, I can't I ...'

'Shhhh...'

Baileys pushed up Tanya's bra to expose her breasts and she moaned as he moved his mouth down to her erect nipples and tenderly kissed them, 'Let's not let those two spoil a good thing. Let me take ye out tonight and we can carry on where we left off.'

Tanya didn't want Baileys to stop but she really did have somewhere to be. She pulled down her bra and buttoned up her blouse, 'Okay, I'll see you tonight. Let yourself out.'

Once she was gone Baileys had a snoop around her apartment and found a photo of James Thorsen in her bedside table. He was a little disappointed, but it reinforced what he already knew, which would undoubtedly play in his favour...Tanya was not over him!

At seven pm sharp, Baileys picked up Tanya. Instead of taking her to a restaurant, he had set up a small table on the balcony of his hotel room so they could have an intimate dinner and an opportunity to talk. Tanya was pleasantly surprised to see how much effort he had gone to. She noticed the small touches, the rose petals on the table, the champagne chilling on ice and the softly glowing candles. She looked at Baileys and wondered how she had been so lucky to come across such a thoughtful, attractive man.

Dinner was wonderful; the conversation was light and fun. Tanya had temporarily pushed the thought of James with a whore out of her mind and was fully present with Baileys. When they moved inside and sat on the sofa, the conversation turned more serious, 'John, tell me a little more about your life, I don't really know anything about you except for your work.'

'There's nothin' to tell really…the usual, work too much, play too much,' Baileys smiled.

'What about family? Have you ever wanted children?' she ventured.

'Yeah, one day I suppose, with the right woman.' He looked down with a sad look on his face, 'I guess that's why I was so upset when me ex called it off. For the first time in me life I could see meself havin' children. Then after she left, I found out she was sleeping with other men on the side.'

'Oh John, that's awful! You poor thing,' said Tanya sympathetically.

'That's not the worst part.'

'Whatever could be worse than that?'

Baileys looked down as if embarrassed, 'She was getting paid for it!'

Tanya was shocked, 'What do you mean? As in…a prostitute?'

Baileys put his face close to Tanya and stared into her eyes, 'As in…whore!'

Baileys was hoping that Tanya would put two and two together and understand what he was telling her, but his comment went over her head. Instead, she gave him a sympathetic look and took his hand, 'Oh gosh, that really is a disgusting thing to happen to you. I completely understand how it broke your heart, especially if you loved her enough to want children with her. All I wanted for years was to have children with James, and then one day out of nowhere he tells me that he is in love with someone else. All those years I believed nothing could break us,' tears stung her eyes, 'and suddenly it's all gone, just like that!'

'Just like that,' echoed Baileys.

He leant in and kissed her, and this time Tanya took the initiative and started to undo his trousers. When she got down on her knees, Baileys let his head fall back onto the sofa and thought about the one thing that really turned him on…fucking Beth.

Just before Baileys felt he was going to come, he asked Tanya to stop. Standing up, he took Tanya's hand and pulled her up to her feet. He walked her over to face the wall and placed her hands above her head. As he ran his hands down the side of her body, he used his feet to gently part her legs.

'What are you doing? I feel like I'm being frisked.'

Baileys put his mouth up to her ear, 'Shhh, trust me.'

He placed a blindfold over Tanya's eyes and then pulled her dress over her head. Standing with only her panties on, Tanya felt exposed and vulnerable, but most of all she felt excited. Baileys put his hand inside her panties and caressed her behind, and then he slowly ran his tongue down her spine until it found its way between her legs. Tanya couldn't take it, she wanted to touch him, but he kept telling her to stay still. As she was about to reach climax, she cried for him to stop.

Baileys pulled away and Tanya wondered what he was going to do next. Suddenly she jumped as his tongue was replaced with cold ice. As Baileys ran the ice up the inside of her thigh, she shivered. When he ran it over her breasts, she shivered more. He followed the curves of her body with the ice and when he reached her panties, he put the ice in his mouth. The combination of cold ice, hot breath and a warm tongue drove Tanya wild. This time she didn't tell him to stop, she screamed in ecstasy as her orgasm took over her entire body.

Baileys was really enjoying himself and was surprised that he had another erection so soon. He ripped off Tanya's panties and took her from behind, moving his hips slowly, allowing himself to feel her until he got his release.

'Wow,' said Tanya when Baileys pulled away, 'that was incredible. You really are a good lover.'

'I know,' replied Baileys with a cocky smile, 'and there's plenty more where that came from.'

When they fell asleep snuggled in each other's arms, Tanya dreamt about Baileys, while he dreamt about destroying Beth.

30

THE TRUTH WILL SET YOU FREE

'I'm goin' to stick around for a few days,' Baileys said to Tanya as they lay in bed after another long sex session.

'Really? Don't you have work to do?'

'Of course, but I'd rather be here ravishin' yer sexy, little, arse,' he replied nuzzling his face into her neck.

Tanya felt like a teenager. She couldn't believe how much she was falling for John, or how lucky she had been to find love again so soon. He had already extended his stay and besides a quick trip to Hong Kong, they hadn't left each other's side for a month.

'I'd love you to stay,' she said as she let her hand slide between his legs. He was hard again, so Tanya ducked under the covers.

'What time do ye finish ye meetin' today?' Baileys asked once Tanya resurfaced.

'Six o'clock. Why, what do you have in mind?'

'I want to cook for ye tonight, have a nice night in. What do ye say?'

'Cook?' Tanya was surprised, 'A handsome, sexy man, who can cook too? How did I get so lucky?'

'God was obviously feelin' good the day he made me, and ye are the lucky woman that gets to enjoy it.'

Tanya smiled, 'I forgot to add cocky to my last sentence.'

'Well, if ye want cocky, I can show ye cocky.' Baileys grabbed Tanya and turned her onto her stomach. He wasted no time and pushed inside her. He was more forceful and aggressive this time, making Tanya scream as he grabbed her hips and thrust deeply into her.

Baileys was smiling. He knew that he had Tanya just where he needed her. Over the past month, she had proved how emotionally invested she was in the relationship. He had really gone out of his way to make her feel safe, so she would open up about her relationship with James Thorsen. The guy sounded like a boring bastard as far as Baileys was concerned. He didn't appear to have any skeletons in the closet and Baileys was disappointed that he hadn't found out anything he could use against "Mr James Borin' Bastard Thorsen."

As Baileys thrust harder into Tanya, he imagined Beth. He remembered how she felt and how she made him feel, and he had to stop himself from calling out her name when he came.

Baileys looked at the clock, 'Almost show time.'

He had been rehearsing his lines all day. He knew he had to get them right in order to make his story convincing enough to get Tanya on board, and when she walked through the door he was ready.

'Wow, something smells wonderful,' she said as she hung her bag on the back of a chair. 'Let me just get out of these clothes and I'll join you.'

Baileys poured them both a Pinot and waited for Tanya on the patio. Once she arrived, they ate dinner and engaged in some light-hearted chatter.

'John, I'm very surprised by your culinary skills. Dinner was amazing.'

Baileys smiled to himself. Although he only knew how to cook one dish, he was impressed by his own effort to pull off his little charade, 'Now why would ye be surprised? I told ye... I'm a man of many talents.' Baileys ran his hand up Tanya's leg and smiled when he realised she wasn't wearing panties. He slipped his finger inside her before putting it inside his mouth, 'Before we get into this sweetness, let's eat dessert.'

Tanya closed her eyes and tried to calm herself when Baileys went to the kitchen. She had never been so turned on by anyone in her life.

Once dessert was finished, Baileys poured them both another drink and took a slow deep breath, 'Tanya, I've been meanin' to talk to ye for a while, but never felt the time was right until now.'

Tanya was concerned by the sudden change in Bailey's demeanour, 'John, whatever is the matter? You look sad.'

'Well, that's because I have to tell ye somethin' and I'm sure ye aren't goin' to be very happy about it.'

Tanya stiffened. Her instinct told her that Baileys was about to tell her something about James and the whore!

'I know ye don't want to hear this, but I think ye deserve to know.' He held her hand, 'Ye know I was in love and ye know how I felt about her?'

'Yes.'

'Well, her name was Beth.'

Tanya looked at him and saw the tears in his eyes. Baileys took another breath and continued his story, 'I thought our love was mutual and I honestly thought we would be together forever. Then one day, with no warnin', she walked out on me. She told me she didn't want a relationship and definitely didn't want marriage and kids.'

Tanya listened, resonating with his pain

'A few months later, I found out from her best friend Ruby, that Beth was pregnant with me baby, but she had an abortion.' He let the tears fall down his cheeks, 'She did it all without tellin' me. I was heartbroken. *My* baby…gone!'

Tanya was shocked but allowed Baileys to talk.

'I asked Beth if it was true and she said she did it because she didn't love me. She said she didn't want to bring a baby into the world with a man she didn't love. I was so confused because up until the day she walked out, I thought everythin' was goin' great.'

Tanya gave Baileys a tissue, 'I'm so sorry John. That must have been devastating.'

Baileys blew his nose and nodded.

Tanya wanted to know more, 'What about sleeping with other men? When did you find out about that?'

'About two weeks after Beth moved out of our apartment I saw her with another man and I followed them.' Baileys pretended to look embarrassed, 'I know it was the wrong thing to do but I needed answers. I wanted to know if they had been havin' an affair.'

'And had they?'

'I wish they had.' Baileys looked down, 'I waited for them to say goodbye and then I approached the man. He was actin' really strange and I noticed that he had a weddin' ring on his finger. Turns out, he thought I was a cop and that I'd tell his wife! Anyway, after I assured him that I wasn't a cop, the scumbag told me that he paid Beth for sex every week! All he knew was that she was a high-class hooker who *apparently* calls herself Kat.'

Tanya gasped.

'Can ye believe it? I confronted her and of course she denied it. So, I asked Ruby and she denied it, but I could see by her face that it was true. Those lyin' bitches are probably in it together. That Ruby is pure evil.'

Tanya shook her head, 'This is incredible.'

'It gets worse,' Baileys paused for effect. 'Three months later, I'm at the airport and I see Beth walking towards me with a ring on her finger. Not just any ring…a huge, diamond engagement ring! Biggest I've ever seen. She looked so happy… *they* looked so happy.' He let his words linger in the air and then looked directly at Tanya, 'I'm so sorry!'

Finally, what he was telling Tanya registered. Tanya's eyes grew wide, 'James?' she muttered.

Baileys nodded his head, 'Yes.'

'Are you sure?'

'Yes.'

'Engaged to be married?'

'Very!'

Tanya felt like a knife was cutting through her heart.

Why hadn't James told me about this? I knew that he had fallen in love with someone, but I had no idea that he had asked her to marry him.

She looked at Baileys, 'But you said she's a whore. What if that man was lying because they were having an affair?'

'I thought that too, so I hired a private detective. It appears that she is havin' sex with *a lot* of men for money. Here I was thinkin' she was just a flight attendant...'

Tanya gasped, 'A flight attendant?'

'Yes.'

'Does she work for James' airline?'

Bailey's nodded his head, 'Yes.'

Anger flashed across Tanya's face, 'He fell in love with one of his *flight attendants?*'

Baileys waited for Tanya to process what he was telling her before continuing, 'It turns out she also offers her *"services"* at a private club in New York.'

'Good lord! Are you absolutely sure?'

'Yes! I flew out there meself to get some answers.'

Tanya was visibly angry, 'This is unbelievable. James has to be told! He has a reputation to withhold. His airline has a reputation to withhold. She could destroy everything he's ever worked for.'

Bailey's smirked, 'Would that be so bad?'

Tanya suddenly looked sad, 'Despite what he has done to me, James doesn't deserve that...and even worse, he certainly doesn't deserve to find out that he is engaged to a prostitute from one of her pathetic clients, or God forbid, the press.' Tanya felt the blood draining from her face, 'We can't let this happen. The press will have a field day.'

'Let them,' said Baileys callously. 'They both deserve to suffer. Especially him! Ye gave him ye life!'

Tanya looked away.

'Tanya, he left ye for a *whore!*'

'Stop it!' she snapped.

Baileys realised he had pushed Tanya too far and softened his tone, 'I'm sorry, it's so unfair for *both* of us. I just feel they should at least be made accountable in some way for the pain they have caused.'

Tanya finally looked at Baileys, 'Two wrongs don't make a right John. What good will it do to destroy another two lives?'

Bailey's eyes pleaded with her, 'Tanya, we have found happiness and we deserve it. They don't!'

Tanya's patience was wearing thin, 'What on earth are you proposing we do John?'

Bailey's felt a tinge of hope, 'I'm glad ye asked. Ye *should* go to the press.'

'To do what exactly? Expose Beth…or Kat…whatever her name is! Embarrass James…destroy them both?'

'Yes!' replied Baileys enthusiastically.

Tanya looked into his beautiful eyes, which had turned almost black, 'I can't see what there is to gain, except misery and more heartbreak; it's a pretty ruthless thing to do John. It doesn't feel right.'

Baileys placed her hand in his, 'Tanya, look at what they've done to us…to you! Can ye at least sleep on it?'

'You are actually serious?'

'Yes!'

Tanya wasn't sure why, but she nodded, 'Yes.'

Bailey's cupped her face in his hands and kissed her.

After they made love Tanya couldn't sleep, all she could think about was Beth. Tanya couldn't understand what kind of woman would lead such a deceitful life. She sounded cold and selfish, definitely not the kind of person James would want to be with. And, what bothered Tanya the most, besides not being able to fathom how James could fall in love with one of his flight attendants, was the fact that he asked Beth to marry him so quickly.

Trying to make sense of it, Tanya replayed the last few months of her relationship with James through her mind and she wanted answers. She wanted to meet Beth and she wanted to know everything; when they met, how they met, did James know the truth, and worst still…had he paid her for sex?

Tanya turned to look at the clock, it was 2 am. She wasn't angry anymore, she just felt sad. Despite what Baileys had told her, she didn't want to hurt James. Worse still, this new revelation had made her realise something…she still loved him!

'I've made a decision. I know what I'm going to do,' Tanya declared to Baileys at breakfast. 'I'm going to meet Beth face to face, and I'm going to tell her to end it with James.'

Baileys smirked, 'That's nice in theory Tanya, but she won't do it.'

'What makes you so sure?'

'Because I've already tried it.'

'Then I'll give her no option!'

Baileys was pushing her, 'How?'

'If she doesn't end it, I'll tell her that I'll go to the press. I'll expose her for the whore that she is and let the cards fall where they may.'

'And what if she doesn't believe ye?'

'I'll make her!'

Baileys walked over to Tanya and kissed her on the cheek, 'That's me girl!'

Inside he was smiling because everything was unfolding exactly as he planned. Baileys knew that Beth wouldn't end it with James. His previous attempt at blackmail and his current scare tactics on the phone had not swayed her at all. Tanya was going to have to come in hard and once she did, Baileys would make his move.

31

TWILIGHT ZONE

'Darling, you are wasting away. Is that dreamy fiancé of yours working you overtime?'

I missed Gran so much. I grabbed her and hugged her tightly, 'Gran, it's so lovely to see you.'

'Gosh dear, you're going to break me in two. Now sit down and tell me what's been going on because you do look frightfully thin.'

'I'm fine Gran,' I smiled. 'Look at you! You look amazing! Obviously living stateside agrees with you.'

'Thank you darling but I actually believe it's all the orgasms I'm having. I do believe it makes one glow.'

I shook my head and smiled, 'How is George anyway, has he fully recovered from his heart attack?'

'Oh sweetie, he's wonderful. We are wonderful. I've actually persuaded him to engage in threesomes now.'

'What?'

'Don't say "what" darling...say "pardon."'

I couldn't think of anything to say.

'Oh dear Beth, look at your face. Seriously, for such a worldly woman you really are a little straight when it comes to sex. I'm talking about Victor!' she laughed.

'Oh,' I said relieved.

'Since Georgie has realised that he doesn't need to work so hard, he's taken quite a liking to my little friend,' she winked. 'Of course I'm absolutely delighted.'

As Gran giggled away, I thought about how simple her life seemed to be compared to mine. Even though I had changed my number, I was getting a lot more phone calls and the calls were getting stranger. The last call played the music from the movie "Twilight," where Bella realised Edward was a vampire. The message was clear to me…they know who I am.

My intimidation wasn't only limited to calls either. Yesterday I received a photo of the club in New York and when I tried to call the mobile number that sent the photo, the line was disconnected. Someone was going out of his or her way to scare me and it was working.

My thoughts were interrupted by Gran, 'Yoo hoo darling, whatever are you thinking about? You've gone as white as a ghost!'

'Oh, I'm sorry Gran, it's nothing…let's order.'

During lunch, Gran continued to make me laugh with her stories about life in America. Halfway through our salad, Gran stopped eating, 'Now on a serious note, are you alright darling? You don't look like your usual self, and you haven't told me anything about your wedding plans.'

'That's because there aren't any yet. We've both been so busy, we just haven't gotten around to it,' I lied.

The truth was, Jay was constantly asking me to set a date. He was starting to get upset at my blasé attitude about the whole thing and we even had our first row about it.

'Everybody is always too busy these days! Darling, you simply must make your wedding a priority, especially if you want to have a baby.'

I almost choked on my champagne, 'What baby?'

'Oh come on darling, you must want to procreate with James; your babies will be beautiful. And think of all the practice you will get,' she giggled. 'Besides, I want to be a great grandmother.'

'Well...'

'No "well" about it! I suggest you marry that beautiful specimen of a man as soon as possible and start a family.' Suddenly Gran gasped, 'Oh my heaven's above, how insensitive of me. His swimmers can swim can't they?'

'I don't know. I assume so. Anyway, can we please change the subject?'

'Well, if you insist, but promise me you'll get on with the wedding arrangements as soon as possible. Before I die, I would like to see my favourite granddaughter married off, and barefoot and pregnant in the kitchen.'

I rolled my eyes, 'I'm your *only* granddaughter!'

'That's irrelevant darling...you are still my favourite. Now let's get some yummy dessert, we need to fatten you up.'

As we ate our way through a deliciously dark chocolate cake, Gran told me all about her upcoming trip to Saint Raphael in the Cote d'Azur, 'You and James simply must come. We can leave the men at home and sneak off to have fun like we used to.'

I had to admit, it did sound like a great way to escape my troubles, and spending some quality time with Gran would be just what I needed, 'It does sound like fun. I'll check my roster and speak to Jay tonight.'

On the way out of the café Gran hugged me, 'Darling, please say you will come. I miss you.'

I kissed her cheek, 'How can I say no to that face? Okay I'll come, but I can't vouch for my "dreamy fiancé."'

Jay came home from work a little earlier than usual and surprised me. I was looking out of the kitchen window when he came up behind me, 'I've missed you, sexy.'

'Hey,' I smiled as he nuzzled his face into my neck, 'this is a surprise.'

His hand lazily drifted under my skirt, his fingers gently teasing the inside of my thighs. His other hand softly brushed against my breasts, 'A nice one I hope?'

I closed my eyes as he slowly lowered my panties, and I could feel how hard he was when he brushed up against my back. Jay turned me around and kissed me, 'I love you,' he whispered as he slowly and deliberately entered me. As our bodies moulded into one another, Jay's hips moved as slowly and sensually as his kiss, and just when it felt like we were both going to climax, he pulled away, 'Come with me.'

Jay led me to the rug in front of the fire. Laying me down, he kissed me while his fingertips gently caressed my neck, breasts, and stomach, until they reached between my legs. As his fingers explored inside me, I ran my hands through his hair and moaned. My whole body was aching for him, 'Jay...'

'Shhh,' he said as his featherlike kisses moved down my body.

When Jay's warm breath and tongue reached my sex, I lost control and screamed out his name. Jay took me swiftly and as he thrust deeply into me, I could feel waves of pleasure pulsating through my body again. Jay's tongue darted inside my mouth as our bodies clung tightly to each other, each thrust delivering a new sensation, until finally we rose together and gave in to our internal ecstasy.

Jay rolled onto his back, 'Oh my god, I've never come like that before.'

Breathlessly I agreed, 'It was pretty erotic.'

He looked at me tenderly, 'I love you Beth.'

I ignored the pain in my heart, 'I love you too.'

After we had showered, I remembered Gran's invitation, 'Gran has invited us to San Raphael for a holiday.'

'What a fantastic idea Beth! Is it just Tilly and George?'

'Yes, and Victor...quite the threesome, I hear.'

Jay laughed, 'We should definitely go. I'll check with Anna to see if she can free up my schedule for a week.'

Three days later Jay and I boarded his private jet, and we were on our way to France. When the plane landed, I turned on my phone and gasped when I saw the face looking back at me. It was a photo of, 'Repulsive Roger.'

Jay looked at me concerned, 'Beth are you okay? You've gone white.'

I quickly put my phone in my bag, 'It's nothing.'

'Talking about phone calls, that reminds me...I forgot to tell you that I've had a couple of calls from Ruby's friend John Davenport.'

Oh shit.

'And?'

'It's all a bit strange really. He left a message with Anna saying it was an urgent matter, and then each time I've attempted to call him back he hasn't answered. He doesn't even have voicemail. Does that seem odd to you?'

I shrugged my shoulders; I was feeling faint and doing everything in my power to concentrate on walking. I had no idea who was plaguing me, but I knew I had to find out. My gut instinct had been telling me that it was that bastard Baileys, and I was almost certain now that it was right. I turned off my phone.

The week Jay and I spent with Gran and George was so much fun, despite the embarrassing sounds of the threesome next door.

'Beth, it's not like you to be so prudish about sex. I know it's your gran, but I think it's great that they are so adventurous.' Jay smiled as he wrapped his arms around my waist, 'I hope we are still hard at it when we are their age. And who knows, if you play your cards right, you may get your own Victor.'

I attempted to make light of Jay's comment; however, due to my increasing fear of my secret life being exposed, I knew that the chances of us being together in old age were getting slimmer and slimmer by the day.

When we landed back into the UK, I quickly realised that leaving the country and turning my phone off wasn't going to make my problem disappear. I was forced back to reality when I turned my phone back on to see six missed calls, four voice messages and two incriminating photos. The second photo shook me to the core…it was Julia!

32

TRUE COLOURS

B aileys pressed the send button on his mobile phone. *That should do it! If that stupid bitch wasn't scared before, she will be now.*

Tanya walked out of the bathroom, 'I'm going to contact Beth today.'

Baileys feigned surprise, 'Really? Are ye prepared?'

'As prepared as I can be. Are you sure that the number you gave me is correct?'

'Oh yes,' smiled Baileys, 'I'm positive!'

I was getting out of the shower when I heard my phone ringing. I looked over and saw "Private Number" flash on the display. My instinct told me to take the call, so I answered but I stayed silent.

'Hello?'

I waited for the laughter that never came.

'Hello? May I speak with Beth Saunders?'

I relaxed a little, 'This is Beth.'

'I need to speak with you. My name is Tanya.'

I froze. She didn't need an introduction.

'I'm James' ex-girlfriend.'

Silence.

'Hello! Beth, are you there?'

I felt nauseous, 'How did you get my number?'

'I don't think that is relevant.'

'It is to me.'

'Beth, I didn't call to answer your questions. In fact, it's quite the opposite. I want to meet with you. I have something important to discuss. Now, can you meet with me today or not?'

Today?

'Where?'

'Covent Garden.'

'What time?'

'Two o'clock.'

'That's in two hours.'

'Yes, it is! How incredibly smart of you…well done! Now are you coming or not?'

Wow, what a condescending bitch.

'Yes. Where are we meeting?'

'Le Garrick.'

When I arrived at the restaurant, Tanya was already seated. The waiter showed me to her table and when I sat down she scrutinised me with her eyes. The awkward silence that followed was gladly interrupted when the waiter offered me a glass of water. Once we were alone, Tanya finally spoke, 'I've always been curious as to who stole James' heart from me. I envisaged a model, a philanthropist or someone of stature. But you are none of these things, are you?' She gave me a look that could cut through ice, 'You are pretty average really. In fact, I'm even more confused now as to why James would leave *me* for someone like you.' She shook her head, 'I really don't understand it.'

I opened my mouth to talk but she cut me off, 'And what's more, you are a whore!'

Her words took me by surprise, 'Excuse me?'

'Don't play the innocent with me Beth...or shall I call you Kat?'

I felt the blood drain from my face.

Tanya looked at me with disgust, 'I know all about your dirty little secrets and lies.'

Suddenly it all made sense to me, 'It's you!'

'*What* is me?'

It was my turn to be assertive, 'Don't pretend that you have no idea what I am talking about.'

'If you are suggesting that I am the whore...'

'I'm talking about the eerie tune from Twilight and the photos.'

Tanya looked confused, 'I don't have the faintest idea what you are talking about. If this is your way of changing the subject...'

'Give me your phone!'

'I most certainly will not.'

Suddenly I felt angry, 'What's the plan Tanya?'

'Plan? I have absolutely no idea what you are alluding to. Now stop this nonsense and stop trying to derail the conversation.'

'I don't believe you. Now what do you want?'

Tanya looked perplexed, 'I didn't come here to talk about phone calls and photos. However, you are correct...I do want something. I want you to end your relationship with James.'

I stared at her in silence.

'You understand what I'm saying don't you Beth, or do you need me to spell it out for you?'

I glared at her.

'Clearly you do! We both know that James deserves better than being humiliated in the press,' she looked at my engagement ring, 'and... heartbroken. Never mind what your dirty little secret will do to the business that he has been relentlessly building for years. What do you think it will do to him when he finds out that his fiancé is whoring herself around the world?'

'He won't find out,' I said defiantly. 'Besides, I don't do that anymore.'

'Don't be so bloody naïve Beth! I found out, and it's only a matter of time before one of your disgusting clients recognises you in the media and comes forward.'

'How did you find out?'

Tanya was clearly agitated, 'Stop trying to change the subject.'

I took a chance on my gut instinct, 'It was Baileys wasn't it?'

'Baileys? Who on earth is Baileys?'

I realised my mistake, 'John...John Davenport.'

Tanya blushed and looked away.

Oh my god...he didn't!

'You are sleeping with him aren't you?'

'Keep your voice down,' scolded Tanya, 'it's none of your business.'

'I'm making it my business. You don't understand...'

'How dare you! You left him. He's not yours anymore!'

Mine?

I let her comment go for the moment about him not being mine, 'That bloody bastard! Tanya, he is pure evil. You can't…'

She cut me off, 'Don't you ever tell me what I can and can't do. What kind of woman are you? First you take away the one thing he wanted most in the world, and then you break his heart!'

It was my turn to be confused, 'What on earth are you talking about? What exactly did I take away?'

'Wow! You really are a good actress. Don't pretend you have no idea what I am talking about. You are a disgusting person Beth Saunders. In fact, I don't even want to waste any more of my time with you.'

Tanya stood up to leave. She turned to look at me and her eyes were full of hate and pain, 'Do it Beth. End it with James!'

In a futile attempt to stop her leaving, I grabbed her arm, 'Tanya, you must listen to me.'

'Get your hands off me,' she hissed. 'The only words I want to hear from you are, "It's done!"'

'But Tanya…'

'You have one week to finish this Beth.'

'And if I don't?'

'Then you and James will reap the consequences.'

'How exactly?'

'Well, I'm sure the press will have a field day with your dirty little secret life.'

'But you just said Jay deserves better than that. Surely you wouldn't do that to him?'

'I lied.' She leaned in close to my face and almost spat the words at me, 'You would know all about that wouldn't you Beth?'

As Tanya turned and walked away, I could feel my blood boiling. I was livid. That bastard Baileys was lying to Tanya and manipulating her like a puppet on a string. I took a few deep breaths to calm myself down and then dialled Ruby's number. I was thankful that she picked up, 'I need to see you…now!'

As Beth left the café, Baileys smiled to himself. Neither Tanya nor Beth had been aware of him watching the whole interaction unfold.

I'm a feckin' genius.

Baileys finished his wine and waved to the pretty waitress who had been serving him. When she returned with his credit card, he handed her his business card. The pretty waitress read what he had written and smiled, 'I'll call you later…sir!'

33

GIRL POWER

'Ruby he's filled her with lies. He's manipulating her!'

'So! What do you care? You know you have to end it with Jay, so maybe this is the perfect opportunity.'

'I know,' I replied sadly. 'But that's not the point. No woman deserves to be treated so badly. You of all people should understand that.' Ruby looked away and I could see that my comment had hit a nerve, 'Sorry Rubes, but look what the bastard did to you. Now he's going to do it to Tanya and she's only just getting over a broken heart.'

'Why is that *our* problem?'

'Because we need to stick together, so narcissistic bastards like Baileys don't get away with all the lying, cheating and manipulation.'

'Oh, but it's okay for you to lie, manipulate and sleep around with married men? A bit of a double standard wouldn't you say "Kat"?'

'The only married man that I have ever slept with is Baileys...and I regret that.'

Ruby snapped back, 'Do you?'

'Yes! Rubes, this is about an evil man taking advantage of a vulnerable woman. We both know he has another agenda;

this isn't only about me ending it with Jay. Tanya's clearly in love with him and he's going to break her heart all over again!'

Ruby thought for a moment, 'That poor woman in Hong Kong won't have any idea that her low life husband is fucking someone else.'

'Exactly! And I strongly believe that the poor woman I met today has no idea that he's married with kids.'

Ruby looked at me, and her steely resolve softened, 'So there is some of the old Beth in there.'

'Rubes, it's always been there. I've made mistakes, but I'm still me.'

Ruby sighed, 'Okay, let's put our heads together and give that fucking lying bastard his karma.'

Two hours later we had drafted a plan, but none of it would work without another ally. Ruby and I both knew that what we needed to say to Tanya would hurt her, but we also knew that she deserved much better. I dialled her number.

'This is a surprise. I didn't expect to hear from you so soon.'

I ignored Tanya's icy tone, 'Can you meet me today? It's important.'

I could almost hear her thinking down the phone line, 'Is it absolutely necessary? You better not be wasting my time.'

'Yes it is. I need to talk to you.'

Tanya sighed, 'Very well then.'

'Thank you,' I said relieved.

'Where?'

'Same place, same time?'

'Yes, that's fine!'

I gave Ruby a thumbs up, 'And Tanya, one more thing.'

'What?' she snapped.

'I need your word that you won't tell John.'

'Why?'

'Please Tanya. I'll explain when I meet you.'

She hesitated, ' Very well, you have my word!'

2.05 pm

Ruby was giving me a lecture on why I shouldn't eat croissants when I saw Tanya approaching.

Tanya pulled out a chair and sat down, 'You must be Ruby. John has told me all about Beth's sidekick.'

'I doubt it,' responded Ruby coldly.

I could sense Ruby tense up, so I placed my hand on her leg as a sign to ease up. Tanya looked directly at me, 'So what is so important?'

I looked at Ruby, who seemed more relaxed, until she opened her mouth, 'What has that fucker told you?'

Tanya seemed taken aback by Ruby's tone, so I squeezed Ruby's leg in an attempt to get her attention, but she ignored me, 'Tanya, I don't know you, but I do know that lying bastard John Davenport. Now let's get one thing straight before I go on, I whole fucking heartedly agree that Beth should end it with Jay, but that has nothing to do with why we asked you here today.'

Tanya looked totally confused and despite my eyes pleading with Ruby to keep to the plan, she continued to rant, 'We need to know what he's told you. Beth mentioned something about her breaking his heart and…'

Tanya interrupted Ruby, 'I don't think it's any of your business what John and I discuss.'

Ruby leant in closer to Tanya and almost spat out the words, 'Trust me Tanya, you want this to be my business. The only fucking heart that's been broken around here to do with John fucking Davenport...is mine!'

Tanya looked at me, but I was looking at Ruby. She was visibly upset, and it made me realise just how much he had meant to her and how much he had hurt her. It fired me up, 'Tanya please. I know it's difficult, but you have to put your differences with me aside and listen to us. We believe John is lying to you and manipulating us both in some way.'

Tanya suddenly seemed a little overwhelmed, 'I need a minute. I'm going to the bathroom.'

As soon as Tanya was out of earshot, I turned to Ruby, 'Rubes, what on earth was that?'

'I don't know, sorry! I just got worked up at the thought of that bastard.'

'Okay, but we have to stick to the plan. Can you try to reign it in a little?'

'Well, it's done now. Let's see what she has to say when she comes back.'

I looked towards the bathroom, '*If* she comes back.'

Thankfully, Tanya returned and sat down, 'I want to hear your story first Ruby.'

For the next hour, Ruby told Tanya everything that had happened from the minute she met Baileys; His reaction when he joined her and Beth in the bar in Hong Kong, his time in London and his fake promises, how he reacted when he saw Beth and Jay at the airport, the day she met his wife and kids, to finally flying back to the UK with a broken heart. By the time Ruby had finished talking Tanya was clearly upset.

Tanya looked at me, 'He actually paid you for sex?' she asked horrified.

'Well, technically we didn't have sex until the second time but...' Ruby elbowed me, 'Oh, yes...sorry...twice...sort of.'

Ruby rolled her eyes at me.

Tanya looked shocked, 'I can't actually believe this. It all sounds like a soap opera, not real life. He hasn't told me any of this.'

'Well, there's no fucking surprise!' Ruby said bitterly.

Tanya looked at Ruby, 'And he is a father? He has children?'

'Yes.'

'And his wife is pregnant?'

'Yes.'

Tanya turned to me, 'So Beth, you didn't have an abortion?'

'Abortion? No, absolutely not!'

'And I'm assuming that you never had a long term relationship with him?'

I cringed, 'Definitely not.'

'But you did?' Tanya asked Ruby.

'Yes, until I found out about his family.'

We all sat in silence while Tanya tried to make sense of everything. Finally, after a few minutes she spoke, 'It's like we are talking about two different men. Are you both sure we are discussing the same person?'

Ruby had deleted all the photos of Baileys from her phone except one, which she showed to Tanya. Tanya didn't need to say anything, we could see from her reaction that we were all talking about the same John Davenport.

Ruby gave me a nudge to continue, 'I'm sorry Tanya, but that's not the worst of it.'

Tanya looked up, her eyes brimming with tears, 'What the bloody hell could be worse than all of that?'

I told Tanya about the blackmail and my recent bout of eerie phone calls and picture messages.

Tanya went pale, 'And you think it is John?'

'In light of our current situation, I am almost certain of it. I thought he had gone away, but clearly he's been doing a lot of work behind the scenes to get revenge for me not paying his second blackmail attempt.'

Tanya put her face in her hands, 'Oh my god, how could I be such a poor judge of character? He's making a complete fool of me.'

'Don't beat yourself up Tanya,' said Ruby, 'I can usually smell a bastard a mile off, but I fell for it.'

Tanya looked at me, 'What do you think he wants? He's gone to an awful amount of trouble, for this to simply be about breaking up your relationship with James.'

'I don't know his end game,' I said honestly, 'but I do know that he wants money.'

Tanya suddenly remembered something, 'He did ask me last week about my settlement from James. He was wondering whether I could extort more money from James if he knew about you Beth. Maybe he's going to suggest that I blackmail James?'

Ruby was intrigued, 'What else did he say?'

'He said that Beth would never agree to ending it with James,' Tanya looked embarrassed, 'and he encouraged me to apply pressure by threatening exposure.'

'It sounds like he is covering all bases,' said Ruby.

I had a thought, 'Why don't we play him at his own game?'

'What do you mean?' asked Tanya.

Ruby was excited, 'Yes, good one Beth. Let's play along and see what he is going to do after you say no to Tanya.'

Tanya looked wistful, 'I'm still not totally convinced he is up to anything.'

Ruby poured another wine, 'Trust me darling, that fucking narcissist is up to something.'

I looked at Ruby, and then Tanya, 'Are we doing this ladies?'

Ruby raised her glass, but Tanya hesitated, 'What if I can't do it?'

'What do you mean?' I asked.

'What if I can't pretend? I don't even know if I can look at him.'

I looked hard into Tanya's eyes, 'Tanya, you can. You are a strong woman. You won't be alone; *we* can do this...together!'

Ruby put her glass down, 'We are not saying it's going to be easy Tanya, but you *can* do this. Like Beth said, *we* can do this!'

Ruby raised her glass again and looked at Tanya, 'Let's get the bastard!'

I gave Tanya a nod of encouragement, raised my glass, and after a moment's pause, Tanya followed suit. Ruby's face broke into a triumphant smile, 'Here's to fucking Charlie's Angels... and to girl power!'

'To girl power,' I said.

'To girl power,' echoed Tanya.

34

THE PLAYER GETS PLAYED

Baileys smiled at Tanya when she stepped into his car, 'Hey sexy, how was yer day?'

'I met Beth again.'

Tanya could see an instant change in Bailey's demeanour by the way his hands gripped the steering wheel. He kept his gaze forward as he put the car into gear, 'Oh, and how did that go?'

Tanya sighed, 'Well you were right!'

Baileys looked at her with a grin, 'She said no?'

'She said no!'

'So what did ye say to her?'

'I told her she was a fool and that I have no option but to go to the press.'

'And she still said no?'

'Her actual words were, "Do what you like. I'm not giving up this life because you are jealous. No one will believe you anyway, you are just a scorned ex."'

Baileys roared with laughter.

Tanya looked at him, 'I'm sorry, I'm failing to see what is so funny?'

'Tanya, it's great. She's playin' right into yer hands. What the little gold digger doesn't know, is that I have exactly what ye need to convince her otherwise.'

'Which is?'

'You'll see,' he said cockily.

Back at Tanya's apartment, Tanya told Baileys to pour the wine while she changed her clothes. When Tanya hung her bag on the back of a chair, she quickly checked her voice recorder to see if it was still turned on and was pleased that it was.

Tanya came back into the lounge and Baileys pulled her close. She looked into his beautiful eyes that were full of lies, 'So what do you have in your little bag of tricks?'

'Well, I can show ye what's in here first,' he said as he put Tanya's hand on his crotch.

Tanya was about to pull away and then remembered what the girls said about playing the game. She kept her hand on his erection, 'How about we talk about the "other tricks" before we play with this one?'

'No way! I need this sortin' out first, otherwise I won't be able to concentrate.' He unzipped his trousers and sat down on the couch. Tanya placed herself on top of him and gave a performance worthy of an Oscar.

'Whoa, someone is feelin' frisky aren't they?' Baileys said once they had finished.

'I guess it's all this talk of destroying Beth,' Tanya replied with a grin.

'Well, we'd better get on with it if it turns ye on so much. I wouldn't mind another fuck like that before the night is through.'

Tanya smiled but inside she felt sick. She poured herself another glass of wine while Baileys went to get a folder from his suitcase.

'What's all that?' she asked innocently when Baileys put the folder on the table.

'This, me love, is all ye need to have Beth beggin' for ye not to expose her dirty little secret life.'

Baileys pulled out a catalogue of notes, photos, and press cuttings and Tanya was genuinely shocked, 'Where on earth did you get all this information from?'

Baileys smiled, 'Let's just say I've been doin' a little due diligence.'

Baileys told Tanya about how he had coincidentally met a flight attendant who was friends with Beth. However, he failed to mention how he seduced her and stole Beth's number from her phone, or the fact that he was still having sex with her occasionally. Baileys then showed Tanya a photo of the nightclub in New York, along with photos of Julia and Roger.

'So these people just told you everything you needed to know about Beth without question? Surely they wanted something from you?'

'Let's just say a little threat goes a long way,' he smirked, 'and a college tuition fee can really make a girl talk.'

Tanya picked up Julia's photo, 'You paid for her tuition?'

'What else was I goin' to do?'

'Couldn't you just have had sex with her?'

Baileys laughed, 'Tanya, she is a prostitute. I can't imagine who she's slept with, and to tell ye the truth I don't find her attractive.'

Tanya studied Julia, 'I find that hard to believe. She is beautiful. Look at the size of her breasts!'

Baileys smiled at the memory, 'How can I lie to ye? I'm embarrassed to say that I did sleep with her once. But in my defence, that was before I realised she was a prostitute.'

'Oh,' said Tanya playing along, 'well I don't blame you really. She is very attractive and very sexy.'

Baileys was impressed with how well Tanya was taking everything, so he opened up a bit more than he had planned to, 'Since I'm being honest with ye, there is somethin' I need to tell ye.'

Tanya felt a mixture of uneasiness and excitement, 'Go on.'

'Well, let's just say that I have been usin' a few intimidation tactics with Beth meself.'

'Intimidation tactics, why on earth would you do that?'

'Well, since I met ye, I couldn't bear the fact that borin' arse Thorsen would choose a whore over someone like yerself. I was tryin' to get Beth to end it with him.'

Tanya feigned disappointment, 'Oh, I see.'

'Don't think ill of me Tanya. I only did it because I care about ye.'

'What kind of things have you been doing?'

'Are ye sure ye want to know?'

'Yes. I want us to have an honest relationship.'

Baileys held her hand and kissed it, 'Sendin' her photos, callin' and not sayin' anythin'... that kind of stuff.'

'And is it working?'

'Clearly not! She is still with him!' Baileys replied dryly.

'So what now?'

'Well, now that ye have stepped in, maybe ye should lay on some more pressure. Make her sweat a bit, and somehow make her believe that ye are serious about goin' to the press. I can give ye some incriminatin' photos that I have and ye can send them to her.'

'You want *me* to intimidate Beth?'

'We can do it together if it makes ye feel better. Work as a team,' he smiled. 'I'll keep on with the phone calls and let's see how long it takes her to run scared!'

'And do you think it will work?'

'I'm not sure, but unless we apply as much pressure as possible, we'll never know.'

Tanya pretended to be thinking and then turned to Baileys, 'I'm not sure that I'm totally comfortable with the plan. It's basically blackmail and it all sounds a bit dramatic to me, not to mention a little unconventional.'

Baileys looked disappointed.

Tanya put her hands on his face, 'But I do love that you want to do this for me. It makes me feel very special. Thank you.'

'Well, ye are a very special woman Tanya.' Baileys stood up and pulled Tanya into his arms, 'James Thorsen is a fool for lettin' ye go.' He started to undo the zip on her dress, 'Will ye at least give it some thought?'

She looked into his eyes, 'Okay.'

Tanya's dress fell to the floor and while Baileys kissed every part of her body, Tanya closed her eyes and kept repeating Ruby's words in her mind, 'Let's get the bastard!'

The following morning Tanya called Ruby to give her an update, 'What a fucking low life,' said Ruby. 'Great job keeping it together and awesome work on the recording. I think there's more to his plan, so hold tight for a couple of days if you can, and we'll call you if there are any developments this end.'

Tanya felt surprisingly powerful, 'Thanks Ruby. Will do! I'm actually going away for a couple of days on a work trip, but I'll send you the recording as soon as I have edited it.'

'That will be great. Oh, and Tanya.'

'Yes?'

Ruby sounded pumped up, 'Stay strong!'

'Thanks...I will.'

Tanya hung up her phone and couldn't believe how liberated she felt. She smiled to herself at the turnaround of events. She would never have imagined that she would be in cohorts with Beth... and like Ruby so much. She felt great.

35

THE DEVIL IS IN THE DETAILS

It didn't take long for Ruby's theory about Baileys to be proven right. We were at her place when the call came through, 'Well, well, Kitty Kat, ye picked up?'

I went cold at the sound of his voice. I put the call on speakerphone and nodded to Ruby to turn on her voice recorder.

'I doubt this call is social. What do you want?'

'There's no need to be so hostile. I'm actually callin' to do ye a favour.'

'I doubt that. How on earth can *you* possibly help me?'

Baileys sounded amused, 'Now now, let's be nice…put the past behind us and move on shall we?'

'Like I said, what do you want?'

'Oh dear, I'm findin' ye tone very hostile Kitty Kat. Now, it's come to me attention that a certain "ex" is tryin' to ruin ye, "lifestyle of the rich and famous," he laughed.

'How the hell do *you* know about that?'

'I have me sources.'

'Well, for someone who was recently blackmailing me for the same thing, I'm a bit confused as to how you can possibly help… unless of course you are calling to blackmail me again!'

'Ye know, for a flight attendant ye really are switched on sometimes. However, I'd rather ye looked at it as, "You scratch my back and I'll scratch yours." Blackmailing sounds so cold, don't ye think?'

I took a deep breath to control the anger that was rising within me, and when I looked over at Ruby she looked like she was about to punch something, 'You really are a condescending, arrogant, bastard aren't you?'

He laughed, 'Sticks and stones Kitty Kat. I can make all this go away but ye will have to stop the name-calling. Despite how the sayin' goes, you really are startin' to hurt me feelin's.'

'How are you going to make it go away? Do you have a magic wand in your narcissistic bag of tricks?'

'Now that's just mean, but I'll let it slide. Let's just say that love does stupid things to people *and* used correctly it can give you power. *You* of all people understand that.'

'How would you know about love? I doubt you've ever loved anyone in your life, except yourself!'

Baileys pretended to sound hurt, 'Really Kitty Kat, ye are being very personal. I've called ye because I know I can make Tanya leave ye alone, and all ye are doin' is attackin' me. If ye don't cut it out, I may just put the price up.'

'How much this time?' I said bitterly.

'We can talk about that later. First ye have to agree to let me help ye.'

'Not without knowing what it's going to cost me.'

'Details, details…the devil's always in the details. I think the question ye should be asking is, what it's going to cost ye if ye don't pay me?'

I was losing my patience, 'It was only a few months ago that you were blackmailing me for the same reason. I find it very hard to believe that you won't go to the press once you have your money?'

'Such little faith. Money is money, it doesn't matter how it comes.'

'Clearly not to you,' I said sarcastically.

Baileys laughed.

'How will I know that you'll keep your word?'

'Well, ye just goin' to have to trust me aren't ye?'

It was my turn to laugh, 'Are you serious? How can I trust you after all you have done?'

His tone changed and he was suddenly angry, 'So far as I see it, ye don't have a choice do ye? Now go check ye email.'

He hung up the phone and I looked at Ruby who was doing push ups, 'Rubes are you okay?'

'Not now Beth!' she snapped. 'If I don't do these push ups I'm going to fucking explode! Ten…eleven…'

I made a cup of tea and waited for Ruby to calm down. When she had finished venting, she sat next to me and was visibly shaking with anger, 'We have to finish this fucker off Beth. He's never going to go away.'

Resignedly I agreed with her, 'I know.'

'We have to do whatever it takes to make sure that bastard spends some quality time getting arse fucked behind bars.'

I put my hand over Ruby's clenched fist, 'Don't worry Rubes, we'll get him.' And as I said the words…for once, I actually believed it.

36

KEEP YOUR FRIENDS CLOSE... AND YOUR ENEMIES CLOSER

Tanya put her glass down, she was gobsmacked, 'He wants how much?'

'Two million pounds,' I replied.

'Greedy fucking twat,' said Ruby.

Tanya looked at me, 'And you got all your phone conversation on tape?'

'Yes.'

Tanya listened to the audio recording and by the end she was smiling, 'This is fantastic Beth! We are compiling quite a bit of evidence against him. I was talking to my private detective...'

'You have a private detective?' I asked impressed.

'Yes, he's a very old friend, very discreet, and he has offered to help.'

'We are fucking Charlie's Angels,' laughed Ruby, 'his name isn't Bosley by any chance is it?'

Tanya smiled at Ruby and then looked at me, 'Beth, do you have any emails from the last blackmail attempt?'

'Yes, I kept everything. Baileys is always referring to flight attendants being dumb; I think he's quite the dumb arse himself. He even sent them from an email address with his initials in it.'

'Well, he does do most of his thinking from his dick, so no surprise there,' said Ruby.

Tanya raised her eyebrows, but then we all broke into laughter.

'Okay,' said Tanya bringing the conversation back down to earth, 'what's the next step? Shall I try to get more information out of him about the blackmail?'

'I'm not sure that he'll open up about this current attempt, because he's doing it behind your back,' I said.

Ruby had a thought, 'Yes, but don't forget that he thinks you are in love with him Tanya. So, he may even think that you would do something similar for him, and then he'd have both of you blackmailing Beth.'

Tanya looked confused, 'Sorry I'm not following you. What do you mean?'

'Well, we all know how narcissists think. They like to come up with the idea themselves and thrive on control, so maybe *you* have to direct the conversation about blackmailing Beth, so he thinks it's his idea.'

Tanya looked puzzled, 'How on earth would I do that?'

Ruby was in full PI mode, 'Well, if you can somehow convince him that you do love him, and that you really want Beth to suffer because you hate her for what she has done to both of you, he may suggest for you to blackmail Beth.'

'You really think he would do that?' asked Tanya.

'It wouldn't surprise me because that's exactly how his mind works. He wants money and this way he'll get a lot more. I say it's worth a try.'

I felt excited, 'That's genius Rubes! Tanya, do you think you could convince him that you have fallen in love with him? (I paused) I know the other part about me may not be so hard to do.'

Tanya looked very serious for a moment, 'It will be difficult, and I'll have to really put on my acting skills,' then she smiled and looked at me, 'in both cases.'

Ruby raised her glass again, 'Fucking girl power…I love it!'

Tanya rolled over and gave Baileys a passionate kiss. They had just finished another mammoth sex session and despite Tanya not finding it any easier to submit to her role as the doting girlfriend, she was very convincing, 'John can I tell you something?'

'Yeah, anythin'.'

'I know it's very soon…' she brushed his hair back from his face, 'but I think I've fallen in love with you.'

Bailey's face broke into a wide grin, 'Well now.'

'I realise it is a bit quick and please don't feel that you have to respond. I just want you to know that you have made me very happy these past few months. I never thought I would feel this way about anyone again.'

Baileys pulled her in close, 'Well if it makes ye feel better, I feel exactly the same way,' he lied.

Tanya kissed him again and whispered, 'I'm glad that whore left you.'

Baileys laughed and mimicked Tanya's accent, 'I'm glad that boring arsed bastard left you.'

Tanya giggled and then looked serious, 'I have to say, I'm not usually a very judgmental person but after meeting Beth and witnessing her self-righteous attitude, I can safely say that I hate her guts.'

Baileys roared with laughter, 'Hate is such a strong word! I think I love ye a little bit more.'

'Really? Well in that case I hate, hate, hate her!'

Baileys wrapped his arms around Tanya and closed his eyes, 'Like I said, ye are a very special woman.'

Tanya smiled to herself and drifted off to sleep.

The following morning, Tanya woke to the sound of the coffee machine. She walked into the kitchen to find Baileys in full chef mode, 'Sit down gorgeous, I've made ye breakfast.'

'Wow, it smells amazing. What's the occasion?'

'No reason.'

Tanya smiled, 'I could get used to this.'

Baileys pulled out her chair and as Tanya sat down, he caressed her breasts, 'I could get used to these.'

'Seriously John, do you take Viagra? Your sex drive is insatiable.'

'Ye are me Viagra,' he laughed. Baileys joined Tanya at the table, 'Do ye really hate Beth's guts?'

His question took her by surprise, 'Yes.'

Baileys grinned, 'Good!'

Tanya could almost see his mind ticking away so she took her opportunity, 'It almost feels like getting Beth to break up with James isn't enough. It will most likely break his heart more than hers, especially if she is with him just for his lifestyle.'

Baileys listened but kept quiet.

'She is such a cold bitch. What she has done to you is unforgivable, and who knows how many other people she has hurt soliciting herself. It doesn't seem right that she is getting off so lightly.'

Baileys took a sip of coffee, then looked at Tanya, 'I couldn't agree more.'

Tanya waited for him to say something else, but he didn't, and they ate the rest of their breakfast in silence.

A couple of hours later, Baileys popped his head into Tanya's bedroom, 'Hey Tanya, I won't be around for a few days, I have some business in Hong Kong that I have to take care of. Maybe when I get back we can chat some more about what ye said at breakfast.'

'Beth?'

'Yeah, I may have an idea,' he winked.

Tanya walked over to him and put her arms around his waist, 'Do we have time now?'

Baileys cupped Tanya's bottom in his hands, 'If I had time, I wouldn't be talkin' about *her*. I'd be doin' somethin' much more interestin'. But that'll have to wait too. Me flight leaves in less than two hours.'

Baileys drove his car into the driveway and when she opened the door she was naked, 'Well hello handsome. What time is your flight out?'

Baileys picked her up and walked towards her bedroom, '8 pm.'

'Good, we have a lot of time to play then. Now lay down, I want to sit on that beautiful face.'

When Baileys waved her goodbye, he couldn't believe that he had stumbled upon such a sex fanatic. She had more toys than a sex shop, was outrageous in the bedroom and had even taught him a few tricks. Baileys smiled when he thought about how she had tied him up, and he made a mental note to discuss a new career path with her when he got back from Hong Kong; her talents were wasted as a waitress!

Two days later

Baileys called Tanya, 'Hey sexy, just checkin' in to let ye know I've had to extend me trip for a few days. Bloody clients are takin' forever to close a deal.'

'That perfectly fine,' Tanya said feeling relieved. 'I am missing you though.'

'Ah babe, I miss ye too.'

'I've been thinking about Beth.'

'Ye have?'

'Yes, and the more I think about her, the more I dislike her.'

Baileys laughed, 'So what do ye want to do about it?'

'I want her to suffer...the way you have... and the way I have.'

'Ye do, do ye?'

'Yes, I do.'

'What do ye have in mind?'

'That is the problem... I have no idea.'

'I'm no expert meself either, but let me have a think over the next couple of days and we can put our heads together when I get back.'

'Thank you, that would be good.'

Baileys turned to see his wife walking towards him, 'I better go. I have a meetin' in a couple of minutes.'

'Okay, don't work too hard.'

'I'll try not to.'

'I love you.'

'I love ye too.'

Just as Baileys hung up the phone, his wife tapped him on the shoulder, 'Darling, you seriously work too hard, can you turn your phone off now? Our table is ready.'

37

TURNING THE TABLES

Monday

My phone rang and Gran's photo flashed on the display, 'Darling do you have a vibrator?'

I couldn't help but smile, 'Hi Gran.'

'Mine has broken and I'm in the market for a new one. I was wondering if you can recommend something that you youngsters prefer.'

'Victor has died?'

'Oh heavens no, he's fine! It's the small one that I take travelling with me. It doesn't seem to create such a fuss when I go through customs.'

'Sorry Gran, I don't actually own a vibrator.'

She gasped, 'Seriously darling, you need to get on top of your sex game. You don't know what you are missing! And trust me, James will thank you for it.'

'Thanks for the advice, but I think James and I are fine.'

'Poppycock! I'm going to send you one.'

'Gran, there's no....'

'Nonsense, now I must go. Chat soon. Love you darling!'

Ruby was waiting for me to finish my phone call, 'Your gran hasn't changed.'

'Actually, she's getting more outrageous with age.'

'Sounded interesting! I can't believe you don't have a vibrator!'

I shook my head, 'Seriously, *what* is the big deal about vibrators?'

Ruby smirked, 'Well darling...if you had one, you'd know!'

We arrived at the address Tanya had sent us, and saw Tanya sitting in an office with her private detective. Ruby tapped on the window and Tanya beckoned us in, 'Marty, may I introduce you to Ruby and Beth. Girls, this is Marty, my long-time friend and one of the best detectives I know.'

'How many does she know?' Ruby whispered to me, making me giggle.

Marty shook our hands, and then got straight down to business, 'Ladies, I've reviewed the evidence. Let me commend you on such an organised operation. Very smart, I must say.'

Ruby whooped and slapped me on the back.

Marty cleared his throat, 'Now that being said, we do still have a little work to do.'

I looked at Marty, 'Do we have enough evidence to get him charged?'

'Not quite, however you girls are doing great with what you have compiled so far.'

Tanya looked a little disappointed, 'What more do you need Marty?'

'We really need more concrete evidence of his intent to blackmail, some solid proof.'

'What about his emails?' I asked.

'They will help, but he can say that someone sent them from his address. It would be advantageous if you can get him on voice record asking for the two million, and his plan for the exchange of the money.'

'How long will the bastard get?' asked Ruby.

Marty suppressed a smile, 'If he is charged in the UK, blackmail carries up to fifteen years and extortion carries up to a twenty-year prison sentence.'

'What is the difference between blackmail and extortion?' asked Tanya.

'Extortion is the act of obtaining money by using force, you know, threats or intimidation tactics.'

'He is definitely intimidating,' I said.

'Well Beth, if you can record him being aggressive or threatening, we have a much stronger case.'

Tanya looked at Ruby and I, 'He's back in two days, let's come up with a plan to antagonise him.'

Ruby sniggered, 'Just tell him he has a small dick. That should do it.'

Marty coughed and Tanya stifled a laugh.

I turned to Ruby, 'Rubes you said that narcissists like control and to feel important. What if I try to take control somehow? That will make him mad.'

'Are you certain that he is a narcissist?' asked Marty.

All three of us replied at once, 'Yes.'

Marty smiled, 'Well ladies, then I do feel we have to be clever. Why don't you put your smart heads together and come up with a plan and I'll do what I can from this end. Let's keep the channels of communication open and let's get this scoundrel.'

Tanya decided to stay behind to chat with Marty, so Ruby and I said our goodbyes and headed to a local bar for a drink.

I passed my notebook to Ruby, 'How about this?'

Ruby passed it back, 'You know he's never going to agree to that, he'll just rip it up. He wants two million Beth, five hundred grand isn't going to cut it.'

'It'll make him mad though.'

'Or die laughing. Look, let's sleep on it and revisit it tomorrow.'

'I thought you had a flight tomorrow?'

Ruby smirked, 'Called in sick. This is far more important.'

Jay followed me into the kitchen, 'You seem to be spending a lot more time with Ruby these days. I'm glad you girls have your friendship back on track.'

'Yes, it is lovely,' I said honestly.

'Is she still dating that John guy? I haven't heard back from him and was thinking that maybe we should invite them both to dinner.'

Think Beth.

'Sorry! I forgot to tell you that she isn't seeing him anymore.'

'Oh, that's a shame.'

'Actually, it isn't. Ruby found out that he is married with young children.'

Jay looked appalled, 'You are joking!'

'No, apparently he is quite the schemer and obviously a very good liar. Maybe you should avoid his calls.'

'Yes, most definitely. How is Ruby taking it?'

'Not good actually. In fact, I've never seen her like this before. She was in love with him.'

Jay looked genuinely sad, 'Poor girl. I've never understood how people can be so downright deceitful, especially to the person they supposedly love. He must have something seriously wrong with his moral compass if he thinks it's okay to lie and cheat to his wife.'

I turned away so Jay couldn't see my face.

Jay came up behind me and wrapped his arms around my waist, 'Lucky for us, we don't have to worry about that.'

My heart sank, 'Yes, lucky for us!'

Tuesday

After another catch up with Ruby I went home and sent Baileys an email.

To: JD69
Subject: Counteroffer
From: BS
Date: October 10, 2019 19:30

I've been thinking about your proposal...aka your blackmail!
I can give you five hundred thousand pounds.
Two million is simply out of reach.

To: BS
Subject: Joke
From: JD69
Date: October 10, 2019 19:40

Don't waste my time!
I said 2 million!
You have 3 days!

To: JD69
Subject: ?
From: BS
Date: October 10, 2019 19:43

Or else???

To: BS
Subject: No Games
From: JD69
Date: October 10, 2019 19:50

Don't be a smart arse. You know what else.
I go to the press...you go down... he goes down!
This is the stuff movies are made of Kitty Kat...only you aren't going
to get your happy ending like "Pretty Woman."

Let's face it, you aren't Julia Roberts, and something tells me that
boring arsed Thorsen isn't going to come and rescue you from a
fucking balcony.
Now check your phone!

As soon as I finished reading his email, my phone buzzed.
I opened the message to see a photo of Jade's mansion in LA.
The second photo was Jay's friend Charles kissing Jade good-
bye on the steps. I ran to the bathroom and threw up.

Wednesday

Sitting in Marty's office with Ruby and Tanya I giggled to
myself because I actually felt like one of Charlie's Angels
waiting for the voice to appear, 'Good morning Angels.'
When Marty walked in and said, 'Good morning ladies,'
Ruby must have been thinking the same thing as me because
she replied, 'Good morning Charlie.'

It took a minute for Marty to register, then a wide grin
spread across his face, 'Yes, it is a bit like that isn't it?'

Once Marty sat down, it was straight back to business.
I showed everyone my email correspondence and latest text
messages from Baileys.

'My god, that's Charles!' said Tanya shocked. 'What on
earth is he doing in that disgusting place?' She looked at me,
'Oh, I'm sorry Beth.'

'It's okay. I only went there once and it was a disaster, so no harm done.'

'Oh, and that makes it okay?' said Ruby sarcastically.

I ignored Ruby and explained to everyone who Jade was and what happens at the mansion.

Tanya looked sad and Marty noticed, 'Tanya dear, are you alright?'

'I was just wondering if I actually knew James at all. I mean, what if he went there?' She looked at me with big, sad eyes, 'Beth, did he go there? Is that how you met?'

'No!' I shook my head, 'Tanya, Jay would never do that.'

'Well, Charles obviously did, and they are like brothers.'

I could see her pain, 'Tanya, he never went there,' I lied. 'And he would never have cheated on you...ever! Jay is a man of high morals, you know that!'

Marty looked a little concerned for Tanya, 'Shall we postpone this meeting until tomorrow perhaps?'

Tanya smiled at him, 'Marty, you're a sweetheart but it's okay. Thank you! Let's carry on.'

Marty nodded at Tanya and then he looked at me, 'Beth have you had any luck antagonising the fellow?'

'No sorry! It's like he's the king of making something intimidating or threatening sound charming.'

Marty's gaze moved to Tanya, she shook her head, 'Me neither, sorry!'

'Then we only have one option,' said Ruby, 'we have to get proof of him taking the money.'

Marty clapped, 'Right you are Ruby, well done!'

Ruby looked jubilant, however sudden panic rose within me, 'How am I going to get two million pounds in two days? I can't ask Jay for it.'

Tanya smiled, 'I can give it to you.'

Ruby and I both looked at her a little shocked.

'What?' said Tanya. 'James wasn't the only successful one in the relationship you know!'

'See!' Ruby elbowed me, 'Fucking girl power! I love it!'

I looked at Tanya, 'Are you sure?'

'Absolutely. It's not like he's going to get away with the money.' She looked at Marty, 'Marty I'm assuming that you are going to swoop in and arrest him as soon as he walks away aren't you?'

Marty nodded, 'Right on the mark Tanya.'

I looked at Marty, 'So you want me to physically hand him the cash?'

'Yes dear, just like they do in the movies,' he smiled. 'Now there is no need to be afraid, I'll have a photographer taking photos, and I'll obviously be there to witness the transfer and arrest the scoundrel.'

Ruby was clapping, 'Fucking YES! Forget being a flight attendant – Marty, how do I become a Private Detective? This shit is so much more fun.'

Marty and Tanya both laughed at Ruby's enthusiasm, I on the other hand felt sick to my stomach.

After we said goodbye to Marty and Tanya, Ruby offered to take me for a drink, 'Don't worry Beth, he won't do anything to you, and besides, I'll be right there with you.'

'You are coming with me?'

'Of course I fucking am. Female solidarity and all that,' she smiled. 'And besides, I want to see that bastard's face when Marty puts the cuffs on him.'

'He's going to cuff him in broad daylight?'

'Well, they do on T.V. and aren't we currently in an episode of Charlie's Angels?' she laughed.

'You are loving this aren't you Rubes?'

She smiled, 'I've never felt more alive!'

38

KARMA IS A BITCH

Thursday

To: JD69
Subject: Exchange
From: BS
Date: October 12, 2019 11:00

I have your 2 million. You can have it on the following conditions:
I want your word that this is the last time that you blackmail me for money.
I want you to tell Tanya to back off. If I end my relationship, it will be on my terms… nobody else's.
I want you out of my life for good! No more games!

To: BS
Subject: Impressed
From: JD69
Date: October 12, 2019 11:10

Smart girl after all…you have my word. I'll send bank details!

To: JD69
Subject: Meeting point
From: BS
Date: October 12, 2019 11:15

No bank details! I don't want an electronic trail.
I'll be at "Le Garrick" in Covent Garden tomorrow at 2pm.

To: BS
Subject: Confirmed
From: JD69
Date: October 12, 2019 11:19

You are exceeding my expectations!
Your brainpower is impressive...and here I was thinking you were just a dumb flight attendant!
I'll be there.
P.S. Wear something sexy!

Ruby punched a pillow, 'How could I ever have fallen for that chauvinistic fucker?'

'Rubes it's okay. We're going to get him!' I grabbed her shoulders to make her look at me, 'You have to let it go! He's the dumb one, and pretty soon his dumb arse is going to be in a lot of pain...in more ways than one!'

Thursday night.

Baileys ran his fingers down Tanya's back, 'Tanya, I've been thinkin' about all this stuff with Beth and borin' arse Thorsen.'

Tanya rolled over to look at him, 'And?'

'I'm startin' to think that maybe we should let it go.'

Tanya sat up in bed, 'That's a sudden turnaround. Why on earth would we do that?'

Baileys rubbed her thigh, 'Don't get upset. Hear me out.'

Tanya relaxed a little, 'I'm listening.'

'It just hasn't been sittin' well with me. After all, we are both good people, right?'

Tanya nodded her head, 'Yes.'

'And I'm a big believer in Karma.'

Tanya had to stop herself from laughing out loud, 'You are?'

'Yes, absolutely! I think that maybe we should let all this nonsense about tellin' the press go. I'm pretty sure that the Universe will deliver their Karma in one way or another.'

Tanya feigned surprise, 'John, I had no idea you were so spiritual... or forgiving, for that matter.'

Baileys pulled Tanya to him and kissed her nose, 'There's a lot ye don't know about me. It keeps it excitin'.'

Tanya pretended to be thinking, and after a couple of minutes she spoke, 'It pains me to say this but maybe you are right. Maybe it's not our place to mess with destiny.'

'Exactly! They have made their own choices; let the cards fall where they may. It's their problem, not ours.'

'What should I do? It'll be difficult to backtrack now.'

'It'll be easy. Send Beth a message tellin' her that ye are takin' the high road and don't care what she does.'

'Is that it?'

'And that she doesn't have to worry about ye goin' to the press.'

'What if she doesn't believe me?'

Baileys smiled, 'Don't ye worry, she'll believe ye all right.'

Tanya let his comment sit for a moment then sighed, 'Are you sure? I was rather looking forward to spoiling her happy little life.'

Baileys smiled and wrapped his arms around Tanya, 'I know ye were, but it's like they say…"Karma is a bitch!"'

She sighed, 'Fine, I'll do it tomorrow.'

Baileys kissed her, 'That's me girl!'

Friday

Tanya walked into the kitchen to find Baileys looking at his phone. He looked up when he heard her approach, 'Hi gorgeous, I'm glad ye are up as I have some bad news.'

'Oh?'

'I've got to fly to Hong Kong this afternoon. Urgent business to take care of.'

'When are you coming back?'

'That I can't tell ye. It could take at least a week or two to sort out the bloody mess.'

Tanya was becoming an expert at pretending to look sad, 'Oh dear, what time is your flight?'

'Two o'clock.'

'Is it absolutely necessary for you to leave today?'

'Unfortunately, I don't have a choice.'

'Oh well, I suppose you have to take care of business.'

Baileys grinned to himself, 'I'll definitely be takin' care of that. Now come here so I can take ye one last time.'

Tanya raised her eyebrows, 'Last time?'

Baileys realised his mistake, 'Well ye know what I mean, last time for a while.'

As Baileys slipped off her robe, Tanya closed her eyes and smiled.

Last time for a long time.

Five minutes after Baileys left Tanya's apartment, she called Ruby to give her an update. Ruby sounded excited, 'That bastard must be planning on doing a runner to Hong Kong with the cash.'

'That's exactly what I suspect,' replied Tanya. 'Anyway, are we all set to go?'

'Yes! Beth and I will pick you up at 1 pm sharp.'

12.30 pm

I was relieved to see Ruby's car pull up outside my apartment. I had been feeling nervous all morning and waiting for Ruby had seemed like an eternity.

'You okay?' asked Ruby.

I took a deep breath, 'Yes, now that you are here.'

'Don't worry Beth; he's not going to do anything. He wouldn't dare.'

'I know, I just can't even bear the thought of seeing his face.'

'His face is bloody beautiful! It's the evil lurking behind it that's the problem.'

I looked at Ruby, 'Are you okay?'

She never replied.

We picked Tanya up at her meeting point and I didn't even recognise her, 'Nice wig,' I said once Tanya got into the car.

Ruby glanced at Tanya in the rear-view mirror, 'I'm impressed. That coat completely changes your body shape. Seriously, we are in a fucking episode of "Charlie's Angels."'

Tanya laughed, 'That reminds me, I better call Marty.'

Once Tanya hung up the phone, she tapped me on the shoulder, 'All set ladies. Marty is in position; the table is ready...It's almost show time!'

2 pm

Ruby and I were sat at our table when Baileys walked into the cafe. When he saw Ruby his face broke into an evil smile, and I noticed Ruby stiffen instantly, 'Rubes, stay cool,' I whispered.

Baileys approached the table and stared at Ruby, 'Well, well, well, look what the Kitty Kat dragged in.'

I spoke before Ruby had a chance to react, 'We are not here for idle chit chat *Baileys*.'

His eyes moved to me, 'Please Kitty Kat, call me John.'

I forced myself to look at him, 'I have your money.'

Baileys clapped, 'I didn't doubt ye for a second.' He smirked as his eyes moved from my face down to my chest, 'I know how creative ye can be.'

I could feel my adrenaline kicking in and forced myself to remain calm, 'Did you tell Tanya to back off?'

'Yes. *That* little problem is taken care of.'

'Good.' I glared at him, 'I want your assurance that I won't hear from you ever again. This is the last time I ever want to see your face.'

'That hurts me feelings Kitty Kat, but yes, ye have me word. Now, even though I'd love nothing more than to have a little tête à tête with ye both, hand over the bag and I'll be on me way.'

Ruby finally spoke, 'Don't you want to count it?'

His eyes bore into Ruby's, but she held his gaze, 'No, I trust it's all there. Anyway, two million pounds is a lot of money to count.'

I pushed the bag towards Baileys with my foot, he took a quick look inside, 'Well ladies, it was a pleasure doin' ye both.' He laughed and then looked directly at Ruby, 'I've really got to go. I'm about to be a Daddy any minute now, and I wouldn't want to miss that, now would I?'

I put my hand over Ruby's clenched fist as we watched Baileys walk away. When he reached the entrance to the café he stopped to say something to the maître de before he turned to see Marty and two men standing in front of him. Marty held up his badge and read Baileys his rights, simultaneously, one of the men seized the bag, while the second man placed handcuffs on him.

The look on Bailey's face was priceless; from confusion to anger, and then to surprise when he noticed Tanya walking towards him. This was our cue to join the group and Ruby wasted no time getting straight into Bailey's face, 'Now *that* was something I wouldn't want to miss.'

Baileys was livid, 'Ye feckin' bitches! This isn't over.'

Tanya took off her wig, 'Darling, wasn't it you that said karma is a bitch?' She came to stand next to Ruby and I, 'Well, you just got a triple dose!'

Baileys spat out the words, 'Ye will *all* pay for this!'

Tanya ran her hand down the side of Bailey's face, 'I think the only person who is going to pay for this is you! Enjoy prison John, I've heard "pretty boys" are *very* popular...and we all know how much you love sex.'

Marty's men had to restrain Baileys as he attempted to launch himself at me, '*You!* Ye scheming whore. Ye have ruined me, ye little bitch. I will get ye for this if it's the last thing I do.'

Seeing both Ruby and Tanya act so strong had given me courage. I looked straight into Bailey's eyes which were ablaze with anger, 'Now, now, Baileys, *that* hurts my feelings.'

Baileys sounded like a wild animal as Marty's men bundled him into a car, and we could hardly contain our excitement. Ruby was singing the theme tune to "Charlie's Angels" while Tanya and I stood on the pavement cheering and clapping like we were on the sidelines of a football game.

When the car was out of sight, I looked at Tanya and Ruby and screamed, 'We did it!'

'YES, we bloody did!' yelled Tanya.

After we all hugged, Ruby linked our arms, 'Let's go for a celebratory drink.'

'Roger that,' I said as we headed in the direction of the pub.

Tanya couldn't wipe the smile off her face, 'Well it's definitely true what they say...karma *is* a bitch!'

Ruby laughed, 'So, what do *we* say ladies?'

We all shouted together, 'Fucking girl power!'

39

THERE IS NO TOMORROW

The elation that I felt over Bailey's arrest was quickly overshadowed by the sense of sadness I felt when I got home. I had promised Tanya that I would end my relationship with Jay, and even though I knew it was the right thing to do for everyone's sake, I was also aware that for Jay it was a no-win situation either way. If I stay with him and he finds out about my secret life, it will break his heart. If I leave him and call off the wedding, it will break his heart.

I tiptoed into the bedroom where Jay was sleeping peacefully and sat at the side of the bed. I wanted to look at the man I loved one last time. I watched his chest rise and fall with each soft breath and then I gazed at his beautiful face, taking in every line and every feature. With teary eyes I whispered, 'I love you…I'm so sorry…please forgive me.'

'Sorry for what darling?' he murmured, startling me.

Bloody hell, I forgot that he was such a light sleeper.

'Sorry that I woke you,' I said brushing away my tears.

Jay didn't seem to notice, 'Come here, I've missed you.' He pulled me into him, 'I want you.'

We made love for what seemed like hours, and it was beautiful and emotional. I tried to savour everything about him and store it in the filing cabinet of my mind. The loving look in his eyes, his smell, the softness of his skin, his beautiful lips, the gentle way he touched me and finally his kiss. Afterwards as we lay in each other's arms, I let the tears roll down my cheeks. I felt completely broken inside, and I knew that tomorrow Jay would be broken too.

Morning came, and I couldn't bring myself to tell Jay. Instead, I avoided him all day, feigning illness so I could hide in bed. As each day passed, "I'll tell him tomorrow" became my mantra. I made excuses to avoid making love and on the rare occasions that I gave in to Jay's pressure, I acted disinterested. This went on for weeks. The more Jay tried to get close to me the more I pulled away, until eventually he stopped trying. It was killing me to do this to him, but I knew it was the only way. I had to make Jay think that I wasn't the right woman for him and that I did not love him anymore. I knew that if I left Jay immediately, without any explanation, he would come after me demanding answers. And I also knew that I wouldn't have the strength to stay away from him if he pursued me.

I could see that acting so cold towards Jay was hurting him, yet it seemed to be working. Jay organised a month-long business trip to New York which gave me the perfect opportunity to leave him. For the first two weeks that Jay was away, I continued to shut him out; calling him when I knew he wasn't able to answer his phone, ending our conversations quickly when he finally managed to get hold of me, and ignoring his pleas to return his calls... it was excruciatingly painful.

And Jay wasn't the only person I was avoiding; I was also trying to keep Ruby and Tanya at arm's length too. Every day Ruby sent me a text message or left a message on my phone asking, 'Is it done yet?' My response was always the same, 'Tomorrow...I promise.'

Her latest reply sounded very angry, 'There is no fucking tomorrow Beth. There is no tomorrow!'

Great, now I'm in a bloody Rocky movie!

With the scene from Rocky III firmly in my mind thanks to Ruby's rant, I started packing my belongings, but it was proving more difficult than I thought; I was emotionally exhausted from crying and physically exhausted from lack of sleep.

Since Jay had left for New York, I had hardly slept. Every time I closed my eyes, images of our time together flashed in my mind. I was haunted by his eyes and his smile. I could smell him next to me in the bed and I could feel him making love to me in my dreams. And if I wasn't dreaming about Jay, I would wake up sweating due to having nightmares about Baileys and the press.

By midday it had all gotten too much, and I called Ruby. As always, she pulled through for me; she held me as I cried, helped me to pack what I needed, and she constantly reminded me that I was doing the right thing. By five pm we were done.

Ruby grabbed my last bag, 'I'll take this down Beth, you take a minute.'

I nodded and walked over to the mantelpiece. With shaking hands and tears streaming down my face, I placed Jay's grandmothers ring box next to a small envelope. My eyes were drawn to the photo of Jay and I standing on top of the mountain when he proposed, I picked it up and put it in my handbag. I took one last look at our beautiful home, closed the door and stepped into the elevator.

Driving back to Ruby's house, I looked at her and felt forever grateful. I loved her like a sister, and I knew that I could not have left today without her help. Ruby had also been doing a lot of work behind the scenes to help me to start a new life. She had been instrumental in securing me a position with a family in Europe that owned a private jet, and although I would practically be on call 24/7, it was exactly what I needed. I would be too far away for Jay to find me and I would be busy enough to take my mind off him.

40

JAY

As Jay stepped inside his waiting car at London Heathrow Airport, he felt a rush of foreboding doom wash over him. He had been feeling anxious ever since Beth had "frozen" him out before he left for New York. During the month that Jay had been away he had hardly spoken to Beth, and when he did manage to catch her, she was aloof and always had a reason to hang up the phone. Jay was frustrated, sad and confused, and he also knew that something very bad was going to happen. He just didn't know when or why, but he did have a very strong gut feeling that today may be the day.

Jay stared out of the window, looking for anything to steer his thoughts away from Beth, but it was no use. Tears started to well in his eyes at the possibility of losing her.

His mind wandered back to the first time he ever saw Beth at a PR event in Sydney, how he was magnetically drawn to her eyes and the cute look on her face when she realised that he had caught her looking at him. Despite the pain in his heart, Jay smiled as he recalled the moment that his world changed. It was the incident on the plane that cemented his intuition about Beth. When Beth fell on top of him and they got entangled at the bottom of the stairs he felt her energy engulf him like an invisible force field; when she opened her eyes and looked at him, her eyes penetrated his soul; when she burnt her hand in the galley, he had an overwhelming urge to protect her and take away her pain, yet he didn't even know her.

Jay still couldn't fathom the magnetic pull Beth had on him, or how his physical body responded when she was close. He had never met a woman who aroused him in a way that he didn't even understand. He wanted to be close to her, smell her and touch her. Their connection ran deep, and Jay knew without a shadow of a doubt that Beth was the love of his life. He had dreamed about growing old with her and he couldn't imagine living without her. When Beth had agreed to marry him, he remembered thinking how lucky he was to have been blessed with such a love, and not one day had gone by that he wasn't grateful.

The pain in Jay's chest became unbearable as he thought about the last few months. How one day out of the blue, Beth simply changed without any explanation. She suddenly became distant and emotionally unavailable. What hurt Jay the most was Beth's refusal to even discuss what was wrong, so they could at least try to make things right. It had infuriated Jay because all he wanted to do was "fix it" and have Beth back. However, Beth's behaviour over the past few months had totally made Jay question his judgment…and had almost made him lose his mind.

When the car pulled up outside their apartment block, Jay felt physically ill. He couldn't remember a time in his life where he had felt so sick to his stomach. With trembling hands, he pushed the button of the elevator and prayed that his instinct was wrong. However, as the elevator climbed to the top floor, Jay's worst fears were realised; he felt Beth's presence gone before he even approached their front door.

Jay stood outside their apartment, hesitant to put the key into the lock. An array of emotions coursed through his body; all he wanted to do was hold Beth and not let her go, tell her that he didn't know how he was going to exist without her. He wanted to reassure her that whatever she was going through they could face it together, and that he would do anything to save their relationship. He wanted to tell Beth how much he loved her and that she was his only reason to breathe.

Jay took a deep breath and turned the key; the door opened to a deafening silence and an eerie emptiness. Jay dropped his bags and ran to their bedroom hoping to find any small piece of evidence that Beth hadn't left. When he looked inside her empty closet, all his fears were realised. He slammed the doors, sat on the bed, and cried. When Jay finally found the strength to walk back into the lounge, he scanned the room, his mind flooding with memories of them together. He thought something was different, but he couldn't put his finger on it, and then he found what he was looking for. Jay's eyes were drawn to a spot on the mantle and he realised that the photo of him and Beth on the mountain was missing. In its place was a small pink envelope, his grandmother's ring box and the keys to the apartment.

With eyes blinded by tears and shaking hands, Jay opened the envelope. The message was simple and clear.

Jay,
I can't marry you.
I'm sorry.
Please forgive me, and please let me go.
Beth.

Jay looked at his grandmother's ring and his mind went back to when he placed it on Beth's finger. He suddenly felt dizzy and fell to his knees, 'Why? God dammit, why?' he yelled.

As Jay allowed himself to succumb to his tears, the stabbing pain in his chest was intolerable. It felt like someone had ripped a hole in his heart. Bile rose in his throat as he tried to catch his breath, and he wrapped his arms around himself, as if doing so would keep him together. As Jay lay on the floor drowning in his emotions, the same thoughts kept running through his mind.

How am I going to live without her?

How am I going to exist?

My reason for living is gone...my Beth is gone!

Hours turned into days, days turned into weeks, weeks turned into months. Jay felt empty, his life felt meaningless. Women didn't interest him; in fact, nothing interested him anymore, not even his work. All Jay wanted to do was come home to *their* apartment and wait. Jay had convinced himself that the connection he had with Beth was too deep to just forget, and he never gave up hope that one day Beth would come home.

Every night as Jay lay in their bed he hugged Beth's pillow as he cried, he watched videos of them together and he relived their love making in his mind. When he closed his eyes to sleep, he would pray that he would have a dream about her, and when he did, he didn't want to wake up.

Jay was aware that his behaviour wasn't helping him to heal, but he didn't care. He didn't want to heal, all he wanted was Beth. Jay also knew in his heart that he would never be able to let her go. The void in his chest was too big, the pain was too real, and Jay was convinced that until he had Beth back he would never be whole again. He was broken!

41

SECOND CHANCES

Eight months later

So much had changed in the past eight months since Bailey's arrest and my leaving to work in Europe. Baileys had been sentenced to a maximum term of ten years in prison, with the possibility of parole after seven years. His wife had met with Marty and after seeing the evidence for herself, had started divorce proceedings straight away. Baileys lost everything in his divorce, including all custody rights to his children.

Ruby had taken a part-time position with the airline and was now working alongside Marty as his apprentice. She was also studying criminology and she absolutely loved it! Tanya and Ruby had become firm friends and despite not seeing each other much, Ruby and I were in regular contact.

'How is Beth?' asked Tanya.

Ruby sipped her wine, 'She's doing okay.'

'Really? Because that didn't sound very convincing.'

Ruby looked at Tanya, 'It doesn't really matter how she is feeling. At the end of the day, she did the right thing...for everyone!'

Tanya's phone rang and she quickly turned it upside down so Ruby could not see the caller ID on the screen.

Ruby was quick to notice, 'Tanya, you're not doing a Beth on me and keeping secrets are you? I've had enough of that behaviour to last me a lifetime.'

'No, absolutely not,' lied Tanya.

Ruby raised an eyebrow, 'New boyfriend?'

Tanya shook her head, 'No, it's a client. I don't want to speak with him because I'm here with you.' Tanya changed the subject, 'So tell me, is Chuck moving to the UK?'

Ruby shivered, 'Please, call him Charlie, I can't stand the name Chuck.'

'Okay! So, when is *Charlie* coming?'

'Next week,' Ruby smiled, 'but he only has a three-month placement. We are going to see if we can actually live together. Apparently, I'm "hard work!"'

Tanya laughed, 'I can't imagine that.'

Since Baileys had broken Ruby's heart, Ruby had found Chuck to be an amazing source of support. They had spent so much time chatting and messaging on the phone, that it didn't take Ruby long to realise that there was something very special about him. They decided to meet up and it became very obvious to Ruby that not only was Chuck quite adventurous inside and outside of the bedroom, but they had so much in common. He was a very positive, caring and loving man who made her laugh. Chuck also had his fingers in a lot of different business ventures, and she loved that about him. He respected Ruby's need for space, yet he was always there if she needed him. Their friendship grew and after six months the dynamics suddenly changed; it was as if they both woke up one day in love with each other.

Tanya's phone rang again. Ruby motioned for her to pick up the call, but she let it ring. Ruby looked suspiciously at Tanya, 'So what's *really* been happening with you lately? Are you still working on that new project?'

'Which one?'

'The new one! The one that has been keeping you up all hours for the past two months.'

Tanya smiled, 'Oh *that* one! Yes, I'm still working on it. Actually, on that note, I have to leave shortly. I have the client coming over this evening.'

'Bloody hell, you need to change your career. It's past eight o'clock. A bit late isn't it?'

'I don't mind,' said Tanya with a glint in her eye, 'I rather like this one.'

'You little minx, I knew you were up to something. Well, off you go, I'm sure you'll tell me one day…enjoy your *client*.'

When Tanya got into the taxi she looked at her phone and she had four text messages and a voicemail. They were all from him. She didn't want to lie to Ruby, but for the moment, she wanted to keep him her little secret. 'Excuse me,' she said to the driver, 'I've changed my mind.' She handed the driver a piece of paper with his address on, 'Can you take me here please?'

Tanya felt a mixture of nerves and excitement when the taxi stopped outside his home. She applied some lipstick, turned off her phone and stepped out of the car. Tanya was halfway up the path when he opened the door, and his smile took her breath away.

'This is a surprise, I thought you had plans to…'

She cut him off with a kiss and pressed herself against him. Putting her hand inside his boxers she looked up at him, 'I do have plans, lots of plans.'

He looked confused.

'With you James!'

42

ALL GOOD THINGS COME TO AN END... OR DO THEY?

One year later

I walked into the bedroom; Antoine was lying on the bed completely naked and propped up by his elbow. He had a beautiful, sculptured body and his eyes twinkled with mischief and anticipation as I walked towards him, 'Purr, hello Kitty Kat. I've missed you.'

I opened my robe and let it fall to the floor, 'Bonsoir Antoine.'

When I left the hotel an hour later, I felt numb. My life as Kat didn't hold the same excitement as it used to. I no longer thrived on the passion and power that I once felt, nor did the money entice me. In the beginning, I thought that holding onto this part of my life would fill the huge emotional void that I had in my heart since leaving Jay, but it didn't. Being with other men just made me miss him more. I longed for his touch, I craved for the intimacy that we shared, and I wanted his love.

I knew when I made the decision to leave Jay that I would never be completely whole again. I knew the day I walked away from our home that it wasn't just the engagement ring I was leaving behind, but also a piece of my soul.

Over time I had convinced myself that my loneliness and heartache were a small price to pay to keep my secret life from being exposed. I knew that the emptiness and sadness that I felt every day was nothing compared to how I would have felt if Jay had discovered the truth about me and hated me for it.

Every day I questioned why I continued to hide behind Kat to escape what I was feeling. Every day I told myself to stop...but I never did. I couldn't stop because I knew that if I gave up Kat, I would be left with just Beth...and I would have to face the truth that I was broken. I had become a prisoner to my own pain and being Kat was my only escape. I now understood and accepted that I was using my secret life as a distraction to numb my pain.

After I showered, I sat down on the sofa with a glass of wine and picked up a magazine that I had bought earlier in the day. I turned the page and there he was. I studied his face, just like I had done with every photograph I had seen of him for the past twelve months. I looked for anything that would tell me he had moved on and was happy, but all I saw were remnants of his brokenness. Jay had lost weight and looked tired, his beautiful green eyes no longer sparkled with mischief, and the smile that used to light up a room was gone. It was clear to me that Jay's light, that once burned so brightly, had gone out...just like mine!

I closed the magazine and turned on the T.V. Jay's face came onto the screen.

Will you ever let me forget?

I turned off the T.V and stared at the emptiness around me. The silence was broken by the sound of my phone ringing. It was Ruby.

'Hey Beth, what you up to?'

'Not much, I just got back from a trip,' I lied.

'Are you okay? You sound a bit flat.'

'I'm fine. I just saw a photo of Jay and it's made me a bit nostalgic, that's all.'

Ruby sighed, 'Beth, how many times have I told you that you have to stop obsessing about him and get on with your life? It's been 12 months now!'

I will if the universe stops putting him in front of me!

'I know, but he looks so lonely and sad.'

'Beth, forget about him. He's a man, his dick will take over one day and he'll be fine!'

When I hung up from Ruby I thought about Jay. She was so wrong about him; he was different to any other man I had ever met. It was never about sex for Jay; it was all about love and having a deeper connection than just the physical. Jay desired and needed a woman who understood him on a soul level, and he found that with me.

With a heavy heart, I climbed into bed and did the same thing I had done every night for the past year. I reached under the pillow next to me and pulled out the photo of Jay and I that I had taken from our apartment. I looked at our happy faces and imagined myself back on the mountain with him. I kissed his face, told him how much I love and miss him, and then I cuddled the pillow as I cried myself to sleep.

Tanya looked at Jay and she knew that for the past six months she had been fooling herself into thinking that he could love her again. Jay was never fully present, and when they made love it was as though he was physically in the room, but his soul was somewhere else. He never laughed or seemed happy, and Tanya could see that the light was no longer in his eyes. She had tried desperately to form intimacy with him, but she realised over time that he wasn't capable of it. Looking at Jay was a constant reminder of what Tanya herself had endured when he broke her heart and she knew from experience that Jay was just going through the motions and trying to exist… he was broken.

Over the past two months Tanya had attempted to get Jay to open up about his feelings, but the more she tried, the more he closed off. Today she decided it was time to intervene as she couldn't bear to see him like this any longer.

Tanya sat down at the dining table, 'James can we talk?'

He looked up from his newspaper, 'About what?'

'About what is really going on here.'

Jay sighed, 'I've told you Tan, there's nothing to talk about. I'm fine.'

Tanya pressed on, 'You're still in love with her, aren't you?'

Jay put the paper down and looked away; sorrow etched on his face.

'You still love Beth.'

Jay turned to look at Tanya, 'How do you know her …'

Tanya cut him off and shook her head, 'I thought I was protecting you, but now I can see that I made the wrong decision.'

Jay looked at her confused, 'Protecting me?'

'You really can't live without her can you? You love her *that* much.'

Jay put his head in his hands and closed his eyes.

Tanya pressed on, 'Please James, I need to know.'

Jay looked up, his face distorted in pain, tears spilling down his cheeks. He didn't need to say anything, his reaction told Tanya all she needed to know. Since they were fourteen years old Tanya had never seen Jay this distraught. She stood up and put her arms around his shoulders, 'James you deserve to know the truth and you deserve to hear it from me.'

Tanya began to tell Jay about Beth's secret life as Kat, and Beth's connection with John Davenport.

Jay's mind flashed back to the incident where he thought he had seen Beth at Jade's mansion in LA, the strange interaction between Beth and John at the airport, and Beth's falling out with Ruby. When Tanya got to the part about John blackmailing Beth, everything began to make sense, from Beth's money problems to her constant nightmares.

Jay looked at Tanya, 'How did you even get involved?'

Tanya blushed as she told Jay about her relationship with John, how he had pursued her for months and how he had tried to coerce her into blackmailing Beth. She went into great detail about her meeting with Beth and Ruby, hiring a private detective, and how together the three women came up with a plan to put John behind bars.

Jay sat back, shocked, his face ashen, 'Did the bastard get put away?'

Tanya nodded, 'Ten years.'

Jay was angry, 'How did I not know any of this?' he turned to face Tanya, 'and how exactly were you *protecting* me?'

Tanya looked down embarrassed, 'I told Beth to break up with you.' She looked up and saw the hurt and disbelief in Jay's eyes, 'Not that it matters, because Beth had already made the decision to leave you. She was terrified that her secret life would be exposed and wanted to protect you from the media. She knew that she was going to break your heart either way. Beth actually believed that leaving you was the kindest option. She wanted to ensure that your business and reputation would remain intact.'

Jay was seething, 'That was not *her* decision to make... or *yours*!'

Tears stung Tanya's eyes, 'I'm so sorry James! We both thought we had your best interests at heart...we *both* love you!'

Jay was visibly shaking, 'Where is she?'

'I don't know exactly,' Tanya said honestly. 'Somewhere in Europe.'

Jay thought about Beth suddenly freezing him out, her note that left him with no clue as to why she left and her request for him to let her go. Then Jay remembered how Beth had taken the photograph of them both on the mountain. He hadn't thought much of it at the time, but he was now questioning why she would take a photo if she no longer loved him. Jay now knew in his heart that everything Tanya was telling him was the truth and he felt overwhelmed. He needed space to think; he stood up and left without saying another word.

Tanya took a deep breath and felt a strange sense of peace. She realised that she no longer wanted or needed Jay; that part of her life was now over. Tanya knew that she deserved a man who would love her in the same way that Jay loved Beth and as she closed the door behind her, for the first time in a long time, Tanya finally felt free.

When Tanya got home she called Ruby, 'I need to speak to you.'

'You sound serious, is everything okay?'

'Not quite, but it will be. I need your help.'

Tanya told Ruby about her conversation with Jay (but omitted the fact he had been her secret lover for the past six months), 'Ruby, I don't think he cares one iota about the repercussions. He is literally a broken man without her.'

'What do you need?'

'I need Beth's address.'

Ruby was silent.

'Ruby are you still there?'

'Yes. Sorry, I'm wondering if it is the right thing to do. I doubt Beth would want her life dragged through the media, even if Jay doesn't care.'

'Do you know that for certain?'

'No.'

'Is Beth still in love with him?'

Ruby thought about Beth's obsession to know everything about Jay's life and the number of times she had told Beth to forget about him, 'Yes she is!'

'Then I'm going to need that address.'

Tanya knocked on Jay's door and his appearance shocked her, 'My god James, have you slept at all?'

'Tan...not today...'

Tanya handed him an envelope.

'What's this?'

'It's for you. A peace offering of sorts.' Tanya kissed Jay on the cheek, 'Can you ever forgive me?'

Jay's eyes were full of sadness, 'There's nothing to forgive…I'm sorry…'

Tanya cut him off, 'Don't apologise James. I had to see if we had anything left.' She touched his cheek, '*And* I'm okay. In fact, I'm more than okay,' she smiled. 'I will always love you James, but I can let you go now.'

Tears spilled down both their faces as they hugged for a life they both knew was over. Tanya pulled away and pointed at the envelope, 'Life is too short James. Finding a love like you two have is rare…it's worth saving, at all costs. So, go and get her!'

Jay stood anxiously on the steps of the apartment building in St Tropez. He had no idea if Beth was even in town and he didn't care, he would wait. A couple of hours passed, and as Jay aimlessly watched the locals meander along the street, he felt Beth's energy before he saw her. He became overwhelmed with emotion as he watched Beth walk up the hill, her arms laden with French bread and vegetables. His smile broke through his tears when Beth dropped her tomatoes and desperately try to salvage them as they rolled down the hill. He was mesmerised.

Bloody tomatoes…stop rolling away!

I managed to rescue two tomatoes and pick up the rest of my shopping before I set off again up the hill. I was almost home when I suddenly had a strange sense that I was being watched. Somewhere in the back of my mind I heard a voice,

"Look up Beth." I raised my head and saw him, his green eyes seeking out mine. I stood still, my mind unable to fathom if I was dreaming, or if it was really Jay standing there.

Despite the look of confusion on Beth's face, Jay could feel her love radiating towards him like an invisible force. When their eyes met, he felt the same magnetic pull that he had experienced the very first time he saw her. With every step he took towards Beth, the broken pieces of his shattered heart started slotting together like pieces of a jigsaw puzzle. Beth did not move.

A tsunami of emotions raged through my body as Jay walked towards me. My heart was bursting with love, but my mind was confused. I wanted to run to him, but I couldn't move. When he stopped in front of me, I was transfixed by his beautiful face, as his energy pulled at me like a magnet. As if questioning reality, I managed to find my voice, 'Jay?'

His piercing eyes penetrated my soul, 'Beth.'

'How did you find me?'

Jay smiled, 'With a little help from your friends.'

'Ruby?'

'Ruby *and* Tanya.'

Just hearing Tanya's name made me nervous, 'What are you doing here?'

Jay studied my face intently for a moment and then he took a step towards me, 'Something I should have done a long time ago.'

I let my shopping fall to the ground as Jay wrapped me in his arms and kissed me. The touch of his lips brought every single cell in my body back to life. All the pain of the past twelve months drained from my heart, and instead of a void, I could feel my insides being replenished with his love.

Jay finally pulled away and held my face in his hands, his voice raw with emotion, 'Don't ever leave me again.'

I looked into his eyes and it was like looking through the windows of his soul. Instead of emptiness, I saw a flame, burning fiercely, as he looked back at me.

Fear and guilt ripped through my body at the realisation that I couldn't promise Jay anything. I had to tell him the truth, 'Jay, there is something you need to know.'

Jay could feel me trembling, he pulled me tighter into his arms, 'Beth…it's okay. I know everything.'

I dropped my head in shame, 'You don't know everything.'

He put his mouth to my ear and whispered, 'I know *everything*.'

I started to cry, 'But…'

Jay silenced me, 'But…none of it matters.'

'What about the press? Your reputation?'

'We can deal with that. We can get through anything… *together*.' He raised my chin with his finger, 'Beth, please look at me. I love you! I know who you really are. I know your soul.' Jay kissed my tears and he held me like he was never going to let me go, 'I have been lost without you Beth…broken inside. You are my reason to breathe, my reason to exist. *Nothing* else matters…only you…only *us*!'

I dissolved into Jay's arms as my mind registered what he was saying to me. I was finally safe; Jay knew about my secret life, and he didn't care. He loved me unconditionally and nothing could ever tear us apart again.

I looked up into the beautiful eyes that mirrored my soul, 'Someone told me once that my life wasn't a movie, and that I wouldn't get my happy ever after.'

Jay reached into his pocket, his eyes sparkling with mischief, as a sexy, wicked look flashed across his face. He placed his grandmother's ring onto my finger, 'Well…they were bloody wrong weren't they!'

THE END

Made in United States
North Haven, CT
20 November 2021

11324863R00174